AUNT BESSIE LIKES

AN ISLE OF MAN COZY MYSTERY

DIANA XARISSA

D1528587

For happy couples everywhere.
And happy single people, too!

AUTHOR'S NOTE

I'm surprised and delighted when I think that this is the twelfth book in the Aunt Bessie series. I'm still enjoying writing about Bessie and her friends. Thank you for coming on this journey with me.

If you are new to the series, Bessie first appeared in my romance novel, *Island Inheritance*. She was the source of the inheritance, however, so we learned her life story mostly through diaries and letters. Unable to let go of the character, I decided to give her her own cozy mystery series. It was one of my better decisions in life!

Because of the whole being dead thing, the mysteries are set around fifteen years before the romance. The first Bessie book took place in March, 1998, and they've continued on from there. I always suggest that you read them in order, as the characters do change and develop, but I write each one to stand alone as well.

This is a work of fiction and all of the characters are fictional creations. Any resemblance they share with any real person, living or dead, is entirely coincidental. The Isle of Man is very real and a truly special place. The historical sites mentioned within the story are also real. The various businesses in the story, however, are fictional and any resemblance that any of them bear to real businesses is also coincidental.

I've used British (and Manx) spellings and terminology throughout the book, and there is a short glossary of terms in the back to help readers from outside the UK with anything that might be unfamiliar. The longer I live in the US, the more likely it is that more Americanisms will sneak into the texts. I'm sorry about that, and if you let me know, I will try to correct them.

The picture on the cover of the book is of St. Lupus Church in Kirk Malew on the Isle of Man. It is situated near Castletown. Built in the twelfth century, it is one of the oldest churches on the island still in use as a church.

Remember, I love hearing from readers. Please feel free to get in touch in whatever manner most suits you. There are contact details in the back of the book. (I would especially love snail mail, as my daughter usually checks my post office box with me, and she's always disappointed when it's empty!)

CHAPTER 1

"I don't know. Maybe the blue one is better," Doona said, turning slowly in front of the shop's largest mirror.

"I liked the blue one better," Bessie said firmly. "And the blue hat is nicer than that one, as well."

Doona patted the hat she was wearing and frowned. "This one is sort of, well, unusual," she admitted. "I'm still not totally certain that I should wear a hat, anyway."

"It's a wedding," Bessie replied. "It's only proper to wear a hat to a wedding."

Doona nodded, but she still looked uncertain.

"That's great on you," the shop assistant said as she wandered past with an armful of dresses for another customer. "I love the hat. It's such an unusual style."

"I'm not sure I was going for unusual," Doona muttered, turning around even more slowly. "Maybe I'll try the blue one again."

"Yes, do that," Bessie agreed.

Doona nodded and disappeared into the changing room while Bessie settled back in the comfortable chair that the shop had thoughtfully provided. It was probably meant for long-suffering husbands, but Bessie was quite happy to take advantage of it. This was

1

the fifth shop she and Doona had been in, and while she hated to admit it, Bessie was getting tired.

"After this, tea and cakes," Doona said as she stuck her head out of the curtained cubicle. "My treat, since I'm dragging you through every shop in Douglas."

Bessie chuckled. "You don't have to treat, but I won't say no to a tea break, or a slice of cake, for that matter."

Doona nodded and then withdrew behind the curtain once more. With nothing to do but wait, Bessie amused herself by watching the other customers. Douglas sometimes felt quite far away from the small village of Laxey where Bessie had lived for all of her adult life. While she often felt as if she knew nearly everyone in Laxey, when in Douglas she was far less likely to see friends or even acquaintances. The shop they were in had a nice mix of styles that seemed to appeal to everyone from the teens giggling at the front of the shop to the woman near the back who must have been close to Bessie's own age.

No one who knew Elizabeth Cubbon, known as Bessie to nearly everyone, was brave enough to ask her exactly how old she was and Bessie certainly wasn't telling. She rarely gave her age a thought, preferring to focus on how she felt, which was mostly fit and healthy. If pressed, she'd admit to having had her free bus pass for many years now, but would also point out that she was some years away from receiving a telegram from the Queen. Having a cottage on the beach meant that she took plenty of exercise each day and breathed in fresh sea air while she walked. She credited both the air and the exercise for her continued good health.

"It's just a bit matronly," Doona complained as she pushed aside the curtain and stepped back out in front of the mirror. "I feel too young to look this old."

Bessie studied her friend for a moment and then nodded reluctantly. "You're right. I think I like the dress so much because it would suit me, but you're too young for it, really."

"I suppose that means more shopping after our tea break," Doona said with a sigh.

"I'll definitely need a slice of cake, then," Bessie told her.

Doona nodded before she went back into the changing rooms. Bessie and Doona were unlikely friends, but after knowing each other for nearly three years, they'd become extremely close. Doona was in her mid-forties, with two failed marriages behind her. She and Bessie had first met at a Manx language class as her second marriage was ending, and Bessie had provided the right mix of tough love and caring sympathy to get Doona through the worst of her heartbreak. Over the past year Doona had been the one providing support for her friend as Bessie had found herself caught up in multiple murder investigations. Now they were both happy and excited about the impending nuptials of one of their mutual friends.

"What are you going to wear to the wedding?" Doona asked as the pair settled into seats at the nearest café.

"I don't know," Bessie replied. "I suppose I should go shopping, really. I don't have any hats anymore, and if I'm going to buy a hat, I may as well buy a dress to go with it."

"You don't have much time," Doona pointed out. "It's already the first of February, although where January went, I simply don't know."

"Time does seem to be moving very quickly lately," Bessie agreed. "But the wedding isn't until Valentine's Day. I have plenty of time to shop."

"We should have been looking for dresses for you as well. I didn't even think, sorry."

"I was looking for me as well, but I didn't see anything I liked. I'll probably do my shopping in Ramsey. There are a few shops there that I quite like."

"We can stop there on the way home, if you'd like," Doona offered.

"It isn't really on the way home," Bessie said. "Anyway, I can go shopping any time. This is your only day off this week. Let's just focus on you."

"I don't want to ask for any time off at the moment. Things are a bit tense at the station and I don't want to add to the atmosphere."

Bessie nodded. Doona was one of the civilian front desk staff at the Laxey branch of the Isle of Man Constabulary. Inspector John Rockwell ran the station and he was a good friend to both women.

3

His second-in-command, Anna Lambert, was sometimes more difficult to work with.

"Did I mention that Hugh's invited Inspector Lambert to the wedding?" Doona asked as their tea was delivered.

"Yes," Bessie said, pressing her lips together firmly to prevent herself from adding anything to her reply.

"I know he felt he really had to, as he'd invited everyone else at the station, but I do wish he hadn't," Doona said in a quiet voice. "I hope I don't get stuck sitting with her at the reception."

"Oh, that would be awful," Bessie exclaimed. She blushed and shook her head. "That's not fair. I don't much like how the woman does her job, or like her as a person, but I'm sure we can find a way to get along for a few hours if we have to, for Hugh's sake."

Doona nodded unenthusiastically. "Maybe Hugh can put her with some of his more distant relatives," she suggested. "You know, the ones you don't really like but have to invite anyway."

Bessie laughed. "As I understand it, it's going to be a fairly small wedding. I'm not sure he's invited his more distant relatives."

Hugh Watterson, a young police constable in Laxey, was marrying his pretty blonde girlfriend, Grace Christian, on Valentine's Day. As a primary schoolteacher, Grace wasn't any wealthier than her husband-to-be, so they were keeping the wedding as small and affordable as possible. Neither set of parents had the money to throw the couple a lavish affair, either, although Bessie had heard that both sets were giving the couple what they could to help them make a deposit on their first home together.

"Hugh's taking a week off after the wedding," Doona said. "That's one of the reasons why things are a bit tense at work."

"Why would that cause tension?"

"Constables are meant to book their holidays well in advance," Doona explained. "Asking for an entire week off on such short notice didn't sit well with Inspector Lambert."

"They did plan the wedding in something of a hurry," Bessie said. Hugh had finally worked up the nerve to ask Grace to marry him after a difficult murder investigation where Hugh had actually been a suspect. All of that had taken place at the very beginning of the new year, and once Grace had said yes, Hugh had been determined to make her his wife as quickly as possible.

"Yes, well, John gave Hugh permission for the week off without asking Inspector Lambert for her opinion. I gather if she had been asked, that she wouldn't have been as quick to agree."

"It's Hugh's honeymoon. Anyway, he deserves a break after everything that happened last month. A great deal of the stress and strain he was put under was down to how Inspector Lambert handled the investigation."

"She said she doesn't want to start a precedent, but I don't think any of the other constables are giving any thought at all to getting married. They all seem to be enjoying the single life, sometimes a bit too much."

"There's nothing wrong with being single," Bessie said stoutly.

"Of course not," Doona agreed. "Although weddings are fun, too."

"Yes, and I imagine honeymoons are quite nice," Bessie, who'd never been married herself, said.

"Yes, they can be," Doona replied. "Although Hugh and Grace are just going to Ramsey for the week, I gather. Hugh said something about getting a special price for a week at the Seaview, which is lovely, but it's not exactly the most romantic honeymoon destination."

"The Seaview is one of the nicest hotels on the island, but it would be nicer for them to get away properly," Bessie said thoughtfully.

The delivery of thick slices of Victoria sponge ended that particular conversation. Refreshed by tea and cake, the pair headed back out into the high street to continue searching for the perfect dress for Doona.

"This might be it," she called from behind a fitting room door an hour later. "I really love this one."

Bessie studied her friend for a short while before she spoke. "It's almost perfect," she said eventually. "But not with that hat."

Doona frowned. "I have to agree. This hat isn't working with this dress. But I love the dress. I'll just have to look for a different hat."

"Remember the hat in the second place we went to?" Bessie asked her. "That would be perfect with that dress."

Doona thought for a moment and then nodded happily. "You're absolutely right," she said. "I'll just pay for the dress and then we can go over and get that hat."

Bessie sat back with a happy sigh as Doona went to change. Her best friend was going to look lovely at Hugh's wedding, and Bessie wouldn't be the only woman wearing a hat, which was sometimes the case these days.

"Let's go and get lunch," Doona suggested a short time later as the pair made their way back to Doona's car with the dress and hat safely purchased.

"I'm not all that hungry after that huge slice of cake," Bessie replied. "What did you have in mind?"

"Oh, something extravagant and decadent," Doona laughed. "But we can skip lunch and go somewhere for dinner instead, if you'd like."

"I can, if it's an early dinner," Bessie said. "Hugh's coming over at half six so I'll need to be home by then."

"Is he bringing all of his case files?" Doona asked. "He's become quite obsessed with some of them."

While Hugh had been suspended during the recent murder investigation, John Rockwell had given him some cold case files to study. "He's bringing over the files that he's most interested in," Bessie replied. "He's hoping I can help fill in more background information and maybe help him find a starting point for reopening at least one or two of the investigations."

"If anyone can help him, it's you," Doona said. "You know everything there is to know about everything that's ever happened in Laxey."

Bessie laughed. "Not exactly, but I have lived there for a long time. I'm really hoping I can help. It would be nice to see some of the old cases solved."

To fill the time before dinner, Doona drove them to Ramsey, where they had a wander around the large bookshop and then did some grocery shopping. That meant a stop at Bessie's cottage to drop off groceries before heading out for their evening meal.

As they'd skipped lunch, Bessie didn't feel at all guilty about having something indulgent for dinner. The new fish and chips shop that had just opened in Laxey was getting rave reviews from Bessie's friends, so she was eager to try it.

"I can see why everyone is saying such good things about this place," she said to Doona after her first bite. "This is delicious."

"The best fish and chips I've had in ages," Doona replied.

"I understand the owners have come from across," Bessie remarked. "I'm glad they decided to open in Laxey instead of Douglas."

"We didn't have much choice," the man in the white apron who was walking past said. "We couldn't afford anything in Douglas. We barely scraped together enough for this place. Now that we've been here a few weeks, though, I can see why the island is so popular. It really is something special, isn't it?"

"It is," Bessie agreed. She and Doona introduced themselves to the man, who looked to be in his late forties. He was short and a bit plump, but that was hardly surprising considering his occupation.

"I'm Dan Houseman," he told Bessie. "My wife is called Sadie and she's in the kitchen, frying fish as fast as she can. I'm strictly front of house, as I can burn water on a good day."

"Well, she's very good at what she does," Bessie told him. "I'm sure you'll be very popular here in Laxey."

"We'd love it if you'd become regulars," Dan told her. "We're thinking about starting some sort of loyalty scheme, you know, like the supermarkets do. Every ten meals you buy, you get one free, or something like that."

"That sounds like a great idea," Doona said enthusiastically. "Not that I need any excuse to eat more fish and chips."

When a large group of people entered the shop, Dan excused himself to help the girl behind the counter with their orders. Bessie crunched her way through the last of her fish with a satisfied smile on her face.

"I think we should try to eat here at least once a week," Doona said after she'd swallowed her last chip.

"I don't think I should eat fish and chips that regularly," Bessie replied. "Maybe once a fortnight?"

Doona laughed and patted her tummy. "You're right. I shouldn't eat fish and chips that often, either. I've finally lost a few pounds but I'll put them right back on if this gets to be a habit."

Doona was curvier than Bessie, who'd always kept herself fit and slender, but recent stress had caused Doona to lose some of the extra weight she'd carried for years. The dress Doona had purchased for the upcoming wedding was two sizes smaller than what she normally wore, which worried Bessie slightly.

"You can afford to put a few pounds back on," she told Doona as the pair got up to leave. "You've lost quite a bit of weight."

"With everything that happened with Charles, I sort of lost interest in food," Doona replied. "I'm feeling a lot better now, but I'm determined to keep the weight off."

"Just make sure you're still eating healthily," Bessie said.

"I am," Doona told her. "Tea and cake for lunch and fish and chips for dinner. What could be healthier than that?"

The two women laughed together as they walked back to Doona's car. The drive to Bessie's cottage was a short one.

"I won't come in, as you're expecting Hugh shortly," Doona told her friend.

"Today was fun," Bessie said. "And you're going to look wonderful at the wedding." Bessie climbed out of the car and walked into her cottage, pausing to run her fingers over the plaque at the door.

"Treoghe Bwaane," she murmured. The Manx words meant widow's cottage, which had felt particularly apt when she'd purchased the property at age eighteen. She wasn't a widow, but she'd felt like one. While she'd been born on the island, she'd spent nearly all of her childhood in America. She'd been surprised and angry when her parents had insisted that she move back to the island with them when she was seventeen. Leaving Matthew, her first love, behind had been difficult, but he'd promised to follow her. She'd been planning for their future together, back in the US, when she was told he'd succumbed to illness on the difficult sea crossing.

Inside the small kitchen of her cottage, Bessie put down her handbag and looked out the window at the beach and the sea. She'd spent many hours sitting in this room, watching the waves and wishing she could change the past. Now, so many years later, she was content that everything had happened for a reason. She felt as if she was exactly where she was meant to be in her little home by the sea. If she had married Matthew, her life would have been very different, and she loved the life she'd built for herself.

She shook her head to clear away the memories and then looked at the clock. Hugh would be there any minute, and knowing Hugh, he'd be hungry. She needed to get the kettle on and start piling biscuits onto a plate.

A few minutes later, just as she was adding a few fancy chocolate biscuits to the pile, Bessie heard a car pull up outside her cottage. The kettle began to boil as she headed for the door.

"Hugh, you look wonderful," she exclaimed as the man bounced out of his car and crossed the short distance to Bessie.

"Ah, thanks, Aunt Bessie," he said, blushing brightly.

While Hugh was in his mid-twenties and engaged to be married, to Bessie he still looked like the awkward teenager who had frequently taken refuge in her spare bedroom after disagreements with his parents. He was over six feet tall now, but even though he towered over Bessie, who was only a few inches over five feet, she still found herself wanting to treat him like a child.

He enveloped Bessie in a hug before following her into the cottage. Bessie laughed as she watched his eyes light up when they spotted the plate full of biscuits.

"You did have dinner, didn't you?" she asked before she put the plate on the small kitchen table.

"Oh, yes," Hugh assured her. "A bunch of us who were working until six had sandwiches delivered from the shop across the road."

Bessie nodded and handed him a small plate to put his selections on. While he was busy stacking as many biscuits as he could onto it, Bessie prepared tea for them both.

"How are you?" she asked after she'd joined him at the table, her own plate, with only a few biscuits on it, in front of her.

"I'm mostly good," Hugh replied, quickly sipping some tea to wash down the mouthful of biscuit he'd spoken around. "I'm really happy most of the time, and then I start to worry about, oh, everything and my mood crashes. Getting married is scary."

"I wouldn't know," Bessie said. "But from what I've heard, your feelings are perfectly normal. You're making a big life change, after all."

"I love Grace so much," Hugh said, reddening slightly. "I'm really worried that I won't make her happy."

"And you won't, at least some of the time," Bessie replied. "As long as you're both happy most of the time, you're doing well."

Hugh chuckled. "That sounds closer to achievable," he said.

"I think you two are just right for each other and that you'll have a wonderful life together. You do have to remember that it won't always be easy, though."

"After what we went through last month, it should feel easy, at least for a while," Hugh said.

Bessie nodded. "The events at Thie yn Traie were difficult for you both. I do hope you've learned something about communication from them."

"I have," Hugh told her. "We both have, really. We've talked a lot since then and I know we understand each other better. In a strange way, I'm almost glad we had that trouble, because it's helped us both learn a lot."

"Good, just make sure you keep learning, about each other and yourselves. I think you're going to live happily ever after for sure."

Hugh grinned. "I hope you're right," he said. "I just wish I could afford to spoil Grace as much as I'd like."

"Grace isn't marrying you because she wants to be spoiled."

"I know," Hugh sighed. "I saved up for months to buy her the perfect ring, but now I think I should have saved up for our honeymoon instead. When I bought the ring, I was thinking we'd wait a year or two to get married, but once she said 'yes' I simply couldn't bear the thought of waiting."

"Doona tells me you're going to spend a week at the Seaview in Ramsey," Bessie said.

"Yes," Hugh shrugged. "It's a really nice place, but it isn't exactly a romantic getaway. I investigated a theft there not long ago and the owner was really pleased with how the investigation went, so he's giving me a great rate for the honeymoon suite, but I'd still rather take her to Paris or New York City or something."

"Never mind, you'll be together and that's what matters."

"I know you're right," Hugh said with a small frown. "But I feel as if I'm letting Grace down."

"But what have you brought tonight?" Bessie asked, changing the subject before Hugh got too miserable.

"You know I've been going through the cold cases," Hugh replied. "John's letting me reopen the investigations on a couple of them and we've agreed that I should start with this one."

Hugh pulled a large folder from the bag he'd brought with him and opened it carefully. As Bessie watched, he pulled out a few old photographs and laid them on the table in front of her.

"The missing Kelly girls from Lonan," Bessie said as she looked at the top photo. "I haven't thought about them in years."

Hugh nodded. "From what I've learned so far, no one has thought about them in years," he told her. "Please tell me everything you can about the girls in these pictures."

Bessie studied the pretty young girl who was laughing in the top photograph. "Susan Kelly was sixteen when she'd disappeared one night in the spring of nineteen-seventy," Bessie recalled. The photo was black and white, but Bessie could remember the girl's beautiful red hair and sparkling green eyes clearly.

"She was beautiful, was Susan Kelly," Bessie said to Hugh. "The photo doesn't do her justice." She slid Susan's picture to one side and looked at the next snapshot.

"Karen Kelly," she murmured. "She was about a year younger than her cousin, Susan, and had a very different personality."

"Tell me more," Hugh said. "The information in the files is dry and dull. You're already bringing the girls to life for me."

"Susan was a very sweet child and she'd turned into an equally sweet teenager," Bessie said, casting her mind back over the years. "Her father had a market stall here in Laxey in those days and she used to help out once in while. She's the only one I really knew, as they all lived in Lonan."

"Lonan isn't that far away," Hugh pointed out.

"No, but I don't drive," Bessie said. "And even if I did, there isn't much in Lonan. I rarely went there in those days and I only go there now to eat at that gorgeous restaurant that opened last autumn."

"Just tell me whatever you can, then," Hugh suggested.

"As I said, Susan was sweet and sometimes helped out with her father's market stall. Karen was younger, but even at fifteen she had a bit of a reputation. I don't know that I ever met her, but she was talked about quite a lot after she disappeared."

Bessie turned Karen's photo over and looked at the last picture. "And Helen Kelly," she said with a sigh. "She was talked about even more than the other two, even before she disappeared."

"Why?"

"She was the oldest of the three cousins and she had a wild streak in her," Bessie replied. "It was nineteen-seventy and she got a lot of ideas from watching what was going on in America. She wanted to be a flower child and live in a commune or something like that." Bessie shook her head. "It was a long time ago. I can't really remember all of the details."

"What about the man with her in the photo?" Hugh asked.

"Matthew Kelly," Bessie said, grinning at the common surname. "He was another cousin, although once or twice removed or some such thing. I think he was eighteen or nineteen at the time, and he and Helen were a couple or had been. I remember the police held him for questioning for a while. Some people were convinced he had something to do with the disappearances."

"Tell me what happened," Hugh said.

"Surely you've read the files," Bessie replied. "You must know the story better than I do."

"I've read the police reports and the newspaper clippings from the time. Now I want to hear your account of the events," Hugh said.

Bessie nodded and closed her eyes. Then she opened them and took a sip of tea before closing them again. "It was spring, maybe May," she began. "The year was nineteen-seventy, I'm quite sure of that. As I recall, it was a quite ordinary spring before the disappearances, which were quite out of the ordinary, of course."

"Susan disappeared first," Hugh said as he flipped through his notes on the case.

"She did. Her parents didn't report her missing right away, as they assumed she was just staying with friends. As I recall, the papers afterwards said that she often spent nights and weekends at her best friend's house, and at first her parents simply assumed that was what she was doing. It was a different time then, of course. And they were a farming family with six or seven children. Susan was the youngest and she was quite capable of looking after herself."

"How long was it before the parents started to worry?"

Bessie thought for a moment and then shook her head. "It was too long ago," she said. "I can't remember all of the details. I think Susan did spend one night with her friend, whose name I can't quite recall, but the pair had a falling out and Susan left the next morning. Her parents reported her missing a day or two later."

"You're right," Hugh told her. "She stayed with her friend, Margot Lane, on the Friday night, and then, according to Margot, decided to go home. Her parents reported her missing when she didn't come home by Sunday evening."

"And the next weekend Karen disappeared," Bessie said. "She'd been grounded for the weekend because of some transgression or another, but she sneaked out some time on the Friday evening. Her parents didn't realise she was gone until Saturday morning."

"They reported her missing right away, but that didn't seem to make any difference," Hugh said.

"And that same Saturday night Helen vanished as well," Bessie added. "Just about the whole village of Lonan was out searching for Susan and Karen. When it got too dark to continue, everyone gathered at the church, but Helen never reappeared."

"I have pages and pages of notes on the investigation," Hugh said. "But I can sum them all up by saying that no trace of the girls was ever found."

Bessie nodded. "I think everyone assumed they'd turn up eventually, at least at first," she said. "We all hoped that they'd just decided to run away for an adventure and that they'd be back one day."

"And they may have run away," Hugh said. "But it seems odd that none of them ever contacted anyone on the island again."

"There was a lot of speculation when it first happened as to why they might have left," Bessie said. "There may be reasons why they went, and why they never came back."

"What sort of reasons?"

"The most popular idea was that one or more of them had fallen pregnant," Bessie said. "Abortion was legal in England, but not here. It wasn't exactly unheard of for girls to go across to terminate an unwanted pregnancy."

"But then they'd come back," Hugh suggested.

"Usually," Bessie agreed. "Or at least ring home to let everyone know they were okay."

"Tell me about Matthew Kelly, please," Hugh asked.

"He was in and out of trouble quite a bit," Bessie said. "Nothing major, but lots of little things. I seem to remember him stealing cars quite regularly, which is funny as he now works in the garage in Lonan."

"According to the police reports, he was interviewed at least a dozen times about the disappearances," Hugh said. "Some of the transcripts from those interviews are missing, though."

"Is that suspicious?"

Hugh shrugged. "Not really. It's been what, nearly thirty years? Bits of paper go missing as files get moved from station to station and office to office. It will be interesting to hear what he has to say when I talk to him, though."

"You're reopening the missing persons cases?" Bessie asked.

"Yes, and I'll be investigating them as probable homicides," Hugh replied.

CHAPTER 2

*B*essie blinked and then took a sip of tea. "Homicide?" she said after a moment. "That seems, well, excessive."

"Three girls disappeared without a trace. It's been almost thirty years and all three have been declared legally dead by their families. I think looking at the case as a murder investigation is long overdue."

"I didn't realise they'd all been declared dead," Bessie said sadly.

"As I understand it, it had something to do with the death of one of the grandparents and his will. Apparently the rest of the cousins in the family weren't happy that three shares of his estate were essentially being held in limbo for the three missing girls. By having them declared dead, they were able to split the shares amongst themselves."

"Horrible," Bessie said with a shudder. "I suppose I can understand it, especially after all of this time, but it's awfully sad."

"All of our cold cases get an annual review, but it doesn't seem as if anything has really been done with this investigation since the early seventies. The inspector who was originally in charge of the investigation retired a year after the disappearances and no one seems to have taken much interest in the case after that," Hugh told Bessie.

"I don't suppose he's still around to discuss things with?" Bessie asked.

"No, he passed away in the late seventies and his wife died not long after. I have his personal notes on the case, which made for interesting reading, though."

"Personal notes?"

"You know how John always takes lots of notes during an investigation? Well, this Robert Harris seems to have done the same thing. About eighty per cent of what he wrote in his notebooks seems to have made it into his official reports. The rest is mostly lists of other areas to explore and his speculation on what happened. He had a short list of suspects that he thought might have been involved and one person in particular that he seems to have been certain knew more than he was admitting, but it seems Inspector Harris could never prove anything."

"And you're hoping to have better luck?"

"I don't know," Hugh said with a shrug. "Some of the witnesses have passed away. I'm hoping that might be an advantage, that people might be more willing to talk now, maybe tell me things they were unable or unwilling to say all those years ago."

"I won't ask who Inspector Harris suspected, but is that person still alive and on the island?"

"He is," Hugh said with a frown. "And I'm not looking forward to talking with him. From what I've read in the files, he won't be happy about the case being reopened, even if he didn't have anything to do with the disappearances."

"I suspect a lot of people won't want the case reopened," Bessie mused. "Although I'm sure the girls' parents will welcome the chance to maybe finally find out what happened to their daughters."

"I'm meeting with them tomorrow," Hugh said. "Please tell me everything you can about all of them."

Bessie refilled her teacup and added a few more biscuits to her plate before she spoke again. "As I said, they all live in Lonan, so I don't know any of them well. Susan's father, I think his name is James, had that market stall here in Laxey, so I knew him more than anyone else. I don't know that I can tell you anything about him really, though. He was a hard-working farmer. I can't remember ever having a conversation with him, although I'm sure I must have said something sympathetic when his daughter disappeared."

"What about Susan's mother?" Hugh asked.

Bessie shrugged. "Her name was Sarah, if I'm remembering correctly. She helped out on the stall once or twice a year, if none of the children were available." Bessie closed her eyes and thought for a moment. "I remember her being there more after Susan's disappearance. As I said, Susan was the youngest and her brothers and sisters were mostly off starting their own lives by the time Susan vanished."

"What can you remember about her reaction to her daughter's disappearance?"

Bessie shook her head. "Nothing," she admitted. "I'm sure she was upset, but as I said, at least for a while we all assumed the girls would be back. Susan's disappearance was something of a surprise. If Karen or Helen had gone first, I'm not sure anyone would have rung the police."

"You make it sound as if teenaged girls disappeared from the island every day," Hugh remarked.

"Not exactly that," Bessie replied. "But it wasn't unusual for teens of either gender to leave the island, often without much warning. I think it was more common in farming families where the children were expected to work hard on the farm whenever they weren't in school. Some simply grew tired of the hard work and decided to make a fresh start in England or even further afield."

"Without saying anything to their parents?"

"If you knew your parents were counting on you to help get in the harvest or keep the cows milked or whatever, you might decide to slip away without talking to them first," Bessie said. "I can't imagine getting permission to go would be easy, under those sorts of circumstances."

"What about Karen's parents?" Hugh asked.

"They were probably ten to fifteen years younger than Susan's parents," Bessie recalled. "Karen was their oldest and they had another three or four after her, at least one of whom was still in nappies when

Karen disappeared. They also had a farm to run and again, I suspect they thought Karen would be back eventually."

"And Helen's parents?"

"They were divorced, which was unusual. Her father ran the family farm and had primary custody of the two children. Helen had a younger brother named Henry. Their mother, I think she was called Amy, had a little flat in Douglas and worked in one of the shops on the high street. Everyone always blamed Helen's mother for Helen's wild streak, but I don't recall the woman being wild at all. A divorced woman who didn't have custody of her children was an oddity in those days, of course."

"Any idea why she didn't have custody?"

"As I recall, and there was a lot of talk about it at the time, it was a very friendly divorce and both she and Helen's father felt that the children were better off in the family home that was familiar to them. They used to spend weekends in Douglas with her and she came up to Lonan to visit quite often as well, at least before Helen's father remarried."

"Was that before or after Helen's disappearance?" Hugh asked. He was taking notes as Bessie spoke, although he was also somehow steadily working his way through his large pile of biscuits.

"It was about a year before the disappearances," Bessie said. "I can't remember his name, but her name was Brandy, and she was closer to Helen's age than his." Bessie sighed. "Wicked stepmothers belong in fairy tales, not the real world, but I always felt that if Helen learned her wild ways from anyone, it was from Brandy."

"You don't remember any of the parents or other family members behaving oddly at the time?"

Bessie thought for a moment. "I'm sure if any of them had been, people would have talked about it," she said eventually. "I don't recall anything being said about anyone in particular."

She sighed and shook her head. "It's odd, really, but I never thought about the Kelly girls as possible murder victims," Bessie said. "Maybe because up until last year murder was something that happened in books and not in my reality. But you're right. At least one of them should have been in touch by now. I feel sorry for their parents."

"I just hope when I'm done I have some answers for them," Hugh said. "I'd hate to put them through another investigation and not get any results."

"If it was murder, the murderer is going to be very unhappy to hear you're investigating," Bessie said. "Promise me you'll be careful."

"Of course I will," Hugh said. "Anyway, it has to be safer investigating cold cases than dealing with Inspector Lambert."

"Are you two having difficulty working together?"

"You could say that," Hugh replied. "I'm just lucky John Rockwell is around. He keeps everything running smoothly and makes sure I don't have to deal with Inspector Lambert very often."

"I understand you've invited her to the wedding," Bessie said questioningly.

"I'd already invited everyone else at the station," Hugh explained. "I couldn't leave her out, not unless I wanted to make things considerably worse. I doubt she'll come."

Let's hope not, Bessie thought. She bit her tongue before the words could come out of her mouth. There was no point in being unkind. Hugh had enough to worry about.

"I don't think there's anything else I can tell you," she said instead.

"I may come back tomorrow night, after I've met everyone, to talk some more," Hugh replied. "I'll have to be very careful, though, as I'm sure Inspector Lambert will be watching for me to make mistakes. Talking with a civilian about things I was told in interviews is definitely out."

"Maybe I'll have to try to talk to a few of the family members myself," Bessie mused. "I'll just have to find an excuse to do so."

"You know John doesn't like it when you get involved in investigations," Hugh said with a frown.

"Yes, I know," Bessie agreed.

"I'd better get home to Grace," Hugh said, standing up and stretching. "She's only staying with me until the end of the week and then she's moving back home with her parents until the wedding."

"That will be nice for her parents."

"Yeah, and the rest of the family. They're all acting like she's moving a million miles away or something. She's been living up here since September anyway."

Bessie chuckled. "But she's getting married. That will change the whole family dynamic," she said. "All change is difficult, even good change."

Hugh nodded. "Which reminds me, I promised to clear out half of my wardrobe tonight so Grace has somewhere to start putting her things. I'd better get home."

"Do stop back tomorrow if you want to," Bessie told him as she walked him to the door. "Now that you've brought it up, I'm anxious to learn what did happen to the Kelly girls."

Bessie locked up the door behind Hugh and then sat back down at the kitchen table. She nibbled idly on a digestive biscuit while she thought about the case Hugh was reopening. What she really needed was an excuse to spend some time in Lonan.

"Mary? It's Bessie. I was wondering if you'd like to have lunch with me tomorrow at that little place in Lonan that you and George invested in," Bessie said when the phone was answered.

"Oh, Bessie, I'd love to," Mary said enthusiastically. "I'm desperate to get out of the house. Packing doesn't agree with me, even though I'm excited about moving."

Mary Quayle and her husband, George, were in the process of moving from their huge mansion in Douglas to the smaller Thie yn Traie, just down the beach from Bessie's cottage. Thie yn Traie was also a large mansion, with several wings and more bedrooms than Bessie could imagine, but for the Quayles it was downsizing. The house had been sold to them fully furnished, which further complicated the move. That Mary was much more eager to relocate than her husband probably didn't help either.

"We can meet there, if you'd like," Bessie suggested.

"Oh, no. I'll collect you," Mary replied. "I'll see you around half eleven, if that suits you."

Bessie was quick to agree. Having never learned to drive, she was always grateful to her various friends when they offered to collect her or drop her back at home, but she never took them for granted. She had a car service that she used regularly and she was always ready to ring them if need be.

With that sorted, Bessie decided to get ready for bed. She curled up under her duvet with a short story anthology she'd recently acquired. The title promised her some of the best detective fiction of the year, but the first two stories disappointed her. Unable to muster the enthusiasm to read any further, she switched off the light and went to sleep.

The next morning was a typical winter one on the island. The beach was windswept and rainy as Bessie stomped across it in her Wellington boots and waterproofs. She walked as far as the stairs to Thie yn Traie, the large mansion perched on the cliff above the beach, and then turned for home. Seeing lights on in one of the holiday cottages that filled the beach between her cottage and Thie yn Traie beach surprised her. It was only half seven, awfully early for anyone else to be up and about.

Feeling slightly concerned, Bessie walked briskly past the lighted cottage, trying to look as if she hadn't noticed the lights. Once past the cottage, she glanced backwards and felt a rush of relief when she recognised Thomas Shimmin and his wife, Maggie, standing in the building's sitting room. She stopped and waited for them to notice her before waving.

"Oh, Bessie, come in quickly," Maggie called after she'd opened the sliding door at the back of the cottage. "Get out of the rain."

Bessie crossed the beach and stepped inside. "I'm dripping wet," she said apologetically. "I won't blame you if you throw me right back out again."

Maggie laughed. "Don't be silly. The floors in here are designed to get wet regularly. It is a beach cottage, after all, and we can't count on our guests to take special care of things, can we? Anyway, we're redoing the floors in this cottage, so drip all you like."

"How are you, Thomas?" Bessie asked the plump man in his fifties.

He blinked at her, seemingly in surprise, before he spoke. "Oh, I'm fine, thank you, Aunt Bessie," he said.

"We're both well," Maggie, equally plump and of a similar age, said loudly. "We're getting ready to do this cottage over and we'd love your opinion."

Bessie smiled to herself. No doubt Thomas was surprised that she'd spoken to him. He was probably used to Maggie dominating the conversation whenever they were together. "But the cottage looks wonderful," Bessie protested. "Why are you changing it?"

"Themed accommodation is the latest thing," Maggie told her. "If we want to stay competitive, we need to adapt."

"Themed accommodation?" Bessie echoed.

"Look, it's in all the magazines," Maggie said. She showed Bessie a pile of magazines on the cottage's dining table. Bessie glanced at a few and saw that they were all open to glossy photographs of expensive-looking holiday homes.

"See, this one has a beach theme," Maggie said, pointing. "And this one is a jungle theme and the third is inspired by Spanish art and architecture."

"Surely you don't need a beach theme with the beach on your doorstep?" Bessie asked.

Thomas laughed. "That's what I said," he told her.

Maggie frowned. "Of course we won't do a beach theme," she snapped, pushing one of the magazines to the side. "But I think we can charge a premium for this cottage once we've found just the right concept for it."

Bessie nodded uncertainly. "Well, good luck," she said.

"Which do you think is better?" Maggie demanded. "Las Vegas or China?"

"That rather depends on the circumstances," Bessie said. "I'd rather go to China, personally, but I know Las Vegas has quite a few fans."

"I mean which would be a better decorating scheme for the cottage," Maggie explained. "Those are my two favourite ideas."

"Well, um, that is, I," Bessie stopped and took a deep breath. "If I were coming on holiday to the Isle of Man, I wouldn't want my accommodation done up like either of those. I'd much rather it have a Manx feel to it. But maybe I'm not like today's young holi-daymakers."

"I think it's safe to say you are not," Maggie said grumpily.

Bessie fought the urge to laugh. "I'm afraid I'm no help at all," she said cheerfully. "I'll just get out of your way. I am looking forward to seeing what you end up with, though."

"Before you go," Maggie said quickly, "what's this I hear about a new investigation into the Kelly girls' disappearance?"

Bessie sighed. She knew that anything she said would be all over the island within an hour. Maggie was a professional at spreading gossip. "As I understand it, young Hugh has been looking into several what they call cold cases," she said. "I think he's going to try talking to all of the witnesses again in the Kelly disappearances to see if he can learn anything new."

"I'm not sure he should be opening up old wounds," Maggie said. "He might be better off choosing a different case to re-examine."

"Why?" Bessie had to ask.

Maggie shrugged. "Todd Kelly, Susan's older brother, married a friend of mine from school. My friend said that no one is happy about the investigation after all this time."

"Surely Susan's parents want to know what happened to their daughter," Bessie protested.

"I think they've just assumed that she's dead and moved on with their lives," Maggie replied. "The investigation caused a lot of grief within the family. I understand that Susan's father hasn't spoken to Helen's father, his own brother, since the girls vanished. A new inves-tigation could cause new rifts."

"I didn't realise the brothers had a falling out," Bessie said.

"As I understand it, Susan's father blamed Helen for Susan running away. When Helen disappeared too, he accused Helen's father of helping the girls leave the island. Helen's father always denied any involvement, but Susan's father didn't believe him and I've been told the police didn't either."

"Surely if Helen's father knew where the girls were, he would have said something by now," Bessie said. "They've been missing for nearly thirty years."

"I don't know," Maggie said. "I'm trying to find out, though. I'm meeting my friend for tea tomorrow afternoon, the one who's married to Susan's brother. Do you want to come as well?"

Bessie opened her mouth to refuse and then stopped herself. She wanted to do everything she could to help Hugh with the investigation and this might be the only chance she'd have to talk to someone from one of the families involved.

"I'd like that," popped out of her mouth before she'd finished thinking her reply through.

"Good. We're meeting at that little tearoom in Jurby, as that's where they're living now. Why don't I collect you and you can ride up with me? I can't imagine how much a taxi to Jurby would cost."

Bessie agreed somewhat reluctantly. Maggie was right, a taxi would be expensive, but Bessie wasn't sure she wanted to spend too much time trapped in a car with the other woman, either.

"I'll see you at two tomorrow, then," Maggie said happily, as Thomas let Bessie back out into the rain.

"I'll look forward to it," Bessie said politely.

Back at home, Bessie settled in at her desk with a pile of papers she'd recently received from her friend Marjorie Stevens at the Manx Museum. Marjorie was the museum's librarian and archivist, and she and Bessie had been friends ever since Bessie had first taken a Manx language class from her nearly three years earlier. While Bessie had never managed to learn more than a few phrases of the difficult Celtic language, her friendship with Marjorie had flourished. The younger woman had encouraged Bessie to conduct research within the island's collection of wills. Marjorie had recently taught a class in reading old handwriting that had left Bessie happily working on transcribing ever older documents from the museum's extensive archives.

The most recent papers from Marjorie were a collection of seventeenth-century wills from a prominent family. Marjorie had suggested that Bessie might like to try transcribing them to see what she could learn about the family and their lives from the documents.

There was a large historical conference coming up on the island in May, and Marjorie was hoping Bessie might be willing to present a paper on her findings. Bessie wasn't certain that she'd find enough to talk about, and the only way to find out for sure was to start transcribing.

When someone knocked on her door, Bessie was startled. She sat back in her chair and blinked several times. The caller knocked again and Bessie was shocked when she looked at the clock on her way into the kitchen. It was half eleven. She'd spent her entire morning transcribing and had completely lost track of the time.

"I'm so sorry," she greeted Mary. "I got lost in a transcription and didn't realise the time. I'm not exactly ready to go out."

"It's no problem," Mary said easily. "You go and get ready and I'll admire the view."

Bessie gave the woman a grateful hug and then rushed up the stairs to change into something appropriate for lunch with her wealthy and always well-dressed friend. A little black dress and matching shoes were quick and easy. Bessie combed her short bob into place and added a touch of powder and some lipstick to her face. "That will have to do," she told her reflection before she headed back down the stairs.

Mary was standing in the kitchen doing exactly what she'd said she would do, looking out the window at the sea.

"You have the same view from Thie yn Traie, or nearly," Bessie pointed out.

Mary smiled as she turned around. "I know, but it feels different here. Maybe it's just because your cottage is so cosy."

There was certainly nothing cosy about Thie yn Traie, Bessie thought as she pulled on her winter coat. The house had originally been built as a summer home for the very wealthy Pierce family. Every room Bessie had ever been in felt cold and impersonal to her, especially in contrast to Bessie's small and cluttered cottage. Bessie loved her clutter; it was what made her home feel like home.

"Ready to go?" Mary asked as she pulled her own coat back on.

Bessie nodded. Mary had to be in her sixties, but she looked younger. As always, she was impeccably dressed in an outfit that Bessie imagined had cost more than her own entire wardrobe. A gold chain around Mary's neck sparkled with a large diamond pendant.

"I've never seen that necklace before," Bessie remarked as she locked the cottage door behind them.

"Oh, George bought it for me for our wedding anniversary," Mary explained. "I'm sure he paid a fortune for it, but I rarely wear jewellery. I feel as if I must wear it, at least once in a while, for a few months, so he knows I appreciate it."

Bessie smiled even as she wondered about married life. It seemed far too complicated, really. She'd been devastated when Matthew had died, but she wasn't sure she'd have done well with the hard work that marriage seemed to be.

Mary had a huge luxury car and Bessie slid into the leather seat with a small sigh. "I think it's almost as comfortable as my bed," she murmured as Mary slid behind the wheel.

"I do love this car," Mary replied. "It's comfortable and wonderful to drive."

Bessie settled back and watched the world go past as they made their way the short distance to Lonan. The road took them past the entrance to the farm where Susan Kelly had grown up and where her family still farmed. For a moment, Bessie was tempted to ask Mary to drive up to the farmhouse, but she reminded herself sternly that she wasn't meant to be getting involved in the investigation as the car purred along. Exactly why she'd felt the need to visit Lonan today was something Bessie couldn't have answered.

Mary parked in the car park for the café and she and Bessie crossed to the door. There was a short queue waiting for tables, a sure sign that the café was continuing to be a success. When Carol Jenkins, her ponytail bobbing as she hurried back and forth, spotted Mary, she gasped.

"You should have rung and told us you were coming," she said. "Let me find you a table."

"We can wait," Mary said.

Bessie was conscious that everyone in front of them in the queue was now staring at them.

"But you shouldn't have to wait," Carol argued.

Mary held up a hand. "Really, Carol, it's fine," she said firmly. "All these lovely people have been waiting and they aren't any less hungry than we are. We'll wait our turn."

Carol looked as if she wanted to argue further, but she was interrupted by a couple who were leaving. By the time they'd made their way through the door, Carol was clearing their table. Within moments she'd shown the first couple in the queue to the vacant seats.

"I hope you don't mind waiting," Mary said quietly to Bessie. "You know I hate getting special treatment."

"As do I," Bessie replied. "Of course I don't mind waiting."

While they waited, Bessie watched young Carol as she took orders, delivered food and chatted with customers.

"She's a very hard worker," she remarked to Mary.

"She is, yes, and so is Dan," Mary replied, referring to Carol's husband, who was the café's exceptional chef.

"You and George were smart to invest in them."

"We were. And they've repaid most of the investment now. I've insisted that we keep a tiny share in the place, as I love it here."

Bessie nodded. "I can understand that," she said.

With Carol working hard to clear tables as quickly as they became available, it wasn't long before she was showing Bessie and Mary to a table.

"I hope this is okay," she said, glancing at the kitchen door that was quite close to the newly cleared table.

"It's fine," Mary said firmly. "What is Dan doing today?"

Carol smiled. "It's American cuisine day," she said brightly. "Our sampler platter gives you a small portion of meatloaf with mashed potatoes and gravy, a piece of boneless fried chicken, a piece of Cajun seasoned cod, and a pork cutlet in barbeque sauce."

Bessie's stomach growled. "Yes, please," she said quickly. The sampler platters at the café were what the place was known for and she'd never ordered anything else when she'd visited.

"Make it two," Mary said. "Should I ask what's for pudding?"

Carol laughed. "We've kept to the theme," she told them both. "Our pudding, or rather, dessert, sampler has a hot chocolate chip cookie, a tiny apple pie, a mini brownie with ice cream and a lemon meringue tartlet."

"Yes, please, again," Bessie laughed. "Although I might need it packing up for takeaway."

"We can do that," Carol promised. "I'll just get your drinks and your food for now."

"So how are you?" Bessie asked her friend as they settled back with cups of tea.

"I'm doing well," Mary replied. "George has been mostly persuaded that we should move to Laxey and sell the house in Douglas. I think it will be good for Elizabeth to have us under the same roof with her, even if she doesn't agree."

Bessie nodded. "She's all recovered from what happened on New Year's Eve?" she asked.

Mary shrugged. "As far as I can tell," she said. "She won't talk to me about it, so I'm hoping she is."

The food arrived to change the difficult subject and neither woman spoke for some time as they devoured the delicious meal.

"That was incredible," Bessie told Carol as she cleared their plates. "I didn't think I'd finish it, but everything was so good that I couldn't stop myself."

Carol nodded. "I know what you mean," she said with a rueful smile. "It's a good thing we're busy or I'd weigh twenty stone. Did you want your sweet course now or for takeaway?"

Mary and Bessie exchanged glances and Bessie laughed. "I'm stuffed, but I can't resist," she said. "I'll have mine now."

"Oh, thank you," Mary said with a laugh of her own. "I wanted to say that, but I didn't want to seem greedy."

"I have something I need to talk to you about," Carol said, looking nervous. "I'll join you for a moment when I've brought pudding, if that's okay."

"Of course it is," Mary agreed quickly.

Carol was back before Bessie and Mary had more than a moment to speculate on what Carol wanted. She set plates in front of them and then pulled over an extra chair. While Bessie dug into her treats, Carol gave Mary an apologetic look.

"What is the matter?" Mary asked. "I'm sure we can work it out, whatever's wrong."

Carol nodded. "I was hoping you wouldn't mind if I took some time off," she said hesitantly.

"Time off?" Mary echoed. "I mean, of course you can. I assume you'll find someone to take your place?"

"Oh, yes, we're actually interviewing candidates starting today," Carol told her. "The first one is due any minute now. I was going to ring you once we'd found someone, actually, so you'd be happy we have things under control."

"This café is your livelihood," Mary said. "I've absolutely no doubt that you have things under control."

Carol blushed and then looked down at the table. "The thing is, Dan and I are hoping to start our family. He thinks waiting tables is too hard work for me if I were to fall pregnant. He wants me to take some time off to focus on that."

Mary beamed at the girl. "What wonderful news," she said. "And Dan is quite right, you shouldn't be hauling trays full of food around, on your feet all day, if you don't have to be. You've both worked so hard to get the business to this point, where you can afford to hire someone else. I'm proud of you both."

Carol looked relieved as she sat back in her chair. "I was afraid you'd think we weren't still committed to the café," she said.

"If you've another little mouth to feed, I'd expect you to be even more committed," Mary replied.

Carol nodded. Behind her the door to the café opened. Bessie looked up and blinked as she realised who was in the doorway.

"Carol Jenkins?" the woman asked, glancing around the room.

Carol stood up and smiled at the new arrival. "You must be Amy Kelly," she said.

"I am," the woman replied. She crossed the room to where Carol was standing and offered her hand. Her eyes met Bessie's a moment later.

"If you'd like to come with me," Carol said, "we can talk in the kitchen."

"That's fine," Amy agreed. "But after we've talked, I'd like a word with Bessie, please."

Bessie flushed as Carol and Mary both looked at her in surprise.

"I'll wait here for you," she said to Amy.

"Thank you," Amy said.

Carol looked from Bessie to Amy and back again and then shrugged. She turned and led the other woman out of the room.

CHAPTER 3

"You don't have to stay," Bessie said to Mary as the other two women disappeared into the kitchen. "I don't know how long Amy will be and I've no idea what she wants to talk to me about, so I don't know how long that will take."

Mary smiled. "I'll stay for a little while," she said. "I can sip my tea and enjoy my extravagant puddings before I worry about anything else."

Bessie dug into her apple pie and took a bite. "This is so good," she said. "The mix of sweet and cinnamon with tart apples is perfect."

"It is good, but I like the brownie better," Mary replied. "I prefer chocolate every time, I think."

Bessie laughed and tried her brownie. "Also an excellent choice," she agreed. "But I can kid myself that I'm eating fruit with the apple pie."

"There is that," Mary conceded. "Which reminds me, or rather it doesn't, but I've just remembered there was something else I wanted to talk to you about."

"I hope everything is okay," Bessie said quickly.

"Oh, everything is fine," Mary assured her. "But George and I have been invited to your young friend Hugh's upcoming nuptials. I think

Hugh may have felt he had to ask us, as we were there to help cele-brate the engagement. Anyway, George and I want to do something special for the pair of them, but I don't feel I know them well enough to get it right. I was hoping you might have some ideas for me."

Bessie nodded and sipped her tea while she thought. An idea had been turning around in her head since yesterday but she wasn't completely convinced that it was a good one. She nibbled her way through her chocolate chip cookie while she thought. Mary worked on her own selection of treats while she waited for Bessie's reply.

"I've been thinking," Bessie said eventually, "but I'm not sure if I've had a good idea or a bad one."

"I'm intrigued," Mary replied.

Bessie laughed. "I don't know that it's intriguing, but I was talking to Hugh last night and he was saying that he was sorry he can't take Grace away on a proper honeymoon. They're booked into the Seaview for a week, but that isn't exactly the most romantic of getaways."

"No, Ramsey wouldn't be on my short list for a honeymoon," Mary agreed quickly.

"I was thinking that I'd love to send them to Paris for a week," Bessie continued. "I'm sure flights won't be too dear, but then there is a hotel and meals and drinks and sightseeing and souvenirs. I wouldn't want to send them to Paris only for them to not be able to properly enjoy themselves."

"It's perfect," Mary said. "If you can manage the flights, I'm sure George and I can find them a nice little hotel. Actually, a few years ago we stayed in the perfect place. It's centrally located and small enough to be cosy but large enough to allow for some privacy. They had a gorgeous honeymoon suite with a huge en-suite with a jetted tub. It will be ideal."

"It sounds wonderful," Bessie said. "Do you think we should talk to Hugh about it or try to surprise them both?"

Mary thought for a moment. "I'd rather surprise them both at the wedding, if we can," she said eventually. "It will be so much more fun that way."

Bessie nodded. "It just seems like a huge undertaking, planning all of it without letting either of them know."

"Do you know Hugh's parents? Or Grace's?"

"I know Hugh's, at least in passing," Bessie said. "I'm afraid I don't know Grace's family at all."

"Then it's time to meet them," Mary said. "They live in Douglas, don't they? Maybe I should talk to them while you deal with Hugh's side of things?"

"Are you sure?" Bessie asked. "I don't want to add more work to your very busy life."

"This will be a distinct pleasure," Mary assured her. "I don't know Hugh all that well, but I like him a lot. He's a fine young man and Grace is a lovely young woman. As my Elizabeth isn't showing any signs of settling down soon, it will be nice to plan something exciting for a young couple in love."

"I'll ring Hugh's mum later today or tomorrow and see if she wants to meet for tea," Bessie said. "The first thing we need to do is make sure they both have passports."

Mary laughed. "That would rather nip things in the bud, wouldn't it?" she agreed. "If we pay for the hotel and you pay for the flights, do you think some of their other friends would be willing to contribute towards meals?"

Bessie nodded. "I'm sure Doona will, and maybe she can get everyone at the station to help out. I don't want anyone to feel as if they have to contribute, though, if they already had a gift in mind."

"But Hugh's had his own place for a while now, surely he has all the household things he needs," Mary pointed out. "I know I didn't have any idea what to get them."

"Both sets of parents are helping with the deposit on their first house," Bessie said. "That's why Hugh and Grace are paying for the wedding themselves."

Bessie scraped the last of her pudding up with her spoon. After she'd washed it down with the last of her tea, she sighed deeply. "I ate too much, but it was totally worth it," she told Mary.

"Snap," Mary laughed.

Carol was there to clear the dishes only a moment later. "Amy is talking to Dan now, so I thought I'd better get back out here," she said as she gathered up plates and cups. "Would you like more tea or anything else?"

"No, I think we're both quite full up," Mary said. "I hope you don't mind if we wait here until Amy is ready to talk to Bessie."

"Of course not," Carol replied. "It's quiet now; you're welcome to stay as long as you like."

Bessie and Mary chatted a bit more about their plans for Hugh and Grace while they waited. It wasn't long before Amy walked out of the kitchen, looking happy. Carol met her as she reached Bessie and Mary.

"Dan has asked me to work a few days as a trial," she told Carol. "I'll start with dinner tomorrow night, if that's okay with you."

"It's more than okay with me," Carol said. "Lunch was busy, but dinner can get crazy, even on a Wednesday. I'll be happy to have the help, but you need to work out whether you could handle the job on your own."

Amy nodded. "That's exactly what Dan said," she replied. "But I love a challenge."

"Good," Carol laughed.

"If I could just have a few minutes of your time," Amy said to Bessie. "I hope it won't take long."

"I'm going to go over the road to fill up with petrol," Mary said. "I'll check back in here before I'm ready to head back to see if you've finished."

Bessie nodded. "But don't feel as if you need to wait for me," she told Mary. "I can get a taxi. It won't be a problem."

Mary nodded and then made her way out of the café, waving to Carol as she went. "I'll settle the bill when I get back," she called.

Carol waved and shook her head. "It's on us," she said.

"It isn't," Mary retorted, disappearing though the door before Carol could reply.

"Have a seat," Bessie told Amy, gesturing to the chair that Mary had just vacated. "Would you like tea or coffee or something?"

"No, I'm fine," Amy said. She took a deep breath and then looked down at the table.

"What can I do for you?" Bessie asked quietly.

"I know you're friends with Inspector John Rockwell and Constable Hugh Watterson," Amy said after an awkward pause. "Everyone knows that you've been involved in some murder investigations with them."

"I have," Bessie replied, wondering where the conversation was going.

Amy took another breath and then looked up at Bessie. There were tears in her eyes. "Please, ask them not to reopen the investigation into Helen's disappearance," she said.

Bessie hoped her face didn't show how surprised she was. She sat back in her chair and studied the other woman. Amy had been a pretty young woman, but she'd aged since Bessie had last seen her. Bessie did the math in her head and realised with surprise that Amy had to be over sixty now. In spite of the lines that stress had added to her face, she didn't look that old to Bessie.

"Why?" she asked softly.

"For the first month after she disappeared I was convinced that she was going to ring me every day," Amy replied, tears beginning to slowly flow down her face. "I kept waiting for the phone to ring, for the door to burst open, for something. The police kept asking questions, acting like they thought something terrible had happened, but I didn't, I couldn't believe it."

She stopped and Bessie quickly dug in her handbag for some tissues. Amy took one silently and wiped her eyes.

"I'm sorry," Bessie said, feeling ineffectual.

"After a while, the police stopped asking questions," Amy continued. "Everything went back to normal, except that Helen wasn't there anymore. Because she had lived with her father mostly, before the disappearance, I could simply tell myself that she was with him and forget, at least some of the time. Forgetting was the only way I could function."

Bessie had never felt like she'd missed out on anything by not having children, but now she felt oddly grateful that she'd never had to deal with the sort of grief she could see in Amy's eyes. "I wish I knew what to say," she said. "I'm so sorry."

Amy nodded. "Thank you. Some people have never even said that. Harold and I were divorced and I let him have custody. Some people thought that allowing him custody meant that I didn't love my children. Giving up custody was the hardest thing I've ever done, but I did what was best for Helen and Henry. They deserved continuity and stability and there was no way I could offer them that, not under the circumstances I found myself in. But I never stopped loving my children. I saw them as often as I could and was as much a part of their lives as I could be."

Bessie patted the woman's arm. "But surely you want to know what happened to Helen?" she asked.

"I really don't," Amy replied emphatically. "It's been nearly thirty years. If she were able to, she would have contacted someone by now. They say not knowing is harder, but I don't want to know. She must be, that is, she can't still be…" Amy trailed off and looked down at her hands. They were tightly clenched.

"I can't stop John and Hugh from reopening the file," Bessie said.

Amy nodded. "I didn't really think you could," she said flatly. "Every night, before I go to bed, I ring Henry to check on him and my grandchildren. Henry indulges me because of, well, everything. In my head, I also ring Helen. I've given her a whole life over the last twenty-nine years. She got married young, but it didn't work out. She was a single mum for a few years before she met the perfect man. They have two kids together and he adopted her son from her first marriage as well. The kids are getting older, of course. The oldest, Jack, is getting married himself soon." Amy stopped and shook her head.

"I'm sorry," she said, swallowing hard. "It's all in my head, but it feels real to me. Maybe I'm crazy, but it's kept me going over all these years. If we find out what happened to Helen, what really happened, I'll lose them all, Jack and the other kids and Helen's wonderful husband and…" She stopped and wiped furiously at the tears that were flowing rapidly.

"I don't think you're crazy," Bessie told her. "I think you've done what you needed to do to survive an impossible situation. Maybe you should talk to your doctor, though, make sure he's aware that the case has been reopened and that you could be in for a shock."

"I have a counselor that I see regularly," Amy replied. "I made an emergency appointment with her after Constable Watterson rang me to make an appointment for an interview."

"When do you talk to Hugh?"

"This afternoon at four," Amy replied, glancing at her watch. "I was going to ring you after my job interview, so running into you was serendipitous."

"I wish there was something I could do to help."

"Talking about it has helped," Amy told her. "I haven't really talked about Helen in, oh, maybe twenty years. Henry gets upset when I bring her up and I don't speak to Harold and Brandy any longer. I moved back up north about fifteen years ago, but I live in Ramsey and most of my friends there don't even know I have a daughter."

"Maybe talking to Hugh will help as well," Bessie suggested.

"As I don't have a choice, I will have to hope so," Amy replied with a wry smile. "I wonder, that is, I keep wondering if he'll find anything after all this time."

"He's hoping people might be more willing to talk after so many years," Bessie told her. "Maybe they'll remember something that they didn't think mattered all those years ago, something like that."

"The whole thing caused so much trouble within the family. Some people haven't spoken to one another since it happened. I really hate to see it all dragged up again for that reason as well."

"I'm surprised it hasn't been reopened in the past," Bessie said. "It seems like something the police would revisit occasionally."

"I'm pretty sure Donald Clucas did his best to keep the file gathering dust," Amy said.

"Donald Clucas?" Bessie asked. "He owned a great deal of property in Laxey, didn't he? Why was he involved?"

"He owned enough of Laxey to be able to influence the police," Amy said. "And his son was the prime suspect."

Bessie sat back in her seat, trying to remember. "Jonas?" she asked after a moment. "It's all coming back to me now."

Amy nodded. "Jonas was spending a lot of time with Karen Kelly before she disappeared. As I understand it, the police inspector in charge of the investigation thought Jonas knew something, but he could never prove anything."

"He was quite a bit older than Karen, wasn't he?"

"He was twenty-something and Karen was fifteen," Amy said. "That didn't raise as many eyebrows in those days as it would today, of course."

"What's Jonas doing these days?" Bessie asked.

"He just sits around living off the money he inherited," Amy said scornfully. "Donald tried to get him interested in the family business, but Jonas wasn't having it. He drank and partied his way through the seventies and then married some really young model-slash-actress that he'd met in London. Eventually Donald cut him off, and he moved back to the island with his wife and a couple of kids. His mother, Laura, supported him for ages behind Donald's back, and then when Donald died about five years ago, Jonas inherited a fortune."

"I was always surprised his father didn't write him out of the will, but Donald had some very ill health at the end, didn't he? I remember someone telling me that Donald and Jonas reconciled just before Donald passed," Bessie said, the conversation stirring up many old memories.

"Jonas was an only child. I believe Donald always hoped that Jonas would change and he was able to convince himself at the end that he had."

"But he hasn't?"

Amy laughed. "You can say that again," she said. "He spends as much time as he can in London, without the wife and kids, of course, but as I understand it, the money is starting to run out so he's been back here for the last few months."

"Do they still have the family home in Laxey?" Bessie asked, trying to remember what she'd heard about the family lately. She had a feeling they'd moved away, but as she didn't know any of them personally, she didn't pay much attention to any stories she'd heard about them.

"Laura sold that when Donald passed. She moved into a retirement community in Douglas and Jonas bought himself a small mansion in Andreas for some reason. He has a flat in Douglas as well, and I gather that's where he prefers to spend his time."

"Does he still own property all over Laxey?"

Amy shook her head. "His father had a few financial setbacks and started selling off pieces of his property years ago. Don't get me wrong, he still left a substantial amount to Jonas, but I gather Jonas is burning through that quite quickly. I don't think Jonas ever understood that in order to spend money, someone has to make some first. He's lucky at the moment, of course, as property prices are soaring. He'll be doing quite well whenever he sells off a house or business now."

"Jonas couldn't have been the only suspect," Bessie suggested.

"Oh, no, his cousin Peter Clucas was also questioned extensively, but Peter was a good kid. He and Helen had some of the same friends, but he did his best to avoid the wildest of the antics. And Matthew Kelly was questioned more than anyone else, but I never believed the people that thought he knew something."

"He and Helen were a couple, weren't they?" Bessie asked.

"I don't think it was anything that serious," Amy replied. "They were spending time together, but I think they were just having fun. Helen was seventeen and she was hoping to persuade her father to send her to university. She wanted to be a nurse. I don't think a serious boyfriend fit into her plans."

"I understand Helen's father had a falling-out with his brother, Susan's father, over the disappearances," Bessie said.

Amy nodded. "Susan's father, James, always thought Harold knew more than he'd admit. He thought that, since Helen was the oldest, she must have planned everything. I'm pretty sure he thought Helen was pregnant and went across to take care of it."

"If that was the case, where do Susan and Karen fit in?"

"James accused Helen of dragging them along because she didn't want to be on her own in Liverpool or wherever, but that never made sense to me. The three girls got along okay, but they weren't particularly good friends or anything. Helen had a couple of friends at school that would have been much more likely to have gone with her if she'd needed to travel across for any reason."

"So what do you think happened?" Bessie had to ask.

Amy shrugged. "I've asked myself that a million times or more," she said. "Late at night, when I'm alone, I imagine that something awful happened to them all. Like I said, mostly I try to convince myself that my little fantasy world is real. In that world, she left because her father wouldn't let her go to nursing school, even though Harold has always said they never discussed the matter."

"Do you believe him?"

"Not entirely," Amy replied. "Helen told me she'd talked with both Harold and Brandy about nursing school and I've no reason to think she would have lied. As far as I know, though, no decisions had been made before she went away. I've never got a chance to ask Brandy about the matter. As I said earlier, we don't speak any longer."

"Do you mind if I ask why?"

"There isn't really a reason that I could give you. Harold and I had to get along while the children were young, for their benefit, but once Henry finished school, we simply never saw one another. I can only speak for myself, but I've no interest in seeing them, either. Henry always invites us to separate events when the grandchildren have birthdays and the like. I have his family for Christmas Eve and they spend Christmas with Harold and also with Henry's wife's family. It was never a conscious decision to stop speaking to them, it just sort of happened."

Bessie nodded. "I feel as if I'm prying," she admitted. "And I shouldn't be. None of this is any of my business."

"You're easy to talk to," Amy replied. "And as I said, it actually feels good to talk about Helen. Maybe I should do more of that."

"Well, you have Hugh to talk to later," Bessie pointed out.

Amy laughed. "You're right, and now I'm not dreading it nearly as much." She glanced at her watch. "But I'd better get home and get myself ready for the interview. Thank you so much for your time."

"I'm always happy to talk, any time," Bessie assured her. "Feel free to ring me or even come to my cottage."

Amy grinned. "I haven't been to Treoghe Bwaane in years," she said. "But I was there once. Do you remember?"

Bessie thought for a moment. "It was when Helen and Henry were quite small," she recalled. "You'd brought them to Laxey Beach for the day and Henry managed to fall off some rocks and bang his head."

"And you provided ice for the swelling and tea for my shattered nerves," Amy continued the story. "That was when things were starting to fall apart between Harold and me."

"You never said a word about that when you were with me," Bessie said.

"I never said a word to anyone," Amy replied. "It wasn't something I could ever talk about. Finding out that my husband had never loved me was a huge and difficult shock, and it was rather embarrassing, as well."

"Again, I'm sorry," Bessie said.

This time Amy laughed. "Oh, it was so long ago now that it really doesn't hurt anymore," she said. "In hindsight, I probably should have tried harder to make things work, anyway. But once I'd learned that Harold had been deeply in love with another woman and had only married me because he'd lost her, I was too proud to stay in the marriage. I've learned a lot about love and loss since then, though. If I had it to do over again, I think I would have stuck with it for a while longer."

"Isn't hindsight an awful thing?" Bessie asked.

"Of course, it's all tangled up with what happened with Helen, as well. I can't help but feel that she'd never have disappeared if I'd been there for her, even though that probably isn't true."

"It isn't true," Bessie said firmly. "Maybe Hugh's investigation can help prove that to you."

Amy nodded and then rose to her feet. "I really must dash. Thank you again, for everything."

Bessie nodded and then watched as the other woman made her way out of the café. Hugh was certainly stirring things up by reopening this case. Bessie could only hope he'd find the answers he was looking for. As the door shut behind Amy, Bessie noticed Mary sitting at a table with Dan and Carol. She got up and crossed the now nearly empty café to them.

"Mary, you should have gone home ages ago," she greeted her friend.

"We started talking and I lost all track of time," Mary said.

Dan stood up. "That must be my cue to get back to work," he said with a laugh. He gave his wife a quick hug and then headed back towards the kitchen, stopping to clear a few tables along the way.

"And I'd better get the dining room ready for the dinner crowd," Carol said. She stood up as well and when Mary rose, gave the older woman a tight hug. "Thank you, as always, for everything," she whispered to Mary.

"Thank you for a lovely lunch," Bessie told the woman. "I would have thanked your very talented husband, but he rushed away too quickly."

"I'll pass it along for you," Carol promised.

Bessie followed Mary outside, where the wind had died down slightly but a steady rain was falling.

"Nothing like winter on the Isle of Man," Mary said cheerfully as she started the car's engine. It only took a moment or two for the car to warm up to a comfortable temperature and Bessie was happy to sit back and enjoy the ride.

"Do you have time for a cuppa?" Bessie asked her friend as Mary pulled into the small parking area near Bessie's cottage.

"I shouldn't," Mary replied. "I promised Elizabeth I'd come over to Thie yn Traie to see what the new designer we've hired has planned for her suite. She's already texted me four times to remind me."

"I'll let you go, then. I'll ring you when I've spoken to Hugh's mum."

"And I'll ring you after I've spoken to Grace's parents," Mary replied. "I'm really excited about our surprise."

"Me, too," Bessie agreed. "I just hope it all works out," she added under her breath as she made her way to her cottage's front door. The problem with big surprises was that they could go wrong in so many ways.

There was no answer at Hugh's parents' house, and they didn't seem to have an answering machine. Bessie let it ring a dozen times and then disconnected. She'd have to try again later. After her large lunch, she was happy to settle for a simple bowl of soup for dinner. She was just curling up with a book when her phone rang. Although she thought about ignoring it, the sound reminded her that she still needed to talk to Hugh's mum, so she answered it instead.

"Bessie, I'm not going to be able to make it tonight," Hugh told her. "The interviews have taken all day and I still have to write everything up for John. There are a lot of things I'd like to ask you about, though, if you're free tomorrow night?"

"I am," Bessie replied. "Will you be coming after work? Do you want me to cook dinner?"

"I thought I'd try to get there around six and maybe try to persuade John and Doona to join me," he said. "I'll bring Chinese, if that's okay with you."

"It's fine; in fact, it sounds wonderful," Bessie told him, suddenly hungry again. "I'll make something nice for pudding."

"Great, I'll see you then," Hugh said before disconnecting.

Since she had the phone in her hand, she went ahead and rang Hugh's mum again.

"Ah, it's Elizabeth Cubbon," she said when the woman answered. "I was hoping we could meet for tea or something. I'd like to talk to you about the wedding."

"The wedding? That's Hugh's affair, not ours," the woman replied. "We'd love to be able to help more, but we simply can't."

"I understand that, but I'd still like to speak to you, if I could."

"No reason why not. Why don't you come for lunch tomorrow? My husband is out all morning at some thing or another. Come around half eleven and I'll make us some soup and sandwiches or some such thing."

"That sounds good," Bessie agreed. "But I do have to be home before two."

"Oh, aye, my other half will be home by that time anyway. You'll be wanting to get away before he gets here."

Bessie laughed, but she knew Hugh's mother was only half-teasing. Hugh hadn't had the happiest of childhoods, although Bessie knew his parents had done their best. Neither of them had been pleased with his plans to join the police, which hadn't helped. Still, Hugh's mother was the right person to consult before Bessie and Mary started working in earnest on their surprise.

Bessie read for a few hours, but she had a busy day planned for Wednesday, so she forced herself to get to bed at a decent time, even before she'd found out who the killer was in her mystery novel.

"He or she will still be there tomorrow," she reminded herself as she washed her face. "That's the good thing about fictional criminals; they stay in place, right on the page."

CHAPTER 4

*B*essie kept her walk short the next morning. It was cold, but clear and with no rain in the forecast, she decided that she'd walk to her luncheon date. It would probably take twenty minutes, but walking sounded better than getting a taxi. She spent her morning working on her transcriptions, this time setting an alarm to remind her that she had other things to do. It was just as well that she had, as she was completely lost in her work again when the alarm sounded.

"Oh, bother," she said loudly. She was just getting to the good part of the will she was working on. But it too would wait patiently for her to return, she reminded herself as she changed her clothes and combed her hair. Hugh and Grace were getting married in less than a fortnight.

Walking to the small semi-detached property where Hugh had grown up took almost exactly the twenty minutes Bessie had predicted. Hugh's mum answered Bessie's knock almost instantly.

"I was just looking out to see if you were coming," she said, blushing brightly. "And there you were, on my doorstep."

Bessie laughed. "Perfect timing," she said lightly.

Hugh's mother nodded and then stepped backwards to let Bessie into the house. "It isn't as tidy as it should be," she said apologetically. "I had good intentions, but I never really found the time."

"I'm sure it's fine," Bessie said, waving a hand.

"Yes, well, I keep the kitchen clean, anyway; let's go in there," the woman suggested.

Bessie followed her down the short corridor to the small kitchen at the back of the house. As she walked, Bessie thought that it was easy to see why Hugh looked as young as he did. His mother didn't look a day over forty, although Bessie knew she was at least a decade older. As Bessie joined the woman at the table that just about filled all of the floor space the room provided, she realised with a start that she couldn't remember the woman's first name.

"Oh, look at me, sitting down like I'm the guest," the woman laughed, jumping up. "I just made sandwiches and the like and I have some soup as well."

Within minutes the woman had filled the limited counter space with plate after plate of dainty-looking sandwiches, scones and biscuits. Bessie's mouth was watering as she considered the various options.

"Do try one of everything," Hugh's mother urged. "Or, better yet, two or three of everything. I've no idea what I'll do with the surplus. Hugh's father won't eat fussy things like this."

Bessie loaded up a plate with as much as she thought she could manage and then sat back down at the table. "It all looks wonderful," she said as the other woman joined her.

"I do hope so. Hugh always talked about your cooking and baking and I always felt like I simply couldn't compete." As soon as the words were out of her mouth, the woman turned fuchsia. "I didn't mean that quite like it sounded," she muttered as she jumped back up as the kettle boiled.

"I never meant to cause any trouble between you and Hugh," Bessie said apologetically.

"Oh, the trouble was never between me and Hugh," the woman replied, waving a hand. "His father isn't the easiest man to live with. I should know, if anyone should. Anyway, I was always glad he had your cottage to head to whenever he and his father had a disagreement. I'm pretty sure Hugh would have been in a great deal more trouble if he didn't have you to look after him."

"He's a very good person and you and your husband should be very proud of him," Bessie said firmly.

"We are. Edward is especially proud of him now that he's getting married. We both think Grace is delightful."

"She's lovely, and I think she's very good for Hugh," Bessie agreed.

"Obviously, Edward and I wish we could help more with the wedding and everything, but, well, we talked to Hugh and Grace and they felt they'd rather have some money towards the deposit on their first home than have a big fancy wedding."

"Which is very sensible," Bessie said. "With the way house prices are rising every day, they should get on the property ladder as quickly as they can."

"But what did you want to talk to me about?"

Bessie swallowed a bite of sandwich and washed it down with tea. "Everything is excellent," she told the woman. "I must tell you that before I forget."

"Oh, it's nothing much," the other woman demurred. "But thank you."

"I wanted to talk to you about the honeymoon," Bessie said.

"Yes, I was disappointed that they're only going to get to Ramsey, but like Edward said, we only went down to Douglas for a weekend for our honeymoon and it didn't do us any harm."

Bessie smiled. "I'm sure it didn't, but I'd really like to see Hugh and Grace have a special honeymoon, and so would my friend, Mary Quayle. We were wondering what you and Edward might think if we surprised them with a week in Paris as a wedding present?"

"A week in Paris?" the woman asked. "It sounds expensive to me."

"I thought I would pay for the flights and Mary offered to pay for the hotel," Bessie explained. "We're hoping maybe a few of their other friends might be willing to contribute towards the cost of meals and the rest."

The woman sat back in her chair, a bemused look on her face. "What an idea," she said.

"But is it a good idea?" Bessie asked.

"It's a lovely idea. It would really mean a lot to both Hugh and Grace if they could have a really romantic break. I'm not sure why you're asking me about it, though. Unfortunately, we can't contribute."

"Oh, no, that wasn't it at all," Bessie said quickly. "Mary and I both felt that we needed to talk the idea through with both families before we started making bookings, that's all. We're hoping to surprise Hugh and Grace, you see. Mary is going to talk to Grace's parents, and the first thing we need to know is whether they both have valid passports or not."

"I hadn't even thought about that," the woman said. "But yes, Hugh has a passport. It's here, actually, with his other important papers. He got it about two years ago when he went on a holiday with some mates to Italy."

Bessie nodded. "That's good to know. They're getting married on a Sunday, so it's probably best if they don't fly out until Monday morning. I'd hate for them to have to leave the party early."

"That sounds about right," the other woman agreed. "And now I'm getting quite excited for them. I've never been abroad."

"I'm excited for them as well," Bessie admitted. "I've never been to Paris, although I've always wanted to go."

"Maybe one day," the other woman sighed.

"You should have Edward take you for your next wedding anniversary," Bessie suggested.

"Right now we're putting away everything we can to help Hugh and Grace," she replied. "Maybe once they're settled, we can talk about it."

With that conversation out of the way, the pair settled into a comfortable chat about nothing much. Bessie was quite full when she left the cozy home at half one.

"We should do this again one day," Hugh's mother said on the doorstep.

"Next time at my cottage," Bessie countered.

"I'd like that," the woman replied.

Bessie was halfway home before the woman's name suddenly popped into her head. "Harriet," she said aloud, startling a man who was walking his dog. Bessie thought about trying to explain, but decided she couldn't be bothered. Let the man think she was prone to randomly shouting people's names in the street. It simply didn't matter.

Back at home, she had only a few minutes to freshen up before Maggie was due. She combed windblown tangles out of her hair and touched up the little bit of makeup she'd applied earlier before heading back to the kitchen to watch for Maggie's car. It wasn't long before a shiny new sporty-looking car pulled into the parking area outside. It wasn't at all the sort of car Bessie would have expected Maggie to drive, but the woman climbed out of the driver's seat and headed for Bessie's cottage.

Bessie grabbed her handbag and hurried to meet her friend. "What a lovely car," she said as she greeted Maggie.

"It was my treat to myself after the long summer season," Maggie replied. "All that running around, fetching groceries and whatnot for our guests, was exhausting. I told Thomas that once it was all over I was going to buy myself a totally impractical car just for fun."

"Well, you've certainly done that," Bessie laughed as she tried to work out how best to get inside the vehicle. It seemed much lower to the ground than what Bessie was used to.

"Getting in and out isn't easy," Maggie admitted. "But it is really fun to drive."

Bessie finally turned around and plopped herself backwards into the car. With her bum on the seat, she was able to swing her legs in as well. "You may have to help me out," she told Maggie.

"It isn't too bad, really," Maggie replied. "As I said, it's really fun to drive. Of course, once summer gets here and I'm back to running endless errands for our guests, I'll have to go back to my old car. That one isn't fun to drive, but it has a huge boot."

"Does this one even have a boot?" Bessie asked, trying to look behind her.

"A tiny one that is totally useless," Maggie said cheerfully. "Here we go."

The engine roared to life and Bessie felt like she wanted to grab something to hold onto as the car sprang forward. Within minutes she was able to relax, though, as the windy roads of Laxey didn't really allow Maggie to drive very fast.

"I hope you don't mind the car," Maggie said after a while. "It's such a long boring drive to Jurby, I thought it would be just what we needed."

"Of course I don't mind," Bessie replied politely. "I'm just happy for you and Thomas that the cottages are doing so well."

"They're doing much better than I ever expected," Maggie said frankly. "I thought Thomas was crazy when he started talking about buying a property on the beach and building holiday cottages, but he was right, there is a real demand for such things."

"I didn't realise they'd be as popular as they are," Bessie admitted. "But you're full to capacity for months on end."

"I hope our guests don't cause you too much bother," Maggie said, glancing sideways at Bessie. "I'm sure your cottage was much more peaceful before we built the holiday homes."

"It was more peaceful, but awfully quiet," Bessie replied. "Although a few of your guests can get a bit noisy, for the most part I don't mind them at all. Anyway, they're only here for a few months of the year. This time of year I have the beach all to myself."

"I went to school with Claire," Maggie changed the subject. "I'm not sure where she met Todd, but they've been married over twenty years now."

"So they got married after Susan's disappearance?"

"Did they?" Maggie asked. "When did Susan disappear?"

"Nineteen-seventy. That's nearly thirty years ago."

"I didn't think it was that long ago," Maggie said with a sigh. "Time moves much too quickly, doesn't it?"

"It truly does."

"Maybe Claire and Todd have been married longer than I thought," Maggie said thoughtfully. "I'll have to ask her."

"She does know I'm coming along, doesn't she?" Bessie asked.

"Oh, I don't know if I mentioned it or not," Maggie replied. "Oh, look at that bird. Do you know what it is?"

Bessie looked in the direction Maggie was pointing but didn't see anything aside from fields. She bit back a sigh. So Claire didn't know Bessie was coming with Maggie. Bessie could only hope things wouldn't be awkward or uncomfortable.

"I hope you don't mind the long drive to Jurby," Maggie said after a few minutes. "Claire doesn't like to go too far from home during school hours, just in case one of the children needs her."

"How many children do they have?"

"Three, but they had them quite late, really. The oldest is eighteen or nineteen and on his own now, but their middle one is only sixteen and the baby is twelve. The youngest has some medical issues that keep Claire busy and make her reluctant to leave Jurby."

"How nice for her to have a chance to have tea with her old friend, then. Do you two get together often?"

Maggie shook her head. "We're both busy. But I thought, with the case being reopened, she might need someone to talk to, so I rang her up."

Bessie nodded. Maggie was the opposite of a fair-weather friend. She'd be the first to ring whenever anything went wrong, eager to gather as much gossip as she could and offer her own firm opinions on what should be done next. Bessie just hoped that Claire knew what she was letting herself in for.

The sporty car seemed to make the journey in record time. Maggie carefully parked it across two spaces in the mostly empty car park. "Can't be too careful with my baby," she explained as she shut off the engine. "I'd be furious if anything happened to it."

Bessie pushed open her door and took a deep breath, ready for the job of getting herself out of the car. Maggie was right, though. It wasn't as difficult as Bessie had feared it might be.

As the pair approached the small café, Bessie looked around. It had been years since Bessie had been here and nothing seemed to have changed much. The café looked as if it needed a fresh coat of paint and its windows needed washing. As Maggie pushed the door open, even the small bell sounded tired. There was a long counter across the back of the room, with a dozen tables scattered around the floor.

The woman behind the counter looked up from a magazine and sighed. "Sit anywhere," she called to them.

Maggie and Bessie exchanged glances and then Bessie followed her friend as Maggie chose a table in the corner. There was a man sitting at the far end of the counter sipping a cup of tea and reading a book. He was the only other customer in the place.

"Menus are on the table," the woman at the counter called. "I'll be over in a minute."

"We're waiting for a friend, so there's no rush," Maggie shouted back.

Bessie picked up the slightly sticky menu and read down the short list of offerings. "I haven't been here in many years," she said quietly. "What do you suggest?"

Maggie laughed loudly. "I think the tea should be safe enough," she hissed to Bessie. "I'm not sure I'm brave enough to try anything else."

The café's door swung open and Bessie watched as a middle-aged woman strode into the room. She glanced around and then crossed to them.

"Maggie? I'm not sure I would have recognised you if there was a crowd in here," the woman said in a low voice.

Maggie stood up and greeted the new arrival with a hug. Bessie noticed that the woman was too thin. She wore thick glasses and her long hair hung down her back in a thick plait. Bessie knew she was in her mid-fifties, but the woman looked older as she awkwardly returned the hug.

"Bessie Cubbon, this is my friend, Claire Kelly. Claire, I was telling Bessie yesterday that I was meeting you here for tea, and she mentioned how she'd been wanting to try the café up here for a long time. I hope you don't mind my bringing her along."

Claire looked at Bessie for a moment and then shrugged. "Makes no difference to me," she said. "You'll be glad you came if you try the Victoria sponge," she added as she dropped into the chair opposite Bessie's.

"Victoria sponge?" Bessie asked, glancing back down at her menu.

"It's the only thing here worth eating," Claire whispered. "They buy everything else from some UK supplier, but Marta makes the Victoria sponge herself. It's really good."

"What can I get you all, then?" the woman from behind the counter had crossed the room and now she stood next to the their table, a notebook and pencil in hand.

"Tea and Victoria sponge for me," Claire replied.

"I'll have the same," Bessie told her.

"Just tea for me," Maggie said.

"Be a few minutes," the woman muttered before she turned and walked back behind the counter. Bessie watched as she switched on the kettle and then went back to her magazine.

"Why did you want to see me?" Claire asked bluntly.

Maggie flushed. "I just thought, with everything going on, you might like someone to talk to. Sometimes it's nice to see old friends, isn't it? We're so busy all summer long with the holiday cottages that this time of year is my only chance to do anything like that."

"That's so kind of you," Claire said. Bessie thought she could hear a trace of sarcasm in the woman's voice, but Maggie didn't seem to notice.

"I wish I had more time for all of my old school friends," Maggie said. "How are you coping with the new investigation?"

"Well, it's nothing to do with me, really, is it?" Claire replied. "I'd been seeing Todd for a while when Susan disappeared, but we weren't even engaged yet. We were both living in Douglas when it happened. Neither one of us were able to help the police at all with the investigation way back then and we certainly can't help them now."

"It must have been a terrible shock for Todd, having his sister vanish like that," Maggie said.

"He was upset, but at the time we all thought she'd just gone across for some reason. He wasn't really close to her. She was the baby of the family, more than ten years younger than him. He was out of the house before she'd hit her teens."

"So what did he think happened to her?" Maggie asked.

Bessie tried not to look as shocked as she felt. Maggie's questions felt awfully rude. The waitress interrupted before Claire replied.

"Three teas and two cakes," she said, setting her tray on the table with a bang. Claire quickly began to remove things from the tray and Bessie and Maggie followed suit. Bessie's mouth began to water as she served herself a plate with a thick slice of cake on it.

"Shout if you want anything else," the woman told them before she walked back behind the counter.

Bessie took a sip of tea and then cautiously tried the cake. "This is really good," she said, embarrassed at how surprised she sounded.

Claire laughed. "Yeah, as I said, it's the only thing here worth eating, but it's really worth it."

"The tea isn't very hot," Maggie sniffed.

"Mine is," Claire told her. "But do let Marta know. I'm sure she'd be happy to make you fresh."

Bessie glanced at the woman, who was again flipping desultorily through her magazine. Bessie doubted that anything they did would make the woman "happy."

"It's fine," Maggie muttered, taking another sip.

"To get back to your question," Claire said after a moment. "Todd doesn't have any idea what happened to his sister or the other girls. We talked about it yesterday before the police constable came over to question us and we don't have any better ideas now than we did in nineteen-seventy."

"How well did you know Susan?" Maggie asked.

"I didn't," Claire said shortly.

Maggie frowned. It seemed clear to Bessie that Maggie wasn't getting nearly as much information from the other woman as she'd hoped.

"I'm sure I remember there being several suspects," Maggie said. "One of the other Kelly cousins was questioned, I think."

"That would be Matthew," Claire replied. "He was involved with

Helen before she disappeared, and that invited all sorts of nasty speculation."

"I remember, back at the time, that someone told me Matthew was going to be arrested. I don't think he ever was, though."

"He wasn't. No one was," Claire said flatly. "Which is why the investigation has been reopened and why every gossip on the island is talking about my husband's family again."

Maggie flushed and drank some of her tea. Bessie washed down the last bite of the delicious cake before she spoke.

"I am sorry that you're all having to go through this," she said to Claire. "But I'm sure everyone would like to see the case resolved. It must be difficult, not knowing what happened to the girls."

Claire shrugged. "It isn't something I think about often. Sometimes, at the holidays, maybe, someone might say something about having all the brothers and sisters together, and then there's an awkward silence while everyone thinks about Susan, but that's really it. But then, Todd and I aren't close to anyone in his family. I don't think about any of his brothers or sisters any more or less than I think about Susan."

"If something did happen to them, it will be nice to see the person responsible behind bars," Bessie said.

"That's certainly true," Claire said. "I can't help but worry just a little bit about that, though. If the girls didn't simply run away, which still seems like the most likely answer to me, then someone has been hiding a secret for a long time and they aren't going to want it to come out."

"Who were the other suspects?" Maggie asked.

"I'm sure I don't know," Claire said tiredly. "I knew about Matthew because he was friends with Timothy, Todd's younger brother. Timothy and Todd were sharing a flat when I first met Todd and Matthew came over sometimes to watch telly or whatever."

"I'm sure Peter and Jonas Clucas were both suspects," Maggie said in a low voice. "But they had Donald on their side. I'll bet the police were paid handsomely to 'lose' any evidence they found that pointed to either of them."

Maggie put air quotation marks around the word "lose" in case the others didn't get her meaning.

"I think I have more faith in our police than you do," Bessie said.

"Oh, the force today is top-notch," Maggie replied. "But in those days, you could buy your way out of all manner of trouble."

"Surely not a triple homicide," Bessie retorted.

Maggie shrugged. "I just know Jonas got away with an awful lot when he was growing up. He stole cars and crashed them, got into bar fights, and I know more than one woman he went out with who ended up with a black eye or worse when she tried to get rid of him."

"I remember him," Claire said. "He went out with a friend of mine a few times. She said he was great fun, and I remember he spent a lot of money on her as well, taking her out for lavish meals and the like. She never said anything bad about him, except that he broke her heart when he broke up with her."

"The key being that he broke up with her," Maggie said. "It was breaking up with him that was dangerous."

"Peter is his cousin?" Bessie asked, hoping to change the sad subject.

"Yes, his father's sister's son, if I'm remembering correctly," Claire replied. "He was just about as wild as Jonas in those days, and I'm sure the police will have taken a good look at him when the girls disappeared, but he's definitely changed now."

"I don't even know what happened to him," Maggie said. "I seem to recall the family moving down south some time in the seventies."

"You're half right," Claire said. "Peter was in his early twenties when Susan disappeared, and he and Jonas seemed to be having a contest to see who could lead the most dissolute life. Jonas was a year older and he set the bad example for his cousin. Around the same time as Susan left, Peter's parents separated. Peter's mum moved to Port Erin and after a while Peter moved in with her. At some point he went back to school, and now he runs the drug and alcohol rehabilitation programme on the island."

"Really?" Maggie asked. "That's quite a turnaround."

"It is," Claire agreed. "He's very effective when counseling young people, because he can talk from his own experience. I gather he hasn't spoken to Jonas in years."

"So you've seen him recently?" Maggie wondered.

"Yes," Claire flushed. "My oldest boy got himself into some trouble. It wasn't anything too serious, but the police recommended that he talk to Peter. It didn't take Peter long to straighten my Jacob out, I can tell you. Anyway, we started talking after one of Jacob's sessions and realised that we'd more or less grown up together. This was all before we heard about the police investigation."

"Well, it's always nice to hear about young people turning their lives around," Bessie said. "I hope the investigation doesn't cause him any trouble."

"I don't think he was ever a serious suspect," Claire said. "I always thought Matthew was the more likely culprit."

"I'm afraid I don't agree with you there," Maggie said. "Matthew's okay. It's Jonas I'd put at the top of the suspect list."

"Oh, I know he was wild when he was younger," Claire said. "But like I said, my friend thought he was wonderful. You should have seen the flowers he used to bring her. I was quite jealous at the time."

"I'd still pick him over Matthew or Peter," Maggie told her.

"I'd better get going," Claire said after a glance at her watch. "I have to get to school to pick up the children."

She reached for her handbag and began to root around inside it.

"Today is my treat," Bessie said firmly. "I'm so grateful to you for introducing me to that sponge that I'm more than happy to pay for everyone."

Claire flushed. "I can pay my share," she said.

"But you'll let me treat, because it will make me happy," Bessie replied.

Claire looked as if she wanted to argue further, but Maggie interrupted.

"I'm happy to let Bessie pay," she said brightly. "We all know Bessie has millions of pounds squirrelled away somewhere."

Bessie turned pink and opened her mouth to protest, but Claire spoke first.

"If you're sure you don't mind," she said hesitantly.

"I don't mind," Bessie assured her.

Claire thanked her profusely and then made her way out of the café. As soon as she was gone, Bessie turned to Maggie.

"I don't mind treating, but I also don't have millions of pounds tucked away," she said crossly.

"I was just teasing," Maggie said, rising to her feet. "Anyway, it got Claire to agree to let you pay, so you shouldn't mind."

Bessie did mind, but there seemed little point in arguing any further. She stood up and crossed to the counter where Marta handed her the bill. Bessie was surprised at how inexpensive it was even after she'd added a large gratuity.

"Thanks," Marta said as Bessie handed her payment.

"You're welcome," Bessie replied. "I don't get to Jurby very often, but I'll definitely stop back for more Victoria sponge the next time I do."

The other woman nodded as Bessie turned and followed Maggie out. The man at the end of the counter hadn't looked up from his book once while they'd been there. Bessie wondered idly if they might have become friends if they had spoken. He seemed like her kind of person.

Bessie and Maggie chatted about the weather and island politics as they made their way back across the island. By the time they'd arrived at Bessie's cottage, it was nearly time for Hugh's visit.

"Thank you for an interesting afternoon," Bessie told Maggie as the other woman pulled up near Bessie's door.

"Thank you," Maggie replied. "I didn't mean for you to get stuck with the bill."

"As you did the driving, it was the least I could do," Bessie replied.

"Do ring me if you hear anything interesting about the case," Maggie told her. "I'd love to know who the police suspect, if they really do think something awful happened."

"I'd like to know that as well," Bessie admitted.

She let herself into her cottage, still turning over in her head everything she'd heard over the past few days. There didn't seem to be any shortage of suspects in the case, but as far as Bessie knew, the fate of the girls still remained a mystery. Perhaps the girls had simply run away and all this talk about suspects was unnecessary. Feeling a bit sorry for the men whose names were once more being bandied about as possible criminals, Bessie started working on making a pudding for her guests. The Victoria sponge had been delicious, and it left Bessie in the mood for something completely unlike it. Settling on her favourite American-style brownie recipe, Bessie mixed them up and popped the pan in the oven. That job done, she was left with just enough time to read a few chapters in her book before her friends arrived.

CHAPTER 5

*H*ugh knocked on her door a few minutes early. Bessie was just taking the brownies out of the oven when he arrived.

"I'm probably a little bit early," he said apologetically, as he handed her a box full of takeaway containers. "It didn't take as long at the Chinese place as I thought it would. I was going to drive around for a little while, but the food smelled so good, I had to stop."

Bessie chuckled as she began unpacking the box. "It does smell good," she agreed.

"I'll just go and get the other box," Hugh told her.

"There's another one?" Bessie replied to the empty room. Hugh was back only a moment later with a second box that was at least as full as the first.

"How many people did you invite?" Bessie asked as Hugh began unpacking his box.

"Just John and Doona," he replied. "But I'm really hungry. I didn't get much lunch today."

"I made brownies for pudding, but I don't think we'll have room."

"Oh, I will," Hugh said with a grin. "I always have room for your brownies."

Bessie pulled down plates while Hugh set knives and forks on the table. They were discussing drinks when John and Doona arrived together.

"Oh, it's so good to see you," Bessie told John, giving him a hug. "I feel as if I haven't seen you in ages."

"It has been a while," John said a bit sheepishly. "Things are busy at the station, but I really must start making more of an effort to stop in once in a while."

"You know you're welcome any time, but I do understand about your work. I'm just glad you're here tonight."

John was a handsome man in his mid-forties. He was fit and trim with bright green eyes and brown hair that was just beginning to go grey at the temples. It made him look distinguished rather than older, Bessie thought.

She gave Doona a hug as well and then passed out plates. Everyone was quick to fill them with piles of steaming rice, vegetables and meats. Once they were all sitting around the table, Bessie served drinks and then joined them.

"It's nice to all be here without anyone having found any dead bodies," Doona remarked.

"I am treating the Kelly disappearances as potential murder cases," Hugh pointed out.

"Yes, but they aren't definitely murder, at least not yet," Doona replied. "And they might turn out to be nothing at all. Maybe all three girls are living happily in Canada, with lumberjacks for husbands and maple syrup every day for breakfast."

Bessie looked at her friend. "Are you feeling okay?" she asked.

Doona laughed. "Sorry, this afternoon on my lunch break I was reading a murder mystery set in Canada. The heroine was a transplanted Brit who'd met a lumberjack while she was on holiday and married him after a whirlwind romance. Aside from finding a dead body and showing up the rather inept local police, she also seemed to have maple syrup on every page."

"Didn't that make them stick together?" Bessie asked.

Everyone laughed and dug into their dinner. Bessie ate far more than she'd thought she could manage, but even so, she still found room for a small piece of brownie at the end.

"These are so good," Doona sighed over her pudding. "I'd ask you for the recipe, but I'm afraid I'd get it wrong."

"They aren't difficult," Bessie told her. "I'll copy the recipe for you before you leave."

"Maybe you could share it with me, too," John suggested. "The children are coming over for the February half-term and I'd love to do some baking with them. I'm trying to think of lots of things we can do that aren't too expensive."

"I'm happy to share the recipe," Bessie said. "Don't forget a lot of the historical sites are open during the winter months as well. It would be nice if they could appreciate the island more."

John and his wife, Sue, were in the middle of a very friendly divorce. Sue and the pair's two children had moved back to Manchester following the split. Neither Sue nor the children had enjoyed the time they'd lived on the island, which Bessie thought was unfortunate. She loved the island and hoped that at least the children would come to appreciate it, given time.

"I think Amy misses it," John told her. "When I rang the other day she said she was looking forward to coming. Although that may be more about not getting along with her mum than anything else. She's at a tough age, really."

Bessie thought about the girl, who was just entering her teens. "It is a difficult time," she agreed. "But you'll all get through it, eventually."

John laughed. "Eventually sounds like a long time from now," he said.

When everyone had finished eating, Doona insisted on doing the washing-up. "You start talking about the case," she told the others. "I don't know anything about it at all, so I can't contribute to the conversation anyway."

"So where do we start?" Bessie asked the two policemen.

John looked over at Hugh and shrugged. "This is Hugh's case. It's up to him."

Hugh flushed and then cleared his throat. "Thank you, sir," he said briskly. "As you both know, I've been talking with as many of the involved parties as I could over the past two days. The experience was interesting, but I don't think it was particularly useful."

"I read the article in today's local paper about the case," Doona said from the sink. "So I think I have the background. The three girls all had the same surname, but they were just cousins, right?"

"Yes, all three girls had the same paternal great-grandfather, and Helen's father and Susan's father were brothers. There are a lot of interrelated Kellys in Lonan," Bessie told her.

Doona nodded. "And the three girls vanished over two consecutive weekends and no trace was ever found of any of them. Is that right?"

"It is," Hugh confirmed.

"The paper said that a number of suspects were interviewed and eliminated over the years," Doona said. "Does that mean you don't have any suspects?"

"At the moment we don't even know if we have a crime," John said levelly. "We have witnesses, but it isn't fair at this point to call anyone a suspect."

Doona nodded. "But you do have suspects, right?" she asked.

Hugh grinned. "We do," he conceded. "Maybe even a few too many."

"Who's on the list, then?" Bessie asked.

"At this point, just about everyone," Hugh said with a sigh. "I may have mentioned that some of the interview notes have gone missing over the years. I'm sure that statements were taken from people for whom I don't have statements. And after all this time people's memories are not the clearest. Inspector Harris might have eliminated a number of possible suspects during his investigation, but at this point I can't say for certain that anyone who was connected to the case in any way is in the clear."

"I saw Amy Kelly in Lonan yesterday," Bessie told him. "She doesn't want the case reopening."

"I know," Hugh said. "She made that very clear to me when I spoke to her."

"Which one is she?" Doona asked as she rinsed the last of the plates.

"She's Helen's mother," Bessie replied.

"Oh, the divorced one?" Doona asked. "Along with announcing the reopening of the case, the paper reprinted a couple of its articles from the time. They made a huge big deal out of the fact that Helen's parents were divorced and that Helen lived with her father rather than her mother."

"It was pretty unusual in those days," Bessie said. "But whatever their domestic arrangements, Amy was still devastated when her daughter went missing."

"Of course she was," Doona agreed. "I would have thought she'd have spent the years since pestering the police to keep the investigation open."

"She's afraid that the truth will be bad news," Bessie explained. "She'd rather not know than find out that her daughter is dead."

Doona shook her head. "I'm sure I'd rather know than be left wondering forever."

"I don't know," Bessie said. "Right now she can imagine that her daughter ran away, got married, had children and is living a very happy life somewhere. I can see the appeal in that."

"I suppose," Doona said. "Does that mean she isn't helping with the investigation?"

"No," Hugh said. "I can't repeat what she told me, but she was as helpful as she could be, or at least that's how it seemed. She was far more cooperative than some people, at least."

Bessie nodded. "And you can't tell us who didn't want to cooperate," she said.

"I can't," Hugh agreed. "But I'd love to hear what Amy told you."

"She didn't tell me much," Bessie began. She closed her eyes and replayed the conversation in her head, telling the others everything that seemed at all important. When she was done, she sat back in her seat. "So, is Jonas Clucas a suspect?" she asked Hugh.

"He, like everyone else involved, is a person of interest," Hugh replied. "He's actually in London at the moment, so I haven't had a chance to speak to him, but he's on the top of my list for Monday, when he returns."

"I've met his wife," Doona said. "Or at least I think it was his wife. Is her name Tara?"

Hugh nodded. "I haven't met her, but that is her name. She didn't even know Jonas back then, so I'm not in any hurry to speak to her."

"You might want to talk to her before her husband returns," John suggested quietly. "Just informally, just to see if the man ever mentioned the case to her over the years, that sort of thing."

Hugh pulled out his notebook and made a quick note. "I'll do that," he said.

"Where did you meet her?" John asked Doona.

"On my street," Doona said. "I was taking a walk one day, about six months ago, and she was coming out of the house three doors down from me. You know the one that looks as if it needs some love and attention? That one."

Bessie nodded, picturing the small bungalow. While it wasn't exactly neglected, it didn't look as if it was well cared for either. A fresh coat of paint and a bit of rudimentary gardening would make a huge difference.

"What was she doing there?" John asked.

"I stopped and said hello," Doona recalled. "She told me that she and her husband owned the property and rented it out. The most recent tenants had just left and she was checking it out before turning it back over to their management company to find new tenants."

"I knew they owned a lot of property in the area," Bessie said. "But I always thought it was all commercial. I didn't realise they had residential properties as well."

"Actually, she told me they owned three or four houses on my street," Doona told her. "She looked as if she could afford to buy the rest of them as well."

"Donald was a very successful property investor," Bessie said. "What did you think of Tara? I haven't seen her in years."

"She's stunningly beautiful," Doona replied. "Like model or actress beautiful, but I have to say she didn't look particularly happy. She looked, I don't know, almost too perfect. Her makeup had been done with a heavy hand and I remember thinking that she was overdressed for the weather. It was a warm day and she had on a gorgeous business suit that had to be wool. It fit her perfectly and showed off her spectacular figure, but it had to have been hot on such a nice day."

"You remember a lot from a brief encounter," John remarked.

"It made a real impression on me," Doona told him. "Or rather, she did. There was something not quite right about her, but I don't know what it was. At the time I thought she was just too perfect to be real, but now I'm not so sure. She seemed really invested in making me understand how rich and happy she was and how wonderful her life was. It was odd."

"That is odd," John agreed. "Maybe I should have a little chat with her."

Hugh looked disappointed for a moment and then nodded. "It might be best," he said. "If she's anything like Doona said, she'd probably expect an inspector rather than a lowly constable, anyway."

"I'll ring her in the morning and try to arrange a meeting before her husband returns," John said. "I know from reading through the files myself that her husband's father used to command quite a bit of respect from the Laxey Constabulary. We need to be extra careful when dealing with them, I think."

"It was suggested to me that Donald Clucas paid to have evidence against his son suppressed," Bessie said.

John frowned. "I'd hate to think that's the case," he said. "From everything I've heard, Inspector Harris was a solid investigator. There's certainly nothing in the files that suggests that any evidence was suppressed."

"If Inspector Harris was bought off, he didn't get much," Hugh said. "His widow comes to some of the police family events once in a while, and I know she's on a very tight budget. The inspector didn't leave her much besides his pension."

"Maybe Donald paid off someone higher up in the chain of command," Bessie suggested.

"I can't see Inspector Harris letting anything like that get past him,"

Hugh said. "I've read his notes. He was genuinely at a loss to explain what had happened, and he worked the case, on and off, right up until the day he retired. If there was anything that would have given him the answers, I have to believe that he'd have made a note in his private notebooks, even if it didn't get into the official reports."

"So Jonas Clucas is your favourite suspect?" Doona asked. She rinsed out the sink and then dried her hands and joined them back at the table.

"I wouldn't necessarily say that," Hugh replied. "He's interesting, but he's far from the only person who had means and opportunity."

"What about motive?" Doona asked.

"No one has ever suggested any real motive for either kidnapping or murdering the girls," Hugh replied. "If you have any ideas, I'd love to hear them."

"Maybe someone kidnapped them for ransom," Doona said. "But then they found out the families didn't have any money so they killed them all."

"It's possible," Hugh said, his expression doubtful. "But the gap between the first disappearance and the other two calls that theory into question. Why grab the other two girls if you couldn't get any ransom for the first one?"

Doona opened her mouth to reply and then snapped it shut. After a moment she sighed. "I could offer some possible explanation," she said. "But the whole idea just keeps getting more and more convoluted as it goes along in my head. I think we can forget kidnapping for ransom."

"We can't," John interjected. "It isn't likely, but it's possible. It needs to stay on the long list as we investigate."

"But not on the short list," Doona laughed.

"No, not on the short list," John agreed.

"So maybe they were kidnapped for some other reason," Doona suggested.

"Maybe," Hugh said. "If they were taken off the island, then finding out what happened to them might be impossible. After Susan's disappearance, extra security measures were put into place at the airport and sea terminal. No one matching either Karen's or Helen's descriptions left the island in the week after their disappearances, at least not by plane or ferry."

"But anyone can sail a small boat up to the island, pick up a few passengers and sail away," Doona pointed out.

"Yes, and if that's what happened, I'm probably wasting my time," Hugh said.

"And you don't think you are," Bessie suggested.

"No, I don't," Hugh agreed. "I've heard lots of possible solutions to the case, but they all seem overly complicated. I think the most likely answer is the simplest one."

"And what is that?" John asked.

"I think the girls were murdered and their bodies were buried somewhere on the island," Hugh said. "I'm aiming my questions towards trying to work out where the bodies might be hidden."

"Maybe they really did just run away," Doona said quietly.

"I can't believe that all three of them decided to simply cut all of their ties at the same time," Hugh said. "Running away is one thing, staying away for thirty years is another."

"It's sad to think that they might be dead," Bessie said.

"Nothing would make me happier than for one of them to ring the station tomorrow and tell us that they're all fine," Hugh replied. "That's one of the reasons we were happy with the publicity that reopening the case has generated. I have to believe that someone on the island knows something. I'm just hoping they'll be more willing to talk now than they were in nineteen-seventy."

"And if anyone does know that the girls are alive and well, maybe they'll persuade one of them to get in touch," Doona said.

"I hope so," Hugh said. "I'd love to close the case file with a happy ending."

Bessie nodded, but she couldn't help but feel that a happy ending was unlikely. "All of the Kellys have acres and acres of farmland," she said. "I'm not sure where you'd even begin to look for the missing girls."

"As I said, I'm targeting my questioning towards that issue, although not directly. It's been such a long time, I'm worried that someone has built a housing estate over them or something, though," Hugh replied.

"So, besides Jonas Clucas, who else might know something?" Doona asked.

"All of the girls' parents are still alive," Hugh said. "They were questioned extensively in the original investigation. I tend to believe that none of them knew anything, though. Helen had a stepmother and I'm told they didn't get along, but somehow I can't see her killing three teenagers just to get rid of the one that annoyed her."

"I remember meeting Brandy once, not long after she and Harold got married," Bessie said. "She was quite a bit younger than Harold, not much older than Helen. It doesn't surprise me that the two didn't get along."

"That isn't much of a motive for murder, though," Hugh said.

"No, and Brandy didn't seem the type, at least to me," Bessie added. "She'd dropped out of school and had been working at Ramsey Cottage Hospital as a cleaner. I thought at the time that she seemed to think she'd won the lottery by marrying Harold. He had a bit of money and a big house, and she was able to quit her job. It certainly changed her life. When I met her, she still seemed happy, at least."

"Was that before or after Helen disappeared?" John asked.

Bessie thought for a moment. "It must have been before," she said. "I think she and Harold had only been married for a few weeks when I met her. They were visiting James at his market stall one day and I remember someone teasing her about still being in their honeymoon phase. Helen disappeared some months later."

"For what it's worth," Hugh said. "I talked to her today and I quite liked her. She still seems happy enough with her life, even after all these years. She and Harold held hands while I talked to them and there seems to be real affection between them. I'd hate to think she had anything to do with the disappearances."

"I think you're an excellent judge of character," John told Hugh. "But you can't let your feelings interfere with the investigation. She's still a suspect, no matter how nice she was to you."

Hugh nodded. "I know, sir. I was just saying, she was one of the nicer people I spoke to about the case."

"I had tea with Claire Kelly today," Bessie reported. "She's married to Todd, who was Susan's older brother. She was telling me about Peter Clucas."

"Who's Peter Clucas?" Doona demanded.

"A cousin to Jonas, with far less money," Bessie replied. "He was another suspect at the time. Like his cousin, he drank and caused trouble, and he was in the same social circle as the three girls."

"He's a drug and alcohol rehabilitation counselor now," Hugh said. "And he's very good at his job. I talked to him briefly today, mostly just to schedule a formal interview. He did tell me that he's happy to see the case reopened and that he hopes I can finally find out what really happened to the missing girls."

"Claire spoke very highly of him," Bessie said. "I hope he isn't on your short list of suspects."

"Just because he's turned his life around doesn't mean he shouldn't be held responsible for his misdeeds in his youth," John said. "Inspector Harris always thought he knew more than he admitted to about the case."

"I'm going to keep that in mind as I question him," Hugh said.

"What about Matthew Kelly?" Bessie asked. "Have you spoken to him? I don't think he'll be happy about the case being reopened."

"Matthew Kelly?" Doona asked.

"Another cousin," Bessie replied. "From another branch of the same family. It's said he was involved with Helen Kelly before she vanished, even though he was four or five years older than she was at the time."

"And her parents didn't ground her until she was eighteen?" Doona demanded.

"I don't think it was that unusual in those days," Bessie replied. "And I doubt her parents knew anything about it, anyway."

Doona nodded. "Yeah, that makes sense."

"I have spoken to him," Hugh said. "And you're right, he isn't happy."

"A lot of people at the time seemed to think he had something to do with the disappearances," Bessie remarked. "I'm sure the whole investigation brings up bad memories."

"No doubt," Hugh said. "But that should only make him more eager to find out what really happened. It can't be easy living with the cloud of suspicion over your head for so many years."

"He never moved out of Lonan, did he?" Bessie asked.

"No, which struck me as odd, considering," Hugh replied.

"What's he doing now?" John asked.

"He works at the garage there," Hugh told him. "He's their chief mechanic, which I think means only mechanic, really. When I went to see him he was under an old Renault, changing the oil. From what he said, most of their customers have older cars that he's been looking after for years. He made some comment about fancy people buying new cars and taking them back to their overpriced dealers rather than using good and honest local garages."

"From what I've heard about that place, there's nothing good or honest about it," Bessie said. "I don't pay much attention, as I don't have a car to worry about, but I've never heard anything good about it."

"Me, either," Doona said. "I'm quite happy taking my car back to where I bought it. They've always taken good care of me."

"Well, don't mention that to Matthew Kelly if you ever meet him," Hugh said.

"He doesn't sound happy about anything," Bessie remarked.

"You could say that," Hugh replied.

"Did he ever marry?" Doona asked. "Maybe his wife knows something."

Hugh glanced at John. "I'm not sure how much I should be talking about," he said.

"Marriages are matters of public record," John replied. "As are divorces."

Hugh nodded. "He's married to his third wife," he said.

"Does she make him happy?" Bessie had to ask.

Hugh looked at John and then at Bessie. "I'd guess no, but it would just be a guess."

Bessie nodded. "I can do some poking around there," she offered. "Do you know if his wife is from Lonan?"

"She's not," Hugh said. "Apparently, she grew up in Laxey."

"Did she now?" Bessie said with interest. "What's her name, then?"

Hugh checked his notes. "Joanna Driver," he said after a moment. "She was Joanna Fells for a while, too, I gather."

"I know exactly who she is," Bessie said. "And I know exactly where to find her. She works at the pub in Laxey; she's been there for years."

"I thought she looked familiar," Hugh exclaimed. "Matthew had a wedding photo on one of the tables in the garage and I thought I recognised her, but I didn't know the name." He looked over at John Rockwell and blushed. "Not that I spend much time in the local pub," he added quickly. "But I have lunch there once in a while. It's always good to spend time in the popular local businesses, right?"

"I don't want you questioning witnesses," John said to Bessie. "Or their wives."

"I won't question anyone," Bessie replied. "But I might have lunch at the pub tomorrow. It's been ages since I had a nice pub lunch."

John frowned. "I know better than to try to dissuade you," he said. "If you do go, take a friend with you, please."

Bessie nodded, trying to think who she might invite on such short notice.

"I'm working tomorrow," Doona said. "Otherwise, I'd love to go."

"Is Grace still working as a supply teacher every day?" Bessie asked Hugh.

"At the moment, no," Hugh replied. "She's taken February off to get the wedding planned and then for our honeymoon. She's goes back on the first of March."

"I wonder if she'd like to have lunch with me tomorrow," Bessie said casually.

Hugh laughed. "Do you want me to text her and ask?"

"Oh, yes, please," Bessie replied.

A few moments later Hugh put his phone away. "She'll collect you at twelve," he said. "And she said to tell you she's really looking forward to it."

"Excellent," Bessie said. "So am I."

"And she's also eager for me to get back to the flat," Hugh added. "She's been working with the caterer all day and she needs to know what I think of the various options. Was there anything else we needed to discuss?"

John shook his head. "I think we all have a rough idea of the basics of the case," he said. "From here we'll have to see how things develop."

Bessie insisted that Hugh take most of the leftovers home with him. "Share them with Grace while you go over the catering," she suggested. "Otherwise, you'll just get hungry talking about all that food."

Hugh laughed and quickly agreed. After Bessie let him out, she sat back down across from John.

"Do you think he'll actually be able to find out what happened to the Kelly girls?" she asked the man.

John shrugged. "At this point, after all this time, he needs to hope that someone who wouldn't talk back then is willing to talk now. It does happen, and this case seems like a good candidate for that, which is why I suggested he tackle it first."

"A good candidate why?" Doona asked.

"Whatever happened to the girls, someone has to know something. Three people don't just vanish without a trace. If they left voluntarily, they had help. If something else happened to them, someone saw something or heard something. Maybe that someone didn't realise the significance at the time, but they've had a great many years to think about it. Being asked the right questions now might just get whoever it is to talk," John explained.

"Look at the time," Doona exclaimed. "I'd better get home myself. I have to work early tomorrow."

"As do I," John said.

The pair stood up to go, but Bessie held up a hand. "I want to talk to you about one more thing," she said.

After John and Doona had sat back down, she told them about the plans she and Mary were making for the surprise honeymoon.

"If you think it's a terrible idea, just say so," she said when she'd finished.

"I think it's a great idea," Doona said quickly. "I wasn't sure what to get them for a present, but now I know just the thing. I'll pay for them to have dinner at the restaurant in the Eiffel Tower one night while they're in Paris. It's gorgeous and wonderful and dreadfully expensive, but I can tap into my inheritance and pay for their meal and champagne and everything. It's perfect."

Doona's second husband had named Doona as his heir before his untimely death. While there were a number of complications with the estate, Doona had already received a small windfall from this unexpected source.

"As I don't have any inheritance to tap, I'll have to offer something less extravagant," John said. "But I do know of a terrific little restaurant in a quiet corner of the city that has some of the best food I've ever eaten. I'm more than happy to buy the pair dinner there one night. I have the owner's number. I'll ring him up and arrange it."

"This might actually all come together," Bessie said excitedly.

"I'm sure everyone at the station will be glad to contribute," Doona said. "We were just having a conversation today about how difficult it is to think of what to get them. I'll tell them to put in cash, or maybe they can buy advance tickets for things like the Louvre. I really don't know."

"I think we need a travel agent," Bessie said. "And I think Karen Kelly's younger sister just happens to be one."

John flipped through the pages that Hugh had given him. "You're right," he said. "Kristen Kelly is a travel agent. She works in Douglas. How did you know that?"

"Mary Quayle uses the agency that she works for once in a while. She mentioned to me recently that one of the girls there came from Lonan. She thought I might know the family," Bessie explained.

"What a coincidence," Doona remarked.

"It's a small island," Bessie reminded her. "Don't they say that everyone in the world is connected by no more than six degrees of separation? On the island it's probably more like two or three."

John laughed. "Funny, but probably true," he said. "Take a friend when you see her, too, okay?"

Bessie nodded. "I'll take Mary," she said. "It's half her surprise anyway."

This time, when John and Doona got up to leave, Bessie didn't try to stop them. It was getting late and Bessie was tired. It had been a long day and Bessie had spent most of it with other people. After all her years of living alone, sometimes she felt extra tired when she had to be around others for long periods. With the house locked up for the night, she made her way upstairs, ready to read for a short while and then sleep. She only managed a single chapter before tiredness took over.

CHAPTER 6

*B*essie spent the next morning hard at work on her transcriptions. She'd finished four when she decided she needed to talk to Marjorie.

"Moghrey mie," she said when her friend picked up.

"Ah, Bessie, moghrey mie." Marjorie followed the greeting with a sentence in Manx that Bessie couldn't even begin to understand.

"Pardon?" she asked when Marjorie stopped speaking.

"Sorry," the other woman chuckled. "I haven't had the chance to use my Manx lately. I got a bit carried away."

"And here I was thinking you talked in Manx all day, every day," Bessie laughed.

"I wish," Marjorie replied. "I only get to use it occasionally, and at the moment I've been giving lots of tours to different groups from across. They prefer English for some reason."

"As do I," Bessie said.

"But what can I do for you?" Marjorie asked.

"I've been working on transcribing the wills you sent," Bessie explained. "But I'm not sure what else to do with them."

"Are they at all interesting?"

"I think they're fascinating, especially compared to the later wills that I usually study."

"Then write a paper about that," Marjorie said.

Bessie chuckled. "It sounds rather obvious when you put it that way," she said.

"I've already penciled you into the schedule for the conference," Marjorie told her. "I'll put the paperwork into the post for you in the next few days. The call for papers goes out tomorrow."

"If you get lots of great papers, you know you can leave me off the schedule," Bessie said.

"We'll see what we get. Personally, I find the research you're doing fascinating. I'm looking forward to hearing what you're finding."

"Yes, well, don't turn down any proper researchers on my behalf," Bessie said.

"You are a proper researcher," Marjorie said firmly. "Having a bunch of degrees doesn't mean someone is good at research. And you're especially good at making what you've found relevant and interesting. Some of the best historians in the world can make the most exciting subjects sound deadly dull."

"I won't argue with that," Bessie said. "I've been to enough conferences to know exactly what you mean."

"And who I mean," Marjorie laughed.

Feeling like she had some direction now, Bessie returned to her transcriptions with enthusiasm. She was lucky she'd taken the time to set an alarm, because it rang what felt to her like only a few minutes later.

"Lunch with Grace will be fun," she told herself as she brushed her hair. "The wills will wait."

Grace was right on time and she greeted Bessie with a hug when Bessie opened the cottage door.

"It's so good to see you," Grace said, her face flushed with happiness. "I'm hoping you can take my mind off the wedding for an hour. I'm feeling quite overwhelmed by the whole thing."

Bessie smiled at the pretty young woman. Grace's blonde hair was pulled up into a messy ponytail that suited her. She was wearing a heavy winter coat but she'd obviously buttoned it in a hurry and misaligned the buttons and their holes. Grace was usually calm and collected; clearly planning a wedding was taking a toll on the girl.

"I think your buttons are out of order," Bessie said gently as she gathered up her handbag.

Grace blushed and then undid and refastened her coat. "I'm all at sea," she told Bessie. "I can't focus on anything and I'm sure I've forgotten a dozen very important things for the wedding, but I simply don't know what they are."

"Are you marrying the right man?" Bessie asked.

Grace sighed and stood very still for a moment. "Yes, I absolutely am," she said decisively.

Bessie nodded. "Everything else is just window dressing. Keep your focus on Hugh and the rest will fall into place."

"I hope you're right," Grace said.

"Even if it doesn't, you still end up married to Hugh, so what difference does it make?" Bessie reasoned.

"I know you're right, but I do so want everything to be perfect."

"It won't be perfect, but it will be wonderful," Bessie said. "I can't tell you how much I'm looking forward to it, not for the food or the entertainment or the cake. I'm looking forward to watching two people I quite like agree to spend the rest of their lives together."

Grace nodded. "Quite a few people are looking forward to the food, though, including the groom."

Bessie laughed and then she and Grace made their way out of the cottage to Grace's small car.

"Hugh said you wanted to eat at the Cat and Longtail," she said as she turned the car onto the road.

"Yes, if you don't mind," Bessie replied.

"He also said I'm not to let you question the poor woman behind the bar," she added. "Why would you want to do that?"

"She's married to one of the suspects in the case Hugh is investigating," Bessie explained. "I really just wanted to meet her. That's why I want to have lunch there."

"Hugh doesn't talk about his work with me very much, but I read about the Kelly girls in the local paper yesterday. What a horrible thing to happen, three teenaged girls just disappearing like that. I hope Hugh can work out what happened to them."

"I hope so, too. Their families deserve answers."

The small car park for the pub was mostly empty when Grace pulled in a moment later. They climbed out of the car and Grace gave Bessie a doubtful look.

"It's rather, um, unprepossessing," she said.

"That's a very nice way to put it," Bessie said, looking up at the old building that had been a pub for more years than Bessie could remember. It still looked exactly the same as it always had, tired and in need of a facelift. "But the food used to be good, anyway."

Grace followed Bessie into the building. The bar was to the left and the dining room was to the right. While Bessie would have preferred the dining room, she was more likely to find Joanna in the bar. She turned left.

"Bessie Cubbon? What brings you here?" the man behind the bar shouted across the empty room.

"Peter Yates, I thought you'd long since made enough money to leave the hard work to the hired help," Bessie told him in reply when she and Grace reached the bar.

"Oh, aye, you'd think so, wouldn't you," he replied. "But you can't get good help, that's the problem. Half the kids I have working for me only turn up on payday, you know?"

"Peter, meet my friend, Grace," Bessie performed the introductions. "Grace is getting married soon and she needed a break from all the planning. I thought a nice pub lunch would be good for her."

"You'd be right," he said. "Grab some menus and sit anywhere. We've fish and chips on special today, as well. I'll send Joanna over with your drinks once you tell me what you want."

The women both ordered soft drinks and then crossed to a table in the corner.

"Is Joanna the woman you wanted to talk to?" Grace asked.

"She is, yes," Bessie replied.

The pair had only just started looking at the menu when Joanna appeared.

"Here you are," she said as she put their drinks on the table. "We usually have you order at the bar, but it's quiet so I can take your order now if you'd like."

"Oh, dear, I haven't any idea what I want," Grace exclaimed.

"How are you?" Bessie asked the woman. "I'm not sure if you remember me, but I used to come in a bit more often."

The woman nodded. "Everyone in Laxey knows Aunt Bessie," she said. "I assumed you came in today to ask me about Matthew and those girls that went missing all those years ago."

Bessie flushed. "That's a job for the police," she said.

Joanna let out a shout of laughter. "We all know how you keep getting yourself in the middle of police investigations," she told Bessie. "They must have you on the payroll by now, right?"

"Unfortunately, no," Bessie replied tartly. "I think I'd make a good police officer, actually, but they have rules about age, apparently."

"Let me get your food order and then I'll come back and chat," the woman told her with a grin. "Maybe, if you can solve this case, they'll reconsider their rules."

Joanna was only gone for a moment after the women ordered. When she came back, she was carrying a glass of wine. She put it on the table and then pulled up a chair. After taking a healthy sip, she looked at Bessie.

"So, what do you want to know?" she asked.

"I can't imagine you know anything about the case," Bessie said. "You and Matthew weren't together all those years ago. You've only been married a couple of years, right?"

"We've been married for two years, and I don't think we'll make three," the woman replied.

"I am sorry," Bessie said.

"Don't be," Joanna told her. "It's my second marriage and his third. The odds were against us from the very beginning. It was fun at first, but Matthew has a temper and so do I. This police investigation is just the last straw, really. Matthew is impossible to live with now. He's convinced that the police are going to frame him if they can't work out what really happened."

"That's crazy," Grace snapped.

"Maybe," Joanna shrugged. "But the case has already received a ton of publicity. It would be pretty embarrassing if they had to announce that they'd not actually found anything, wouldn't it? Matthew reckons he'll be arrested in the next few days, just to create new headlines, if nothing else breaks."

"He should be trying to help, then," Bessie suggested. "He was a teenaged boy when it happened. There must have been things he didn't tell the police at the time."

"If there were, he hasn't told me," Joanna said.

Bessie nodded. If the man had kept secrets from the police, he'd probably kept them from his third wife, too. "Do you remember when the girls went missing?" she asked.

Joanna shrugged. "I was around the same age as the girls," she said. "My mum went mad for a few months and wouldn't let me go out anywhere without her, but I didn't know any of them or anything."

"You didn't go to school together?" Bessie asked.

"Oh, aye, we were all at Ramsey Grammar School together, but I didn't go to school very often, if I'm honest. Anyway, it was a big school and I wasn't interested in making friends with the other girls. I was far more interested in the boys," Joanna replied.

"Did anyone you know have any theories about what might have happened to the girls?" Bessie continued.

"We all assumed one of them needed a termination," Joanna replied. "That was the main reason girls went across suddenly like that."

"But surely they wouldn't go without telling someone?" Grace broke in.

"Maybe, but maybe not. It's easier to get forgiveness than permission, you know? If it was Susan, there's no way she'd have told anyone. Everyone thought she was a good girl. If she'd have found herself in trouble, she'd have sneaked away and taken care of it without anyone knowing."

"But that doesn't explain what happened to Karen and Helen," Bessie said.

"No, and I don't really think Susan found herself in trouble, either," Joanna said.

"It looks as if I have to do all of the work around here," Peter grumbled as he delivered two very full plates of food to the table.

"Won't do you any harm," Joanna told him.

He chuckled and went back behind the bar before Bessie could thank him. The food looked delicious, but she didn't want to start eating until she got Joanna to continue.

"So if Susan didn't find herself in trouble, what do you think did happen?" Bessie asked.

"I had an idea at the time," the woman said. "I suppose it could still be possible, but no one wanted to listen to me back then."

"I'd like to hear your idea," Bessie told her.

"I always thought one of the other girls got into trouble," Joanna replied. "You could flip a coin as to which one, really. I think they sent Susan over to find a place and the other two followed the next weekend."

"Would Susan have done that?" Bessie wondered.

"Oh, yeah, she'd have done anything for her cousins," Joanna said emphatically. "They weren't really friends, but they were family, if that makes sense? Ramsey Grammar was a big school and people tended to hang out together in small groups. Their group was kind of anyone with the surname Kelly, really. They were all related in some way to one another and they all looked out for each other."

Bessie's mouth was full when Joanna stopped. Bessie glanced at Grace, who seemed to read the unspoken thought in Bessie's eyes.

"Surely one of the other girls would have said something when she saw how worried everyone was about Susan, though," Grace said.

"Not when they needed to get away the next weekend," Joanna said. "If they told everyone where Susan was, they'd have had to explain everything, and they couldn't do that."

"I can't imagine worrying their parents like that," Grace murmured.

"They were young," Joanna pointed out. "I'm sure they were like all teenaged girls, too self-absorbed to realise what they were doing to other people. Karen and Helen were like that, I'm sure. Knowing them, they thought it was funny, everyone looking everywhere for Susan when she'd only gone across."

"Your solution makes perfect sense," Bessie said. "Except for the ending. If that's what happened, why didn't they just come back after it was all over?"

"Maybe they decided they liked it better over there," Joanna said. "I've often thought that if I ever went across, I wouldn't want to come back. I think I'd love living in a big city where you can be totally anonymous and live your life however you please."

"Oh, not me," Grace said. "I love our island. And, having grown up in Douglas, I really love Laxey. Douglas feels like a big city to me. Laxey is just about perfect."

"I've always felt that way," Bessie told the girl.

"Ha, I'd go tomorrow if I could," Joanna said. "Nothing ever happens here."

"I wouldn't necessarily agree with that," Bessie said dryly.

The other woman shrugged. "I know you've stumbled across a murder or two in the last year, but that isn't exactly the sort of excitement I'm looking for."

"I should hope not," Bessie said.

"Anyway, you wanted to know what I thought; there you are." The woman got up to go.

"I still don't see why none of them have been in touch after all these years," Bessie said.

"If they wanted to be found, they'd get in touch," Joanna told her. "You'll never convince me anything bad happened to them, not unless you find the bodies. Lonan is even smaller than Laxey. If someone murdered three girls and hid the bodies, we'd all have known about it before dawn."

She turned and walked away, taking her empty wine glass with her. Bessie swallowed a bite and then washed it down with her drink.

"Lonan is a small town," she said thoughtfully.

"So someone must know something," Grace said.

"Indeed," Bessie agreed. "The trick now will be getting them to admit to it."

"Hugh will work it all out," Grace said confidently.

"I hope you're right," Bessie told her. "I'd really like to know what happened to those girls."

When they'd both climbed back into Grace's car, the girl turned to Bessie. "I have some wedding errands to run this afternoon. Would you like to come along?"

Bessie opened her mouth to refuse, but Grace looked so hopeful that she changed her mind. "If you'd like me to," she said instead.

"I really could use a second opinion," Grace confided as she started the car. "Or rather a third or fourth opinion. Mum and I have been back and forth a dozen times and I asked my little sister what she thought, but she was no use at all."

"Opinion on what?" Bessie asked.

"You know it's just going to be a small wedding," Grace said. "So I was just going to wear a nice dress, but nothing fancy. When I went shopping, I found this gorgeous wedding gown and now I'm not sure what to do. My mother thinks I should wear the gown, because I'm only going to do this once, but it seems like such an extravagance. Anyway, I'd love to know what you think of it."

Bessie nodded. "I'm happy to offer my thoughts, but ultimately it will have to be your decision."

"Oh, I know," Grace said with a laugh. "But you're so sensible all the time. If you tell me you think it's too over the top for our small wedding, I'll know you're right."

Bessie sat back in her seat and tried not to frown. She didn't want to discourage Grace from getting an elaborate wedding gown if that's what the girl really wanted. But Grace was right; Bessie was far too sensible to encourage her young friend to spend a lot of money on something that would only be worn once, especially if it wasn't really appropriate for the small ceremony that Grace and Hugh were having.

The small bridal shop in Ramsey was only a few minutes away. Grace parked in their small car park and then turned to Bessie.

"I wasn't even going to look at wedding gowns," she said. "But my mother wanted to see if they had anything appropriate for her, and, well, once we were inside, I suppose I just got carried away."

Bessie smiled. "I'm sure that's easy to do," she said. "Now I'm really curious to see this dress."

Grace nodded and led Bessie into the shop. As the bell chimed softly, an older woman with short grey hair walked out of a small doorway at the back of the shop. Bessie looked around in surprise.

"Where are all of the dresses?" she asked. The room wasn't very large and it was furnished like a fancy sitting room, with comfortable-looking couches and chairs arranged in a circle. In the centre of the circle was a small raised platform. A huge three-way mirror stood in a corner.

The woman smiled at her. "We start by talking to our customers to find out exactly what they're looking for, and then we bring out some dresses that we hope might meet their requirements. This used to be a much larger room, with dresses on display everywhere, but I changed things around to help make my brides happier."

"How does this make brides happier?" Bessie asked.

"I used to feel bad when one of my customers would come in and find the perfect dress on display or on the racks and then discover that she simply couldn't afford it. This way we talk about price upfront and I never show my brides anything outside of their budget," the woman explained.

"I went to a bridal shop in Douglas that has dresses on display," Grace said. "When I told the shop assistant that I liked one dress but it was too expensive, she tried to persuade me to stretch my budget. It was awful."

"I'd rather make a little less money but sleep easily at night," the woman said cheerfully. "And you're back to see that dress you love, aren't you? Still trying to decide if it's appropriate for your big day?"

"Yes," Grace said, blushing. "It's just that it's going to be a small ceremony and reception. I don't know if I even want a proper wedding gown. Maybe just a nice dress or suit would be more appropriate."

"So you've brought Aunt Bessie to offer her opinion?" the woman asked.

Grace laughed. "Everyone really does know you, don't they?" she asked Bessie.

"I've lived on the island for a long time," Bessie said. She turned to the woman. "I'm sorry, but I'm not sure that I know you, though."

The woman laughed. "I'm Emma Harrison. I don't know that we've ever met, but everyone knows who you are," she explained. "I moved up north about ten years ago, after living in Port Erin for most of my life. This shop came up for sale and I'd always dreamed of owning my own little business. Anyway, I wasn't here for long before someone pointed you out to me. I believe they said you were an island institution."

"Oh, dear, I'm not sure about that," Bessie said. "But let's see this dress, then."

"You have a seat," Emma told her. "I'll just take Grace and get her changed."

Bessie sat down on the nearest couch, which was every bit as comfortable as it looked. There were a handful of magazines on the table next to her, so Bessie flipped through one of the ubiquitous celebrity gossip magazines that always seemed to fill waiting rooms these days. She was just catching up on the lives of a few total strangers when Grace returned. Bessie watched as the girl climbed carefully onto the small platform and turned to face her.

"Well, what do you think?" Grace asked anxiously.

The dress was fitted without being tight and showcased Grace's slender figure perfectly. After everything Grace had said, Bessie had been expecting something far more flamboyant. This dress was fairly simple, with only a few rows of sequins and beads at the neckline. The short train draped over the platform, and as Grace turned slowly, Bessie was able to appreciate the scattering of embellishments along it as well.

"It's absolutely perfect for you," Bessie said, almost without thinking.

"Really?" Grace asked.

"Really," Bessie said emphatically. "Not only is it perfect for you, it's perfect for a small wedding with friends and family. You look lovely and elegant and bridal, which is exactly how you should look."

Emma handed Grace a box of tissues as her tears began to flow. "I was so worried," Grace said after a minute. "I love this dress so much, but I didn't want people to think, well, I don't know, really, I just didn't want people to think something."

Bessie laughed. "It's your wedding day. You shouldn't care what anyone thinks. You should do exactly what you and Hugh want."

Grace frowned. "That's the other thing. I hate to spend all this money on a dress that I'll only wear once."

"I won't ask how much it is," Bessie said. "But if you can find the money in the wedding budget for it, I think it's worth every penny."

Grace nodded and then stepped off the platform and walked to the mirrors. She studied herself from every angle and then sighed. "I'm not sure I can resist," she said softly.

"I've just started working on getting the new spring line ready to show," Emma said now. "Let me check my books on that dress and see what we can do with the price."

She crossed to the small desk near the door to the back and began sorting through papers. After a moment she looked at Grace.

"Can you read the tag on the skirt? I just need the six-digit number at the bottom."

Grace found the tag and read out the number the woman needed.

Emma nodded and then tapped some numbers into her calculator. "It's just as I thought," she told Grace. "That dress has been discontinued by the manufacturer. No doubt next week they'll send me a flyer with another dress that looks exactly the same, except they'll have swapped some of the sequins or beads around or something, but that dress is no longer available."

"So I can't buy it?" Grace asked.

"On the contrary," Emma replied. "If you're happy to buy my

sample, rather than order a brand new dress, you can buy the one you're wearing at a considerable discount."

"I don't have time to order a new dress, anyway, I don't think," Grace said. "The wedding is on the fourteenth."

Emma laughed. "You definitely don't have time to order," she said. "Are you happy to buy the sample?" She named a price that seemed incredibly low to Bessie.

Grace's eyes went wide. "Are you sure?" she asked. "I mean, that's really inexpensive."

"I have no use for the dress now that I can't take orders for it anymore," the woman explained. "I always sell my samples for my cost price as they've been tried on, sometimes dozens of times."

"I don't care," Grace said. "I'll take it."

Emma smiled. "What about something for your head? A veil or a hat?"

Grace shook her head. "I'm six inches taller than my mother, so wearing her dress wasn't an option. But I am going to wear her head-piece and veil."

Grace went to change back into her ordinary clothes, leaving Bessie to chat with Emma.

"How much was the dress at full price?" she had to ask.

Emma shrugged. "About five times as much," she told Bessie. "But my prices are always flexible. That's another reason why I keep the dresses in the back and don't put prices on the tags. Most of the time I charge about the same as any other bridal shop, but it's nice to have the flexibility to offer a discount now and then, sometimes without the bride even knowing it's a discount."

"That's an unusual way to run a business," Bessie said.

"Eh, I retired early. Owning my own shop was always a dream, and now I have it and I love it, and as long as I break even, I'm happy. This place gives me a reason to get out of bed every day and I love working with brides. They're nearly always happy. The ones that are too demanding pay full price."

"Thank you for helping Grace. She loves that dress but she's on a tight budget."

"I know young Hugh," Emma said. "His mother is friends with my sister. He's a good solid young man. I'm happy to help him and his lovely fiancé out in a small way."

When Grace returned, Emma wrapped the dress up in a huge box. "Now, when you get it home, take it out and hang it up," she instructed Grace. "That will let all of the wrinkles fall out before the big day." She gave the girl some additional advice on caring for her gown before taking Grace's credit card payment.

"I shall have to run down to Douglas and hang the dress somewhere in my mother's house," Grace said thoughtfully as she drove towards Bessie's cottage.

"That's probably best," Bessie replied. "You won't want Hugh to see it before the big day."

"No, I don't."

Back at the cottage, Bessie's message light was blinking as she let herself in. "Oh, go away," she called to the answering machine as she hung up her coat. The machine didn't respond. After she'd made herself a cup of tea, Bessie played her messages. Only one was interesting, and that was Doona, asking her to ring her back at the police station.

"Doona? I hope nothing is wrong," she said when her friend answered.

"No, not exactly," Doona replied.

"Which means what?" Bessie demanded.

"We've had an anonymous caller ring in," Doona told her. "If you're home now, I'll send John over to talk to you about it because the message the caller left was rather cryptic. John's hoping you can help him work out the meaning."

"Me?"

"I'll leave it to John to explain," Doona said. "He's on his way now."

CHAPTER 7

*B*essie refilled the kettle, ready to make tea for the inspector when he arrived. It was just coming to a boil when she heard his knock on the door.

"John, how nice to see you," she greeted him.

"It's always nice to see you, too," he replied.

"The kettle has just boiled. Sit down and I'll make tea."

"Only if you can do it quickly," John said apologetically. "I really need to ask you a few questions, and then, hopefully, I'll have a lot to do."

"Ask away," Bessie suggested as she pulled out teacups. "I can talk and make tea at the same time."

"I don't know how much Doona told you, but we've had an anonymous phone call that has raised some questions."

"That was about all she told me," Bessie replied.

As John pulled out his notebook, Bessie put his cup of tea on the table. She sat down with her own as he flipped through the pages.

"Here we are," he said. "I thought I had it right, but it's too important to rely on just my memory. The caller said: 'If you want to find the Kelly girls, you need to look at the old Grantham place, maybe dig around the garden.' And then he or she disconnected."

Bessie sat back in her chair and took a sip of tea. John looked at her intently. "Do you know where the old Grantham place is?" he demanded.

Bessie nodded, her mind racing. "I haven't thought about it in years," she said. "Michael Grantham was the last in a line of farmers that owned a small piece of land between Laxey and Lonan. He died, oh, I don't know, sometime in the sixties, I think. In his will he left everything to a distant cousin who lived in South Africa, at least I think it was South Africa." She stopped and sipped her tea.

"And then what happened?" John asked. Bessie could hear the impatience in his voice.

"Oh, sorry," she said. "It took a long time to track down the missing relative. The farm became quite overgrown; I remember that. Anyway, when they found the man, he wasn't interested in owning a farm, but he also refused to sell the property for some reason. I suppose he might even still own it, or maybe his relatives do. No one has lived in the old farmhouse for some thirty years or more. I think the man sold off a few parcels of the land over the years, but I'm not sure."

"Do you remember his name? I need to speak to him about going in and digging up his garden."

"His name was Robinson or Robertson or something like that," Bessie told him. "But you should ring Doncan," she added. "He handled the estate and he should be able to put you in touch with the man or his family. Someone has been paying the rates for the last thirty years. Doncan will know who that is."

John pulled out his mobile and punched in a number from memory. A few minutes later, he was talking with Doncan Quayle, Bessie's favourite advocate. Bessie bustled around the kitchen, putting biscuits onto a plate, while she tried not to overhear John's end of the conversation.

Once John explained what he needed, there wasn't much to hear anyway, other than a few muttered "yeses" and the like. When John disconnected the call, he helped himself to a custard cream.

"I hope you don't mind if I wait here for a few minutes," he told Bessie. "Doncan is going to ring a few people and then ring me back."

"You're welcome to stay as long as you like," Bessie replied.

"I'm just going to get something from my car," he told Bessie. When he came back inside, he spread a large map of the area on Bessie's table.

"Can you show me where the farm is?" he asked.

Bessie traced the main road out of Laxey towards Lonan. "It's here," she said, pointing. "This is the entrance to the property and the house sits about half a mile down the drive."

John studied the map and then checked his notes. "It's listed in the public records as being owned by a Marilyn Madison."

Bessie shrugged. "I have no idea," she admitted. "I'm sure Doncan can explain."

"He told me that the property was left to Jacob Robertson and is now owned by his daughter. I suppose that's why I didn't find anything under Grantham when I looked. It was so long ago that none of the constables at the station knew the name either."

It wasn't long before John's phone rang. The conversation was a short one and when he disconnected he looked pleased.

"Doncan was able to reach the owner much more easily than he'd expected. He explained the whole thing to her and she's happy for us to do whatever we need to do," he told Bessie. "Doncan is going to get the paperwork started so it's all official, but I'm going to head over to the property now and see what I can see."

"I don't suppose you want any company," Bessie said, trying to sound casual.

"Have you ever been there before?" John asked.

"Many years ago now," Bessie said. "Michael and his wife used to sell their produce at the Laxey market, but as they got older they stopped farming all of their acreage and just grew a few crops. It wasn't worth getting a market stall for the few things they still had to sell, but if you wanted some of their excellent strawberries you could go and buy them from them during the season. I used to go two or three times during the summer and then make strawberry pies."

"What do you think the caller meant about their garden, then?" John asked.

"Michael's wife, whose name I have completely forgotten, had her own little garden behind the house. She loved flowers and that was all she grew there, mostly roses. Michael used to laugh at her spending all her time and effort on crops that didn't make them any money, but she enjoyed it and she always had beautiful roses in vases all over their house. That's the only thing I can think of that your caller might have meant."

"If I took you out there, could you show me where the rose garden used to be?" John asked.

Bessie nodded. "I spent many a sunny summer afternoon sipping tea in the rose garden and listening to Michael's wife complain about her husband," she said with a chuckle.

John swallowed the last of his tea and stood up. He grabbed another custard cream and then looked at Bessie. "How long until you're ready to go?"

"If you put the biscuits away and wash up the tea things, I'll be ready before you're finished," she promised.

While John started on those jobs, Bessie rushed up the stairs to comb her hair and freshen up. She was back in the kitchen as John rinsed the last teacup.

"This could be a wild goose chase," he remarked as he helped her into his car.

"It could," Bessie agreed. Once John was behind the wheel and the car was beginning its trip out of Laxey, she spoke again.

"It seems as if Hugh's digging has stirred something up, anyway."

"Yes, definitely," John agreed. "Just what we were hoping would happen."

"Is he meeting us at the farm?" Bessie had to ask.

"No, he's chasing down a few other leads," John replied. "We've had a few other interesting phone calls as well. If this turns out to be anything more than a waste of time, I'll ring him to join us."

The road to the old farmhouse was partly overgrown, and "No Trespassing" signs were posted at close intervals. John drove slowly down the very centre of the dirt track, trying to avoid overhanging branches and the worst of the ruts in the road itself. Bessie gasped as they reached the farmhouse.

"It used to be beautiful," she told John sadly. Now the front door was hanging off of its hinges and most of the windows were broken. As Bessie approached the front of the property, she could see where animals had climbed through windows and made themselves at home. Discarded bottles and cans also suggested human trespassers.

John was already on the phone to Doncan as Bessie peeked in windows and sighed over the state of the once gracious home.

"Bethany Grantham must be turning over in her grave," Bessie said after he'd finished the call. "As soon as I saw this, I remembered her name, the poor woman."

"According to Doncan, the current owners aren't interested in taking care of the property," John reported. "He sends them periodic updates on what's happening here, but they aren't willing to spend any money to remedy the situation. He thinks they're just about ready to sell, although what they'll be able to get for this mess is questionable."

"Property prices are going mad," Bessie reminded him. "With the house in this state, new owners will have no trouble getting planning permission to tear the whole thing down and start over. The owners will probably get a great deal more than they deserve for the place."

John nodded. "I'd love to have a look around inside, but I'm not sure it's safe. Maybe we'd better focus on why we're here."

Bessie sighed. She would have loved a chance to explore the house, but John was right. From the windows she could see missing steps and floorboards on the upper level, and the ground floor didn't look much better.

"How do we get to the rose garden?" John asked, looking left and right.

"There used to be a nice path," Bessie told him. "It led right from the front door around to the back of the house."

The path was now completely grown over and Bessie struggled to find any trace of it as she carefully made her way through long grass and tangled weeds. As they reached the corner of the house and turned towards the back, John insisted on going first.

"I'll try to hack my way through," he told Bessie. "If it gets much worse, we'll turn back and get someone up here with the right equipment."

Bessie followed John through waist-high weeds until they reached the back corner of the old farmhouse. The area behind the house looked almost like a jungle as Bessie stood and stared.

"We need men with equipment," John said, sounding frustrated.

"And lots of them," Bessie muttered as she tried to make sense of what she was seeing. Bushes and shrubs battled with small trees and tall weeds as far as the eye could see.

"Where was this rose garden?" John asked.

Bessie took another step forward and then closed her eyes. "Let me think," she muttered. She inhaled crisp February air and tried to imagine that it was a beautiful July day some thirty-five years earlier.

"It was in this corner," she said eventually. She looked back at the house and then nodded. "You can just see the remains of the path that led from the back of the house to the rose garden," she said.

John looked over and nodded. The path that started at the property's back door was only just visible in small patches where the weeds had yet to take over. It clearly headed away from the house and in the direction Bessie had indicated.

"At least it's winter, so the trees don't have leaves," she said, trying to find something positive to say.

"Yes, I suppose that's a help," John muttered. Bessie watched as he struggled a few steps further. "I can just see the path here," he told Bessie. "It's going in the right direction, but we'll need someone to clear it before we can even think about digging anything up."

He pulled out his mobile phone and started ringing people while Bessie tried to spot the old rose garden. Everything was too overgrown. She simply couldn't be sure of anything given the current conditions.

"People are on their way," John told her after a short while. "We should probably just wait in my car."

Bessie sighed and then nodded and led the way back around the house. They'd only just climbed inside when Bessie heard the sound of a car engine.

"That was fast," she remarked.

Instead of the police car or van she was expecting, though, the car that arrived was an expensive-looking sports car. The handsome dark-haired man who climbed out of it frowned as he looked around the outside of his vehicle. John greeted him.

"Doncan, we weren't expecting you out here," he said.

The man nodded. "My father suggested that I come out and act as an official representative of the owners," he replied. "He didn't warn me that I'd end up scratching the paintwork on my new car, though."

Bessie climbed out of the car and gave the new arrival a hug. While young Doncan had been working for his father for some time now, she still thought of him as the child she remembered. His father had been her advocate for many years, but Bessie knew young Doncan was in line to take over for the man eventually.

"The house is in a terrible state," John said.

"It is," Doncan agreed, shaking his head. "And so are the grounds. They've sold off nearly all the land around the house over the years. What you can see is just about all that the family still owns. I can't imagine why they've let it get into this condition, though."

"Are they all in South Africa?" Bessie asked.

"Yes, and as far as I know, they've never visited the island," Doncan replied. "My father sends them regular updates on the state of things, but they don't seem interested."

"Bethany Grantham would be devastated to see it like this," Bessie said.

"It doesn't look as if this has had thirty years to grow up," John remarked, looking around.

"No, at first they did pay someone to look after the property," Doncan said. "I think it was one of the neighbours who came over once in a while and made sure the house was secure and kept the grass cut. My father is going back through his records, but he thinks that neighbour passed away or moved and that was the end of that.

Over the years, my father has offered to find someone else to take care of things, but apparently the owners aren't willing to spend the money."

"It's probably too late now," John said. "The entire property will have to be demolished and rebuilt."

"Which is probably what a new owner would want to do anyway," Doncan said. "Doing up old houses is expensive."

Bessie smiled. "How's the work coming on your new home?" she asked. Doncan had recently purchased a large old mansion that had been sitting vacant for many years.

"Slowly," he said ruefully. "I can't afford to do it all at once, so I'm taking it slowly and steadily and trying to do a lot of the work myself. Ask me that question again in ten years or so and I might have a better answer."

Bessie laughed. "There's no rush," she told him. "I'm just glad you didn't tear the house down and start over."

"It might have been less costly," he replied. "I can't imagine how much everything I need to do is going to cost in the end, but at least this way I'm only spending a little bit of money at a time."

The sound of another vehicle approaching interrupted the conversation. This time it was a crew of gardeners from the village. Two of the men unloaded equipment while the third spoke to John. After a few minutes, John rejoined Bessie and Doncan.

"They're going to start by cutting a path through to the back of the property. Then they're going to work on clearing the path from the house to what was the rose garden. Jake, the supervisor, actually remembers visiting here as a child and he thinks he can remember where the rose garden was."

"I'll just have a quick word with them, if you don't mind," Doncan said.

"Not at all," John replied.

Doncan walked over to the supervisor, leaving Bessie with John.

"I suppose I don't really need you here, not if Jake's memory is reliable," he told her. "I can ring for a taxi for you if you'd rather go home."

"I'd rather stay," Bessie admitted. "I'm curious as to what you'll find."

John nodded. "You can stay, as long as you make sure you're well out of the way," he said. "But I don't think we'll find much of anything today. If we can clear a path to what used to be the rose garden, that's probably all we'll have time for before it starts getting dark."

At John's suggestion, Bessie climbed back into his car. He ran the heater for a few minutes for her before he headed off to check on progress. Doncan joined her a moment later, sliding into the driver's seat.

"I hope John won't mind," he said, grinning at Bessie. "I've always wanted to drive a police car."

Bessie laughed. "I'm sure you'll be fine, as long as you don't actually take it for a drive."

The pair chatted about Doncan's parents, the weather, and local politics while they waited. Nearly an hour later, John joined them.

"Bessie, can you walk back with me and see what you think?" he asked. "Jake is pretty sure he's in the right place, but I'd like your opinion."

Bessie nodded and climbed out of the car. Doncan was quick to follow, and the pair then walked behind John along the narrow path that had been created around the house. The men had cleared a large area behind the house, from the back door outwards, and now Bessie could see the old stone path that used to lead to Bethany's garden. The path curved to the side and then disappeared into the overgrown tangle that the men still hadn't touched.

"Hey, Aunt Bessie," Jake called as she looked around. "I was thinking that the rose garden was just here, right where the path ends."

Bessie walked over to where he was standing and then shut her eyes and tried to think. "The rose garden was to the left," she said eventually. "There was something else to the right of the path here."

"I think they tried different things," Jake said. "I remember pine trees there for a few years, I think."

"You're right," Bessie agreed. "Michael decided to try growing

Christmas trees, so he planted a few rows of them right here, near the house. I seem to recall him saying they were too much work and tearing them out after a few years."

"So the rose garden went off this way?" John asked, pointing.

"Yes," Bessie agreed. "Although there doesn't seem to be any trace of it now, does there?"

The men went back to work, now carefully clearing the area that Bessie and Jake had identified. In spite of the chill in the air, Bessie stayed to watch. After several minutes, Doncan's phone startled everyone.

"Yes, yes, okay," he said into it. "Sorry," he told Bessie after the call ended. "A client of mine has just been arrested and I need to go and sort it out."

Bessie didn't ask any of the questions that sprang to her lips. Instead, she watched the man leave, assuming that she'd hear the whole story before morning thanks to her extensive network of friends, many of whom did little else besides share island news with one another.

After another half hour, the workers had cut back the grass and shrubs and begun working on digging down into the soil.

"Um, Inspector Rockwell? You might want to look at this," Jake called from one corner of the space.

John crossed to him and the pair had a short conversation, staring at something on the ground in front of them. John's face was grim as he turned and headed back towards where Bessie was standing.

"What is it?" she asked as he reached her.

"At this point, I'm not sure," he said. "It could be an animal bone or something else entirely, but I'm not taking any chances. I'm getting a crime scene team out here with floodlights and the proper equipment and they're going to dig up whatever it is."

Bessie nodded and then swallowed a lump in her throat. She knew she was jumping to conclusions on very little evidence, but she couldn't help but feel as if they'd just discovered what had happened to the Kelly girls.

"I'm going to have someone take you home," John continued.

"There's nothing more you can do here and it looks as if it's going to be a long night. I'm of two minds about asking Hugh to join me. He has enough on his plate, really, but he won't want to miss this, either."

Going home suddenly sounded like a very good idea to Bessie. John was already making phone calls as she took a few steps backwards.

"Hey, Aunt Bessie, do you think the inspector still needs us?" Jake asked from behind her.

Bessie jumped slightly and then turned around. "He's never on the phone for long," she replied. "I'm sure you'll be able to ask him in a moment or two."

John dropped his phone into a pocket less than a minute later. Bessie gave herself a mental pat on the back as Jake spoke to him.

"Do you still need me and the guys?" he asked. "We're happy to stay as long as you want, but it's getting on to dinner time, so I'd like to send one of them to get sandwiches or something if we're still needed."

"Thanks, but I can't use you, even though I'd like to," John replied. "You've been great and you're on site and ready to go, but we need trained crime scene technicians now. You're all free to go."

Jake nodded and turned away. He'd only taken a few steps before he turned back. "Aunt Bessie, do you need a ride home?" he asked.

Bessie glanced at John and then smiled at Jake. "I don't want you to go out of your way," she said.

"It isn't really," Jake assured her. "Anyway, I have very fond memories of your little cottage. I wouldn't mind having a cuppa in your kitchen again for old times' sake, if you can spare the time and effort."

"I'd like that," Bessie told him. If pressed, she would have to admit that she barely remembered the man who had to be somewhere in his forties now. So many young men and women had spent time with Bessie over the years, and some had been considerably more memorable than others. After a quick chat with John, she followed Jake to his truck, trying to recall everything she could about the man.

He had a word with the other two men, who were quick to get into their own vehicle and drive away. Then he helped Bessie climb in and shut her door for her.

"You might not even remember me," he said as he slid behind the steering wheel. "My mother was sort of overprotective. She didn't approve of me spending time at your cottage, but she used to go across to see her sister for a week every summer. Dad didn't much care what I got up to while she was gone, as long as I stayed out of trouble. I used to drop by your cottage for tea every day during a single week every August, during my teen years."

Bessie laughed as the memory flooded back. "Oh, my, yes," she said. "I used to look forward to your visits, because you were such a well-mannered child."

Jake chuckled. "I was always on my best behaviour with you, because I was terrified that you'd ring my mother if I did anything wrong."

"I have never had to ring anyone's parents to complain about behaviour," Bessie told him. "And I've only ever had to ask one child to leave."

"We all knew you were strict, but kind," Jake said. "And that you made the best biscuits on the island."

"I used to bake a lot more than I do now," Bessie told him. "I'm afraid I've only shop-bought biscuits in at the moment."

"That's fine with me," Jake said. "My wife is after me to lose a few pounds, so we don't have anything sweet in the house at the moment. Any biscuit will be a huge treat."

While they'd been talking, they'd made their way down the bumpy path back to the main road. As Jake turned to head towards Laxey, something under the car's bonnet made a grinding noise.

"Oh, dear. That doesn't sound good," Bessie said.

"If you don't mind, I'd like to stop at the garage before I take you home," Jake said. "I'd rather not drive too far, just in case it's something serious."

"Of course I don't mind," Bessie told him.

Jake turned the truck around and they slowly made their way into Lonan. Bessie looked with interest at the garage when they stopped.

She'd never been there before, but this had to be the garage where Matthew Kelly worked.

"I'll just see if Matt has time to look at the truck now or if I'll have to leave it with him," Jake said, opening his door. "He's not usually very busy; that's one of the reasons I use him. Anyway, you just wait here a minute, okay?"

Bessie nodded and then settled back in her seat, looking around curiously. At first glance, the place looked almost deserted. There were two petrol pumps near the road, but one had an "out of order" sign hanging on it. The sign looked as if it had been there for a great many years, as the chain holding it to the pump was rusty. Jake was back a moment later, only opening his door long enough to pop open the truck's bonnet. It took Bessie a moment to realise that the man with Jake was Matthew Kelly. He looked far older than Bessie knew him to be.

"I was just leaving the old Grantham place when the noise started." Jake's voice sounded slightly muffled to Bessie from where she sat.

"What were you doing up there?" Matthew asked.

"The police got some tip about something going on up there and they needed us to clear out some of the mess," Jake said.

"What sort of tip?" Matthew snapped.

"No idea. Someone at the station rang the office and asked if we could put a crew together to clear some overgrown land, and we were happy to get the work," Jake replied. "Not much business for gardeners this time of year, you know."

"Who was there from the police?" was Matthew's next question.

"The surname was Rockwell," Jake answered. "I think he was an inspector."

"Not Hugh Watterson?"

"No. I know Hugh. He wasn't there, why?"

"He's digging around into, oh, never mind. If he wasn't there, it must be something else going on."

"We found some bones," Jake said.

Bessie heard a sharp intake of breath from Matthew. "Nothing to do with me," he muttered after a moment.

"I didn't think it was," Jake laughed. His laughter faltered after a moment. "What's this all about, then?" he asked Matthew.

"You've damaged your grunkle sprocket," Matthew replied. Or at least that's what it sounded like to Bessie. She listened intently as the two men discussed car parts for several minutes, understanding none of it.

"You should be okay now," Matthew said eventually. "If it gives you any more trouble, bring her back and we'll change out the whole thing."

"It may be time for a new truck," Jake replied. "This one is starting to fall apart."

"She still has some good years in her. Just treat her right and she'll keep you going."

"We'll see," Jake said. The bonnet slammed down, making Bessie jump. Her eyes met Matthew's and she forced herself to smile.

"Didn't know you'd added Aunt Bessie to your crew," Matthew said to Jake.

"I was just giving her a ride home," Jake explained.

"So she was out at the Grantham place?" Matthew demanded. He took a few steps and then opened Bessie's door. "What's going on out at the Grantham place?" he asked harshly.

"I was asked to point out where the old rose garden was," Bessie said. "Beyond that, you'd have to ask the police."

"Old rose garden?" Matthew frowned. "I understand you asked my wife a lot of questions this afternoon. Stay away from her."

"Now, Matthew, that's no way to talk to Bessie," Jake said.

"She's a meddling old woman. She ought to know better than to meddle in my affairs, though."

"I'd better get you home," Jake said to Bessie. "It's getting late. My wife will be worrying soon."

"Yeah, your wife's always looking for evidence that you're cheating," Matthew muttered. "If only she knew where to look."

Jake flushed and climbed into the car. "Thanks for sorting me out," he said to Matthew. "I'll see you around."

"Yeah, whatever," Matthew replied. He turned and walked back into the dilapidated garage as Jake turned the truck around and pulled away.

"Sorry about that," he muttered to Bessie. "Matthew's a bit, um, difficult sometimes."

"But he repaired the truck quickly," Bessie said, focussing on the positive.

"Oh, he loves motors and mechanical parts. He gets along with them better than people, but if you know Joanna, you already know that."

"I don't really know her," Bessie replied. "I just had lunch at the pub today."

A few minutes later Jake pulled up next to Bessie's cottage. "I won't come in after all," he said. "My wife really does worry if I'm late home."

"You must come another time, then," Bessie told him. "My door is always open."

"Thanks, Aunt Bessie," the man grinned. "I may just surprise you and take you up on that."

Bessie let herself into the cottage and sank down in the nearest chair. It had been a strange and stressful afternoon. Alone with her thoughts, she couldn't help but wonder what John was finding in the rose garden. Matthew had seemed upset, but to her mind he didn't act guilty. She'd have expected him to be a lot more nervous if he'd been responsible for the bones John had found.

Her phone rang, startling her.

"Bessie? It's Mary Quayle. I've spoken to Grace's parents and a few other people and now I think we need a travel agent. I'm not sure how we'll manage otherwise."

"I thought the same thing," Bessie replied. "I just hadn't managed to ring you yet to discuss it."

"What if we go into Douglas tomorrow? I'd rather use the company I always use, if that's okay with you."

"That's fine," Bessie assured her. "Do you want me to meet you in Douglas?"

"Oh, goodness, no," Mary said. "I'll collect you at half nine. We can be there when they open. Hopefully, it will be fairly quiet."

"I'll see you then," Bessie replied.

After a light dinner, Bessie curled up with a book, but found she had trouble focussing. Her thoughts kept returning to the overgrown rose garden behind the derelict property she remembered so well. Eventually, she took herself off to bed early and slept restlessly.

CHAPTER 8

*A*long hot shower followed by a longer than normal walk on the beach the next morning helped Bessie wake up. She was pacing around the kitchen, sipping a cup of tea, when Mary arrived.

"Hello, Bessie," Mary greeted her when Bessie reached the car. "I'm so excited to be doing this for Hugh and Grace."

"Yes, I am, as well," Bessie replied.

"You sound distracted," Mary told her.

Bessie sighed. "I'm sorry. I'm sure you've read about the cold case that Hugh's investigating. I suspect there might be a significant development in the case today."

"But you can't tell me what's going on," Mary said.

"I really shouldn't," Bessie replied.

"So let's talk about Paris," Mary suggested.

As they drove, Mary told Bessie about the various things that she'd already managed to arrange, while Bessie tried hard to pay attention. What she really wanted to do was ring John for an update, but she knew that John would tell her what he could as soon as he was able. The pair arrived in Douglas just before ten o'clock. Mary found a parking space in the large multi-storey car park and then they made their way down the street.

"They've always done an excellent job arranging holidays for me," Mary told Bessie as they walked to the travel agency. "I'm sure they'll be perfect for our needs."

"No doubt," Bessie replied. It had been years since Bessie had taken a holiday, aside from a brief trip across with Doona that hadn't been very relaxing. Maybe she should consider taking a trip herself.

Bessie recognised the woman who was just turning the "closed" sign to "open" as she and Mary reached the door. Kristen Kelly looked no older than thirty, with her blonde hair in a high ponytail, wearing a pair of dark sunglasses. She smiled brightly at Mary and Bessie as they pushed the door open.

"Good morning, ladies," she said. "We're having a special on winter sun destinations. Can I send you somewhere warm and tropical?"

Mary laughed and shook her head. "We need to talk to you about Paris," she said.

"Paris is the perfect getaway," the woman replied. "Close to home, but a world away."

Bessie bit back a sigh. There was no way she was going to be able to talk about the cold case if Kristen kept talking in advertising speak.

Mary didn't seem to mind, though. She followed Kristen to one of the desks and as soon as Bessie joined them, launched into an explanation of what they were trying to do. Kristen nodded and took notes as Mary spoke and then began typing things into her computer. Within minutes she was printing out a sample itinerary.

"We can adjust anything and everything," the woman said. "But let's start from here."

Ninety minutes later, after changing at least half of the items on the list, Mary was finally happy with Hugh's honeymoon. Bessie had made a few suggestions, but she left Mary in charge, as the other woman knew Paris well. The final price was something of a shock to Bessie, but Mary didn't bat an eyelash.

"I'll pay for the whole thing now," Mary told Kristen, handing her a credit card.

"I'm paying for the flights," Bessie reminded her.

"I can put the charges through separately," Kristen offered.

Bessie pulled out her own credit card and within minutes, Hugh's honeymoon was booked and paid for.

"I hope we're doing the right thing," Bessie muttered as she put the receipt into her bag.

"If he doesn't want to go, you can send me instead," Kristen offered. "I think I'm going to need to get away for a while."

"I hope nothing is seriously wrong," Bessie replied.

Kristen shrugged. "You probably know what's going on better than I do," she said. "My father rang me last night. Apparently the police rang to warn him and mum that they'd uncovered some bodies. It's just possible one of them is Karen's."

"I'm sorry," Bessie said.

"I suppose it will be good to finally have some answers," Kristen said. "If they're right. This isn't the first time this has happened. Every time a body turns up anywhere, my parents wonder and worry and hope and pray. It will be hard for them, if it does turn out to be her after all this time."

"I was reading about the case in the local paper," Mary said. "I didn't realise they'd found bodies."

"Just last night," Kristen told her. "I don't know what they actually found, just that they warned my parents that they'll probably want DNA samples to try to match with the skeletons or whatever."

"How awful," Mary said, shivering. "And one of the missing girls was your sister?"

"Yeah, Karen was my sister, and if she isn't dead, I'll never forgive her for leaving," Kristen said. Bessie thought she was trying to sound as if she were joking, but her words fell flat.

"I can't imagine how difficult that must have been for you," Mary said sympathetically.

"I was only six when she disappeared," Kristen said. "I don't really even remember her, but I definitely remember what happened after she'd gone."

"Six? That's very young," Mary murmured.

"Yeah, I suppose. Karen was fifteen and she'd already earned herself a reputation for being a troublemaker. Once she'd gone, my parents decided that none of the rest of us was ever going to get into any trouble, ever. My mother basically never let me out of her sight again." Kristen sighed.

"Your poor mother," Mary said.

"Yes, I suppose so, but as I got older, I didn't see it that way," Kristen told her. "I couldn't wait to finish school and move out of the house. When I think back now, I feel terrible about it, really, but my parents, whether they meant to or not, really smothered all of us. We all moved out as soon as we could and everyone else moved across. I'm the only one still on the island."

"It's such a beautiful place," Mary pointed out.

"Yes, and I do love it here," Kristen said. "But that also means I'm the one who has to try to deal with my parents when things like this happen. It was bad enough that they reopened the case in the first place. If they really have found Karen's body, well, my brother and sisters are going to have to come back and help me. I'm not dealing with my parents on my own if that happens."

"It will be a huge shock for them," Mary suggested.

"Yeah, and they'll blame themselves for not being stricter with her, which is exactly what I heard all through my childhood. 'Your sister was allowed to come and go as she pleased and then she ran away. You aren't going anywhere, young lady,'" Kristen said.

"What do you think happened to her?" Bessie asked.

"I always thought she'd found herself in trouble and ran away to take care of it," Kristen replied. "That was the story that always seemed to make the most sense to me, as I was growing up, anyway. And it was the one my mother always threw at me whenever I wanted to go out with a boy."

"Maybe that is what happened," Mary said. "Maybe what they've found doesn't have anything to do with your sister."

"I don't know," Kristen said. "I can't imagine anyone killing her, that's for sure. She was just a harmless fifteen-year-old girl. Why would anyone want to hurt her? Of course, I can't see why anyone would have done anything to Susan or Helen, either."

"Maybe the three disappearances aren't actually related," Mary said.

Kristen shook her head. "I'm sorry. You came in to book a holiday for your friend, not to listen to me complain about my childhood. Was there anything else today?"

Mary smiled and patted the woman's hand. "You have a lot going on in your life right now," she said. "It's only natural that you'd want to talk about it. Bessie and I are always happy to listen."

"Thank you," Kristen said.

As Bessie and Mary stood up to go, the door to the shop swung open. Kristen made a noise and then spoke quickly.

"Please, sit back down and pretend I'm looking for something for you," she whispered to Mary.

Bessie sank back into her seat and watched as Jonas and Tara Clucas made their way into the shop. She hadn't seen the couple in several years, but they were instantly recognisable. Tara was still stunningly beautiful and her husband still looked arrogant and unpleasant.

"We need a holiday," Tara said hesitantly, looking around the room.

There were three women standing behind the main reception desk and they all exchanged glances before one of them took a step forward, seemingly reluctantly.

"Certainly, we'll be happy to help you with that," she said in a saccharine-sweet voice.

"You'd better do a better job this time," Jonas snapped. "The mistakes that you made last time were almost unforgivable."

"I'm sure we can get things exactly right this time," the woman behind the desk said through gritted teeth. "Where did you want to go?"

Tara glanced at her husband and then back at the woman. "We were thinking about South America, for something completely different."

"South America?" the woman echoed. "I'll have to turn you over to Betty, then. She's our expert on that part of the world."

Bessie could tell which woman was Betty simply from the angry expression that flashed over her face as her coworker was speaking. She had a fake smile in place only a moment later, though, as she stepped forward.

"South America is a big place," she said. "And it's all gorgeous. Come and sit down and let's see what we can work out."

"We don't have time," Jonas barked. "We want to leave tomorrow. Book the whole thing for us and we'll be back to pay for it after lunch."

He spun on his heel and stomped out of the building, leaving his wife to mouth a quick "sorry" before she followed.

"I'm not doing it," Betty said loudly. "I'm not booking them a holiday without any instructions whatsoever. The last time we worked with them, we ended up having to refund most of the trip because they complained about everything. We are not going through that again."

"Ring Jennifer and ask her what she wants you to do," Kristen suggested. "It's her business. She can decide."

Betty nodded and picked up the phone. While Bessie wanted to stay to hear what Jennifer had to say, Mary was back on her feet.

"We'll just get out of the way," she told Kristen. "Thank you for all of your help."

"You're welcome," Kristen replied. "Thanks for bringing us your business."

Out on the street, Mary turned to Bessie and grinned. "I was a bit carried away in there, asking that poor girl all those questions. This playing detective is quite exciting in its own way."

"Yes, but Inspector Rockwell will be cross if he finds out," Bessie warned her.

"Does that mean you don't want to have lunch where I'm sure Tara and Jonas Clucas are having lunch?" Mary asked, winking at Bessie.

Bessie chuckled. "We have to eat somewhere," she pointed out.

"Exactly, and I might be wrong, anyway," Mary replied.

But she wasn't wrong. Bessie could tell that from the tension in the room, before she even saw the couple at the corner table. Mary had a quiet word with the woman at the door and the pair was led to a table right behind Tara and Jonas.

"Thank you," Mary said quietly to the woman.

"Thank you," she replied in a whisper. "No one else wants to sit near those two. They've done nothing but shout at us and each other since they arrived."

"And our second round of drinks is where, exactly?" Jonas demanded, glancing around the space.

"I'll check on that, sir," the woman who'd seated Bessie and Mary said. She disappeared towards the bar as Bessie opened her menu.

"I think I'll have the fish," Tara said softly.

"Have the chicken," Jonas told her. "I don't like the smell of fish when I'm eating. You know that."

"Yes, dear," Tara said. "I just thought, since it's breaded, that it wouldn't smell very strongly, that's all."

"No fish," Jonas replied. "I'm not sure South America is such a good idea. I bet they eat a lot of fish there."

Tara shrugged. "I wouldn't know. I've never been. Where would you rather go?"

"I don't want to go anywhere," Jonas said. "You're the one who's been complaining about needing a holiday. Like I want to spend a week with the children you insisted on having." The man sighed and shook his head. "Maybe you should take the children and go somewhere and I'll stay here and manage the business."

"It's up to you, of course," Tara said. "But the children are getting older. We might not have much time left for family holidays."

"What about China?" Jonas asked. "Do they eat a lot of fish?"

"Again, I don't know," Tara replied. "We should talk to the travel agent. She'll know."

"I don't like them," Jonas said. "And I don't want to waste my time. You can go and talk to them after lunch. Stay all day for all I care. Just get something booked so you can quit nagging me about it."

"Yes, dear," Tara replied.

The pair remained silent after that until Bessie and Mary were almost done with their meals.

"We don't want pudding," Jonas told their waitress. "And I wasn't happy with my food, either. I don't expect to see my meal on the bill."

"But, sir, you ate it all," the waitress replied.

"I was hungry, but it was substandard. I won't pay for it," Jonas replied.

"I'll have to get the manager," the waitress told him.

"No need," Jonas snapped. "Here," he handed the waitress a folded note. "This will pay for our drinks and my wife's meal. That's all you get. Come on, Tara."

Jonas rose to his feet and stomped towards the door, leaving his wife to rush after him. At the door, she stopped. "I've forgotten my bag," she said. "I'll catch up."

Jonas sighed deeply and pushed his way out of the building, leaving Tara to hurry back to their table.

She picked up her bag, and eyes on the door, pulled out her wallet. "Here," she said to the waitress, handing her another note. "I hope that's enough to cover everything. I can't, that is, he tracks, I mean, I hope that's enough." The woman rushed out, leaving Bessie and Mary staring after them.

"What a horrible man," Mary said loudly.

"He is, at that," the waitress said, walking over from the other table. "He comes in once in a while with his latest girlfriend, whoever that might be. He's a bit nicer when he's with one of them than he is with his poor wife. I don't know why she puts up with him."

"That's a very good question," Bessie said. "Maybe the police should ask her just that."

Mary insisted on paying for lunch over Bessie's protests. While Mary was driving Bessie home, Bessie rang the police station.

"Laxey Neighbourhood Constabulary, this is Doona, how can I help?" came the familiar voice.

"Doona, it's Bessie. Is John available?"

"Oh, no. Sorry, Bessie, but he'll probably be out of the office all day today. There's quite a lot happening at that old farm he took you to yesterday," Doona replied.

"I don't want to ring his mobile and disturb him," Bessie said. "But

I wanted him to be aware that Jonas Clucas and his wife are planning a holiday, leaving almost immediately. I don't know if the man is a suspect or not, but based on what I've seen of him today, I hope so."

"I'll pass the message along to John," Doona promised. "I'm sure he'll be in touch later today. As I said, there is a lot going on."

Bessie switched off the phone, feeling sad. It sounded very much like they'd found bodies at the Grantham farm.

"So they've found the bodies then?" Mary asked.

"I don't know anything for sure," Bessie told her. "But it certainly seems like it."

"And nasty Jonas Clucas is a suspect?"

"Again, I don't know," Bessie told her. "Someone told me that he was involved with Karen Kelly before she disappeared, but I don't know if that's true. Anyway, even if he was, as far as I know, there isn't any evidence to link him to the murders."

"But now he's planning a last-minute holiday," Mary pointed out.

"Yes, but he didn't sound too interested in going," Bessie said. "It sounded like his wife wanted a holiday more than he did."

"If I were her, I'd want a holiday from him, not with him," Mary replied.

"Indeed."

There was a car parked outside of Bessie's cottage when Mary pulled up. "You have a visitor," Mary said.

"I don't recognise the car," Bessie replied.

"Maybe we should ring John," Mary said nervously.

"I'm sure that isn't necessary," Bessie said firmly, squashing her own apprehension as she opened her car door. The driver's door on the other car opened as Bessie stood up.

"Aunt Bessie? I don't know if you remember me?" the woman called across the short distance.

Bessie studied her for a moment and then nodded. Last week she might have struggled more to recall the woman's face, but with everything that had happened lately, the woman had been on her mind. "Margot? Margot Lane?" she asked.

"I gather I haven't aged as badly as I feared," the woman said with a small laugh. "I was hoping we could talk, just for a minute, if you have time."

"It's okay," Bessie told Mary. "I know her."

"What's her name?" Mary asked.

Bessie repeated the woman's name and Mary wrote it down on a scrap of paper. "If you don't ring me in an hour, I'll send the police," Mary said.

"Don't be silly," Bessie told her. "I'm sure I'll forget to ring you and then you'll just worry the police unnecessarily. I'll be fine."

"I'll ring you, then," Mary said. "I won't forget."

Bessie wanted to argue further, but Margot was waiting, watching the conversation with a curious look on her face.

"Is everything okay?" she asked as Bessie walked towards her.

"It's fine," Bessie replied. "My friends are just a touch overprotective."

"That's hardly surprising, considering everything that's happened to you in the last year or so," Margot said.

"Yes, well, it's also unnecessary and a little annoying," Bessie replied.

"You should be grateful someone cares," Margot told her.

Bessie flushed and unlocked her door, counting to ten before she blurted out something she might regret later. "Would you like tea?" she asked, changing the subject.

"I'd rather sit on the beach, if that's okay with you?" Margot asked.

"It's a bit chilly," Bessie replied. "Let me get a warmer jacket."

There was a large rock planted firmly on the beach behind Bessie's cottage and it was just the right size for two people to sit on. Once they were both comfortably settled in, Bessie looked at the other woman.

Margot's makeup-free face was lined and careworn, her hair streaked with grey. It was tied back in a sloppy ponytail. Her clothes looked inexpensive and seemed a bit too large for the woman.

"How are you?" was the first thing Bessie thought to ask.

"Tired and old," the woman replied. "Oh, I know, I'm not even fifty yet, but mostly I feel much older. The years have been, well, difficult."

"I'm sorry."

"Not your fault," Margot shrugged. "Not anyone's fault, really. Well, maybe Susan's, if she really did run away. Her disappearance changed everything. I sometimes wonder how different things would be if she hadn't gone."

"I'm sure you've been over the events of the weekend she vanished a million times with the police," Bessie said.

"Maybe not quite that many," Margot smiled. "Actually, I think I only spoke to the police a few times back then. They didn't seem all that interested in what I had to say. My mother did her best to keep them away, as well. She was afraid I'd be scarred for life if they worked out that something awful had happened to Susan."

"It must have been difficult for her too," Bessie suggested. "She must have been terrified that something might happen to you as well."

Margot shrugged. "Anyway, now it's been thirty or so years and I've had to revisit the whole thing, this time without my mother chasing the police away."

"I hope they've been kind," Bessie said.

"Oh, aye," Margot said. "Hugh Watterson is a great guy. He was very gentle with me, really. It isn't his fault that I've had nightmares ever since I spoke to him."

Bessie patted her arm. "I'm sorry," she said softly.

"And then this morning one of my friends rang me to say that she'd heard they'd found Susan's body," Margot said. "I don't know if that's true, but I need to find out. I thought maybe you would know."

"I wish I did," Bessie replied. "I've been hearing rumours myself, but I don't know anything for certain."

Margot nodded. "Of course you'd say that, even if you did know," she said. "You know what's weird? In all these years, after everything that happened, I never once thought that Susan might be dead. That's weird, isn't it?"

"Maybe you just didn't want to consider the worst-case scenario," Bessie suggested.

"We had a fight," Margot said, her voice almost dreamily detached. "She was meant to stay for the weekend, but we had a fight and she decided to go home. We didn't fight very often. We were both nice girls, girls who were young for our age, really."

"Can you remember what you fought about?" Bessie asked.

"Every single word," Margot said bitterly. "Susan had a new boyfriend. She was so excited. Neither of us had ever, well, as I said, we were young for our age. She was first of the pair of us to get a boyfriend and I was jealous. She wanted to sneak out that first night to meet him and I said she couldn't. I told her I'd tell my mom if she went, so she didn't, and then the next morning she told me she was going home. She said she could sneak out of her house without getting caught. She didn't need my help."

"Do you know who he was?"

"She wouldn't tell me," Margot said with a sigh. "I told Hugh that she was very secretive about him. I'm sure he was too old for her or something. She definitely didn't want me to know who it was."

"That wasn't like her," Bessie remarked.

"No, it wasn't," Margot agreed. "I was really angry with her and I told her that she was going to get herself into trouble, but she just laughed and said something about it being her turn to have some fun. I'm sure she was thinking about Karen, who'd already had a dozen or more boyfriends."

"If you had to guess, who do you think the boyfriend was?"

"I don't know," Margot said. "I think, at the time, I thought maybe she was seeing one of the Clucas boys. Peter was okay. I really liked him, actually, and Susan knew that. I assumed, back then, that that was why she wouldn't tell me who she was seeing. I thought she was involved with Peter behind my back."

"What about Jonas?"

"He was busy with Karen," Margot told her. "From what I could see, those two were inseparable at the time. I kept expecting to hear that Karen was pregnant, really."

"If it wasn't one of them, was there anyone else?"

"Oh, Matthew Kelly's name came up when I was talking to Hugh," Margot said. "He was involved with Helen, but they kept splitting up and getting back together every other day. He might have starting chasing after Susan to make Helen jealous. That would have been like him."

"It's hard to imagine anyone killing any of the girls," Bessie said.

"I know. I suppose that's why I never gave the idea any thought. I always assumed she'd run away. When she first went, I thought maybe she'd gone with the new boyfriend, but no one else went missing, well, not until the next weekend."

"If she did run away, why hasn't she been in touch for all these years?" Bessie asked.

Margot shrugged. "There was a time when I thought I knew Susan better than anyone, but when she told me about her new boyfriend, she was different, somehow. I saw a side to her that I hadn't known existed before that night. Now I wonder how well I knew her at all."

"This must all be very painful for you," Bessie said.

"Thinking she might be dead is the hardest part," Margot admitted. "Maybe not thinking about it as a possibility was my way of dealing with it. Now I have to consider that her death was my fault."

"In what way?"

"If we hadn't had that fight, she wouldn't have left my house," Margot said, her eyes filling with tears. "She would have been safe there."

"Nonsense," Bessie said sharply. "You can't blame yourself for what happened, whatever that turns out to be. I understand you feel bad about fighting with her, but you can't possibly believe that that was what got her killed, if she was killed, that is."

"I don't know," Margot said sadly. "I just feel as if I could have saved her."

"She was going to sneak out, you said," Bessie reminded her. "And anyway, Karen and Helen both disappeared as well and neither of them were meant to be at your house."

"I know. And I keep telling myself that I'm being silly, but I can't help but feel as if our fight was what sent her to her death."

"There is only one person responsible for her death, assuming she is dead, and that's the man or woman who killed her," Bessie said stoutly. "Whatever circumstances led up to her crossing paths with the killer, he or she made the decision to commit murder and that's nothing to do with you."

Margot swallowed hard and then nodded slowly. "I'm sure you're right," she said softly. "There's a part of me that wishes the police had just left the case alone."

"I know," Bessie told her. "But it seems as if they might finally be making some progress on it."

"Yeah, I'm just not sure that's a good thing," Margot said.

"If someone did kill the girls, then that someone deserves to be brought to justice," Bessie said.

"I can't argue with that," Margot said. She shivered. "And it's a scary thought, actually," she said. "I can't imagine living with that secret for all these years."

Bessie nodded. "It's scary to think that there might be a murderer on the island who has never been punished for his or her crimes."

"I wish I'd made Susan tell me more about her boyfriend," Margot said softly. "It just didn't seem important at the time."

"And it might not have anything to do with the case," Bessie pointed out.

"But it seems like it does," Margot said. "They say you should live life without regrets, but I'd do anything to get that one night of my life back, especially if they do find Susan's body."

"We'd all do things differently if we had our lives to do over again," Bessie told her. "But as you can't change the past, you must work on making the best of your future. If you think of anything that might help the investigation, let Hugh know as soon as possible."

"I will," Margot promised.

"And remember," Bessie added. "Nothing that happened was your fault."

Margot nodded, but Bessie wasn't sure the woman believed her. As Margot made her way back to her car, Bessie let herself back into her cottage. The phone rang almost immediately.

"It's Doona. Can Hugh and John and I come over for dinner?"

"Of course," Bessie said.

"We'll bring Indian food and something borderline healthy for pudding," Doona told her.

Bessie put the phone down and spent the next hour tidying her kitchen before vacuuming the entire cottage. She was eagerly anticipating what she might learn during the evening ahead.

CHAPTER 9

*H*ugh was the first to arrive, carrying a large box and a small tub. "Doona said to bring something almost healthy for pudding," he explained as he put his parcels on the table and gave Bessie a hug. "Apple pie is mostly fruit and vanilla ice cream is mostly milk."

Bessie laughed. "I'll go along with that," she said as she slid the pie into the oven to warm and then put the ice cream in her freezer.

John and Doona arrived together only a few minutes later. John was carrying a box full of takeaway containers, and Bessie inhaled the delicious scent of Indian food as he put the box down to get his own hug.

"Let's eat before things get cold," John suggested.

Bessie pulled out plates and glasses as Hugh got everyone cold drinks from Bessie's refrigerator. They were all sitting down with very full plates only a moment later. Bessie had only taken a single bite when someone knocked on her door.

As she got up to answer it, John stood up and followed her.

"I can answer my own door," she told him tartly.

"I just need to stretch my legs," he replied, smiling.

Bessie glared at him for a moment and then sighed as the knock was loudly repeated. She crossed to the door with John right behind her.

"Ah, um, good evening." The young police constable at the door was a stranger to Bessie.

She blinked in surprise and then smiled. "Good evening," she said. "Is there something wrong?"

The man shook his head, his eyes moving past Bessie to focus on John. "Oh, Inspector Rockwell, sir. I didn't realise that you were here, sir."

"What's the problem, Constable Jones?" John asked sharply.

"No problem, sir. We were rung by a concerned member of the public and asked to check on Miss Cubbon, sir, that's all," the young man said.

"Mary," Bessie said grumpily. She glanced over at her answering machine and saw the blinking light. "Some of my friends are overprotective," she told the constable. "I'm very sorry that you were dragged down here. As you can see, I'm absolutely fine."

"I'm sorry to have bothered you," the man said. "Have a nice evening."

John followed the man out, walking back to his police car with him. Bessie grimaced when she saw that he'd left the lights flashing on his car when he'd come to her door. Leaving the cottage door ajar for John, Bessie walked back over to the table and sat down. She took several bites before she stopped herself. Too angry to enjoy her food, she sat back and tried to decide what to do. John was back before she'd come to any decisions.

"I'll ring Mary after we've eaten and have a word with her," John said. "What made her think you might be in danger?"

"Margot Lane was here when Mary dropped me off," Bessie explained. "Mary said she'd ring me in about an hour, but I must have missed her calls, maybe when I was vacuuming. I never expected her to ring the police."

"I appreciate her concern," John said. "But she should have tried calling you more than once before calling the station."

There were actually three messages on the answering machine from Mary. Bessie noted the times of the increasingly frantic calls.

"I was still sitting outside with Margot the first time she rang," she told John. "The other two were while I was vacuuming. You can't hear anything over that vacuum cleaner."

"I'll give Mary my mobile number," John said. "The next time she has a concern, she can ring me instead of the station."

"Give her mine as well," Doona suggested. "Or maybe just mine."

John nodded. "Maybe that would be better," he agreed.

Bessie finished her meal, still feeling slightly cross with her friend. While she knew that Mary had acted out of concern, she hated when people fussed over her. Before pudding, John rang Mary and after he'd talked to her, he passed the phone to Bessie.

"I'm so very sorry," Mary said as soon as Bessie spoke. "I don't know why, but there was something about that woman that made me nervous. I know I overreacted and I hope you can forgive me."

"It's fine," Bessie said. "Just don't do it again."

Mary's laugh sounded strained. "I won't," she said.

As the foursome settled down with warm pie and ice cream, Bessie looked at John. "I assume you have lots to tell me," she said. "What's going on?"

"As this is Hugh's case, I'll let him answer that," John replied.

Hugh looked up from his large piece of pie and blinked. "Oh, right, er, sorry," he said. "You know we've been working at what was the Grantham farm. Well, we've found human remains."

"That's sad," Bessie said.

Hugh nodded. "It will take some time to identify the bodies, of course."

"Bodies? Plural?" Bessie asked.

Hugh shoveled a large bite of pie into his mouth and then nodded at Bessie. Bessie took her own mouthful as she waited for Hugh to swallow.

"As of six o'clock tonight, we know we've found the remains of at least four people," Hugh told her.

"Four? But that's one too many to be the Kelly girls," Bessie said. "Who else have you found?"

"As I said, identifying the remains will take time. We've taken DNA samples from all of the girls' parents. We just have to hope we can get sufficient DNA from the remains to perform the necessary tests," Hugh said.

"But four bodies?" Bessie repeated. "I'm sure no one else went missing around that same time."

"We've reason to believe that the bodies were buried there over a number of years," Hugh told her. "And we haven't finished excavating. There may well be more remains still to find."

Bessie shook her head. "That doesn't make sense," she said. "At least not in connection with the Kelly girls' disappearances."

Hugh shrugged. "All we can do is investigate what we've found. Preliminary comments from the coroner suggests that all four skeletons are female and that they were all in their late teens when they died, but that's strictly preliminary."

"So that does fit," Bessie said.

"All of this will be in the local paper tomorrow," John said. "We're hoping that the general public might have some suggestions as to who else we might have found, assuming three of them are the Kelly girls."

"That seems a big assumption at this point," Bessie said thoughtfully.

"We're also attempting to track down dental and medical records for the three girls," Hugh said. "That isn't proving easy, as so much time has passed, but we're doing what we can."

"I know you can match dental x-rays with remains, but what good are medical records?" Bessie asked.

"If any of the girls had any unusual injuries, that can help us with identification," Hugh explained. "An arm broken in more than one place or something like that would leave marks on the bones."

Bessie nodded. "I didn't know any of them well enough to know about such things, but I'm sure the families will remember."

"We've also found some clothing and other items," Hugh added.

"Apparently artificial fibres take a long time to decompose. Anyway, we're working on getting those identified."

"How awful for the families," Bessie said.

"We're hopeful that the DNA results will be conclusive, but they could take a week or more. Even after all this time, I can't help but feel as if we need to keep the investigation moving as quickly as possible," Hugh said.

"Whoever you've found, they must have been murdered," Bessie suggested.

"We're certainly treating the investigation as a murder investigation," Hugh said. "It's hard to imagine any other way the bodies would have all ended up there together."

"Unless the site is an ancient burial ground or something," Doona said. "Maybe you've found an old cemetery?"

Hugh shook his head. "We don't have any definite answer on dating the remains yet, but they've been there less than fifty years, for sure."

"There certainly wasn't a cemetery there when the Granthams owned the property," Bessie said.

"Tell me about them," John invited. "Until we can date things more exactly, we have to consider the possibility that Michael Grantham buried the bodies."

"I barely knew the man," Bessie said. "He inherited the family farm when he was fairly young, around the turn of the century. By the time I started visiting the farm to buy the limited crops they were still growing, Michael and Bethany were quite old. I think they both passed away in the sixties."

"They never had children?" John asked.

"They did," Bessie replied. "But none of them survived to adulthood."

"How sad," Doona murmured.

"I don't suppose they buried their children in the rose garden?" Hugh asked quickly.

"No, they buried their children in Lonan cemetery," Bessie said. "I remember talking to Bethany once about the roses and her mentioning how much she enjoyed taking piles of them to her children's graves in the old churchyard."

"You don't know whether they had boys or girls?" John asked.

Bessie shut her eyes and tried to think. "I simply don't recall," she said eventually. "Bethany used to talk about her children once in a while, but I didn't know at the time that it might be important one day. I seem to remember at least one boy, and maybe two girls, but I may be wrong. Anyway, as I recall, they all passed away fairly young, certainly before their teens. You should be able to find all of it in the old church records, anyway."

"Yes, and we have someone checking into that tomorrow," John said. "I was just wondering what you could remember."

Bessie nodded. "I have to say, I can't imagine them being involved in any murders. They were simply ordinary farmers."

"And sometimes ordinary people commit extraordinary crimes," John said.

"Yes, I know," Bessie said sadly, thinking about some of the investigations she'd been involved with in the last year. "But killing four young women and hiding the bodies seems like the work of a serial killer or something. It doesn't seem possible, really."

"Serial killers don't usually stop," Doona said, sounding a bit nervous.

"It's far too early to be speculating about such things," John said, patting Doona's hand. "It could be quite some time before we can be sure exactly what we've found at the farm. In the meantime, we're taking a good look at all of the possible suspects from the Kelly case."

"Matthew Kelly, Peter Clucas and Jonas Clucas," Bessie said. "Those are the names that keep coming up whenever anyone talks about the case. Are there any other suspects?"

"We're considering a great many other people," John said. "From the family members of the missing girls to local shopkeepers and land owners, but it is true that those three were the original investigating officer's chief suspects."

"And he knew his job," Bessie said.

"But he never managed to make an arrest," Doona pointed out.

"It is hard to arrest someone if you don't have any bodies," John said. "Anyway, we are taking a hard look at those three, as well as considering nearly everyone who lived in the area in those days."

"What about means, motive, and opportunity?" Doona asked.

"At this point we haven't any idea what killed the girls whose bodies we've found," John said. "We have to assume that everyone had access, therefore, to whatever weapon or weapons might have been used."

"Or that they were killed without weapons," Hugh added.

Bessie shuddered. "Whoever it was had to get the girls somewhere alone," she said. "But I don't think that would have been difficult."

"I would have thought that by the time Karen disappeared, Helen would have been on her guard," Hugh said.

"Which suggests that the killer was someone she trusted," Doona said.

"Maybe," John said.

"From everything I know about her, she wouldn't have taken the warnings seriously," Bessie said. "Remember, too, we all really thought the girls had gone voluntarily. I doubt Helen thought she was in any danger, whatever her parents or the police said."

"And that's often true for teenaged girls," John said. "Or teenagers in general, I should say. They feel as if they're immortal and that their parents worry too much about things that will never happen. Even if we have found the Kelly girls, we've also found another girl that fits the same profile."

"So that's means and opportunity," Bessie said with a sigh. "What about motive?"

Bessie looked around at the other three. For a long time no one spoke. Eventually, John cleared his throat.

"As we don't know for sure whom we've found, that's a really difficult question," he said.

"If it was the Kelly girls, I can't imagine any motive, anyway," Bessie said.

"Because of the gender and age of all four sets of remains, we have to consider that someone was targeting teenaged girls," Hugh said. "There are any number of reasons why that might be the case."

"You're suggesting they were sexually assaulted before they were killed," Doona said flatly.

"That's not something we'll be able to determine from the remains," John told her.

"There must be other motives," Bessie said.

"There could be," John agreed. "Sometimes these things escalate as well. Maybe the first girl died accidently, and the perpetrator discovered that he or she enjoyed watching someone die and began to actively seek out victims."

"This is a horrible conversation," Bessie said. "Let's talk about something pleasant instead."

Hugh was kind enough to fill the next half hour with everything he could remember about Grace's wedding plans. The menu for the reception was discussed in great detail, as that was one thing he could recall quite clearly. Eventually, over tea and biscuits, Bessie brought the conversation back around to the Kelly girls.

"Maybe one of the girls found out something she shouldn't about someone," she suggested.

"It's possible," John said. "And the others might have been killed because the killer thought they knew his or her secret as well."

"If we consider our three main suspects," Doona said, "which one would have had a secret that important?"

"It didn't have to be all that important," Hugh argued. "The killer just had to think it was."

"I don't like Jonas Clucas," Bessie said. "And I find it very suspicious that he's planning to leave the island right now."

"I spoke to him today," John told her. "When I suggested that the police would appreciate his cooperation in remaining on the island for the time being, he actually thanked me. He said his wife was desperate to get away but he really didn't want to go."

"That matches up to what we heard," Bessie said. "But I still don't like him. He seems thoroughly unpleasant."

"What about the other two?" Hugh asked. "We all know you're a good judge of character."

Bessie thought back to the different investigations she'd been involved with recently. Overall, she felt as if she'd suspected the wrong person far more often than the right one, but she didn't say that to Hugh. "I saw Matthew Kelly yesterday," she told them. "He's rather unpleasant as well."

"How did you happen to run into him?" John asked.

Bessie explained about Jake's truck and then recounted the conversation she'd overheard. "He didn't seem that interested in what was found at the Grantham place," she concluded. "He just said it wasn't anything to do with him."

"Which is a strange thing to say," Doona argued. "If someone told me that the police had found a body somewhere, I wouldn't even think to bother denying any involvement."

"He's somewhat odd," Bessie said. "And slightly scary."

"Stay away from him," John advised. "And everyone involved in the case," he added.

Bessie shrugged. "Margot Lane came to see me," she reminded him. "And I just happened to stumble across Jonas Clucas twice." She hadn't mentioned that Mary had deliberately suggested lunch where she knew the man would be.

"We haven't discussed Peter Clucas," Hugh said. "What do you think of him?"

Bessie shook her head. "I haven't seen the man in many years," she said. "I know he ran a bit wild back when he was younger, but I understand that he straightened himself out and now works on drug and alcohol counseling. Claire spoke very highly of him."

"I've worked with him and I like him," John said. "I would hate to think he was involved in whatever happened."

"I don't feel as if we've made any progress," Bessie said as she nibbled her way through a biscuit.

"I don't know if we can at the moment," Hugh said. "Not before we're sure exactly who we've found."

"Bessie, I'd appreciate any suggestions you can make as to people I can talk to about the Granthams," John said, pulling out his notebook. "As the bodies were found on their property, they have to be considered people of interest."

Bessie listed the names of a few of the men and women who used to own farms in the area. "Some of them are still farming the same land," she told John. "Others gave up years ago and moved into Douglas or across."

She found her address book and gave John the best contact information she had for each of them. "When you ring them," she told him about one couple, "make sure you talk to her. He's more than a little senile and likely to tell you anything."

John made notes as she gave him similar information about each of the others. When she was done, he smiled. "And that's why I didn't simply start by canvassing the neighbourhood," he said. "Your local knowledge has saved me many frustrating hours of knocking on doors."

"You know I'm always happy to help," Bessie replied.

She let them all out, locking the door behind them. Doona had insisted on taking care of the washing-up before she left. Now Bessie dried the plates and cups and put them back into the cupboard. She was tired, but her brain was racing, trying to work out what the police had found at the Grantham farm. Unable to settle herself enough to read, Bessie decided she needed some fresh air.

Up until she'd found her first murder victim, almost a year earlier, Bessie had never hesitated to walk on the beach at night. Now, however, she didn't feel quite as safe as she had before. She argued with herself for a minute before grabbing a jacket and sliding on shoes.

"Life is too short to worry about nothing," she told herself sternly as she unlocked the door at the back of the cottage. She walked out and breathed in the sea air as deeply as she could. The tide was too far in for her to reach the rock she'd sat on earlier with Margot, so Bessie turned and wandered slowly down the beach, using a torch to illuminate her way. When she reached the bottom of the stairs to Thie yn Traie, she turned around and walked slowly home again.

The walk had been exactly what her body and soul had needed, she decided as she prepared for bed. The fresh air had cleared her mind and the exercise had tired her enough that she was asleep only moments after she laid her head on her pillow. Her internal alarm woke her promptly at six and she sat up feeling refreshed and determined to help John and Hugh with their difficult case.

Feeling as if she were the only person awake on the whole island, Bessie had a quick breakfast and then set out on her usual morning walk. The sun wasn't up yet, but she was happy with her torch as she strode down the beach. The walk to Thie yn Traie seemed too short today, so Bessie continued on, breathing deeply and keeping her mind firmly focussed on Hugh's upcoming wedding and other happy subjects. After some time she found herself on a stretch of beach that ran behind a new housing estate that she was only vaguely aware of. She blinked in surprise at the row of brand new houses in various stages of completion.

"You should really pay more attention to these things," she told herself as curiosity pulled her away from the water and closer to the new homes. They all had large sliding doors at the back of the properties, which gave them gorgeous views of the sea. Bessie stood and stared into one of them, trying to imagine how the property was laid out.

"This must be the dining room," she said eventually, trying to imagine the empty space filled with furniture.

"The one on the end is a model home," a voice said from her left.

Bessie spun around and put her hand to her chest. "I didn't hear you coming," she gasped.

"Sorry, I didn't mean to startle you," the young man said with a laugh. "If you walk down to the other end of the road, you'll find the model home. It's fully furnished so you can see how we think people will use the spaces."

"Oh, I shall have to do that," Bessie said. "I'm incurably nosy."

The man laughed again. "I'll walk along with you, if you don't mind. Maybe I can answer any questions you might have."

Bessie frowned. While the man looked pleasant enough, she was suddenly very aware that they were alone in a very lonely spot.

"I'm Peter Clucas," the man said casually. "I'm the project manager on the site."

"I see," Bessie said steadily.

"I'm also one of the main investors in the project," he told her. "So if you know anyone who's looking for a nice new house with great views, send them my way."

Bessie grinned. "I don't think I do, but I'll keep it in mind."

"I don't have the keys on me, or I'd give you a tour of one of the properties. I think they're pretty special."

Bessie nodded. The young man was very likeable, even if she still wasn't sure she could trust him.

"Let's walk over and peek at the show home," he suggested. "The sales manager will be here after ten o'clock if you wanted to book an appointment to see the inside."

"I'm not house-hunting," Bessie told him. "I'm just nosy."

The man nodded. "Lots of people are, especially the neighbours," he said. "We had an open day last month, and nearly everyone who came by already lived in Laxey and just wanted to get a good look at what we're doing."

He stopped as they reached the last house in the row. Bessie peered in through the large sliding doors and smiled. The room was clearly meant to be a dining room, exactly as she'd thought.

"The kitchen is off to the left," Peter told her. "There's a large reception room at the front of the property and upstairs there are three bedrooms and two bathrooms."

"Peter?" a voice shouted from the opposite end of the street. "I can't work out your coffee maker and I really need a cup of coffee."

The young man rolled his eyes at Bessie. "My father loves to be by the sea," he told her. "So sometimes he stays out here with me. I'd better go and help him with the coffee maker."

Bessie stared at the man who was crossing the beach towards them and then gasped. "Your father is Peter Clucas," she said as she recognised the man.

"You know my father?" the young man asked.

"I knew him many years ago," Bessie explained.

"My goodness, Elizabeth Cubbon," the older man said as he reached the pair behind the model home. "I was just thinking about you, actually."

"You were?" Bessie asked, surprised.

"Your name keeps coming up in my conversations," he explained. He turned to his son and grinned. "You go and rustle up some coffee for all of us," he told him. "I'll just walk back slowly and chat with Bessie as we go."

The younger man hesitated and then nodded and walked quickly away, leaving Bessie with his father.

"I do hope people have been saying nice things about me," Bessie said, trying to keep her tone light.

Peter chuckled. "Actually, everyone seems to think you're incredibly nosy," he said.

Bessie gasped and found herself at a loss for words. Before she could remedy that, Peter held up a hand.

"I didn't mean that quite the way it sounded," he said. "But there are a lot of folks that aren't real happy about the police reopening the Kelly girls' case file, and several of the people I've spoken to seem to think you're involved in the investigation."

"I don't work for the police," Bessie told him. "I have spoken to them about the case, but only because I'm old enough to remember the girls."

"And I'm sure you remember the suspects," Peter said bitterly.

Bessie nodded, unsure of exactly how to reply.

He sighed deeply and then turned and offered Bessie his arm. "We should go and get that coffee," he said. "I'm going to need it today, I think."

Bessie took his arm and they began a slow walk back down the beach.

"I've made a lot of mistakes in my life," Peter said after a few steps. "Getting involved with the Kelly girls was one of them."

"Everyone talks about them as a group, but I didn't think Susan spent much time with the other two," Bessie said.

"Oh, they all ran around in the same crowd," Peter replied. "Susan was sweet and pretty naïve, but Helen and Karen were doing their best to change that. There were half a dozen of us, maybe, that all hung around together."

"Were there other girls in the crowd?" Bessie asked, thinking about the fourth body.

"Margot was part of the group, although her parents didn't give her as much freedom as the others had. And there was another girl. I can't quite remember her name, but she and her family moved away just before the other girls disappeared."

"And you and your cousin Jonas were there," Bessie said.

"Yeah, and Matthew Kelly and Donald Quayle."

"I'd forgotten about him," Bessie said. "His name hasn't come up during the investigation at all."

"He was never a suspect." Peter said. "He was dead before the girls disappeared."

Bessie was silent as she remembered the charismatic young man who'd wrapped a stolen car around a tree on the night before his seventeenth birthday. "His accident was about a month before Susan vanished," Bessie recalled.

"Yeah, it was the first half of the wake-up call I needed to turn my life around," Peter told her. "The disappearances were the other half, of course. Once that happened, I realised I needed to stop drinking and do something with my life."

"I've heard good things about the work you do," Bessie told him.

"Thanks," he said. "I enjoy what I do and I hope I'm helping other kids make the changes they need to make without having to live through the sort of tragedies I experienced."

"I'm sure you've heard that the police have been excavating at the old Grantham farm," Bessie said casually.

Peter shot her a look and then nodded. "I did hear that," he said softly.

"I understand they received an anonymous tip," Bessie said. "And I understand that they've found human remains." John had said that much was going to be in the local papers. Bessie could only hope she wasn't speaking too soon.

"Yeah, that's what people are saying," Peter agreed. "And now I think I'd better be off. I've a lot to get done today."

"But your son will have the coffee ready by now," Bessie called.

"Yeah, tell him I'm sorry. I was too busy chatting with you to notice how late it was."

Bessie watched as he crossed the road next to the site office and climbed into one of the cars that was parked there. He drove away slowly, leaving Bessie with the job of explaining his behaviour to his son.

"I'm sorry," she said. "We were talking about the missing Kelly girls, and then he said he had to leave."

Peter nodded. "He doesn't like to talk about them. He's upset about what's going on at the Grantham farm, too. He used to spend a lot of time out there. He said it was peaceful."

Bessie sipped her coffee and didn't reply. Peter's behaviour had felt somewhat odd and she wanted to report the conversation to John. Was it possible that the man had turned his life around after murdering several young women?

Over their drinks, Peter's son showed Bessie several glossy brochures about the new homes while she tried to pretend she was interested. When she finally managed to get away, she felt as if she'd been stuck in the builder's office for hours. The walk back to her cottage seemed to take a good deal longer than the walk the other way had. Bessie knew that was just because she was eager to speak to John. She found herself hurrying along, anxious to repeat the conversation while it was still fresh in her mind. As soon as she'd let herself into her cottage, she rang the police station.

"John, I'm so glad I caught you," she said. Before he could do much more than say hello, she launched into her report. When she was done, she blew out a long breath. "Sorry, I just had to tell you all of that before I forgot anything," she said.

"I think I need to have a chat with the man," John said. "Thank you for sharing all of that with me. I wonder…"

Bessie never did find out what he wondered, as he stopped speaking. After a moment, Bessie could hear his voice and someone else's, but they sounded far away and muffled. Then John was back.

"I'm sorry, Bessie, but I need to go," John said.

"I hope everything is okay," Bessie said, subtly fishing for information.

"There was an accident at the garage in Lonan," John replied. "I don't know anything beyond that at this point."

He disconnected before Bessie could ask him any questions. She put her phone down and stared straight ahead with unseeing eyes. An accident at the garage in Lonan could only mean one thing, she thought. Something had happened to Matthew Kelly.

CHAPTER 10

*B*essie was surprised when she looked at the clock. She'd been out all morning. No wonder she was hungry. It was already time for lunch. Wondering if John and the others would be coming around for dinner again that evening, Bessie prepared a light lunch of soup and sandwiches. While she'd insisted that Hugh take the rest of the apple pie home with him the previous evening, she'd kept one small slice for herself. Now she reheated it and added a generous scoop of ice cream. She felt better as she did the washing-up and tidied the dishes away.

When Bessie's phone rang, she answered it almost without thought.

"Elizabeth Cubbon? It's Dan Ross with the *Isle of Man Times*. I was wondering if I could get a quote from you about the sudden and untimely death of Matthew Kelly?"

"I'm sorry, what did you say?" Bessie demanded.

"Oh, dear, I am sorry. I assumed that your police connections would have already informed you of the man's death," the reporter said. "I didn't realise that I'd be breaking the bad news to you. How close were you to the dead man?"

Bessie took a deep breath and then spoke in carefully measured tones. "I'm obviously very distressed to hear that something has happened to Mr. Kelly. I understand he was very good at his job."

"Yes, but he was also caught up in the middle of a police investigation," Dan said quickly. "Do you think guilt over his past crimes was what drove him to kill himself?"

"He killed himself?" Bessie echoed.

"Maybe, now that the bodies are starting to turn up, he knew he was going to be caught and he decided to take the easy way out," Dan suggested.

"I'm not sure anyone would consider suicide easy," Bessie said tartly. "And I couldn't possibly comment on any of this."

"Oh, come on," Dan cajoled. "Everyone knows you're privy to the inner workings of the Laxey Constabulary and that you hear about everything that happens in Laxey and Lonan. Give a poor reporter a hint, at least."

"As I said, I couldn't possibly comment," Bessie replied. "Good day."

She set down the phone and then frowned at it. It wasn't the phone's fault that she hadn't thought to wait until the answering machine picked up, of course, but that didn't stop her from feeling unhappy with the device. When it rang again almost immediately, Bessie switched off the ringer and grabbed a jacket. For the second time in two days, she found herself sitting on the large rock behind her cottage, staring at the sea.

It was hard for her to imagine that the man she'd only just spoken to was dead. And suicide? That was even more unbelievable. Matthew Kelly hadn't seemed like the type to take his own life. Bessie watched the waves as the tide slowly moved in. She didn't usually spend much time thinking about death or her own mortality. They were simply unavoidable facts of life. But now she felt slightly off-balance from the unexpected turn of events. As the tide began to creep up over the edge of the rock, Bessie wondered if she ought to head back inside.

After another minute, she climbed down reluctantly, trying to think how she might fill the rest of her day. She was surprised to see a car in the parking area next to her house. The sound of the sea had drowned out any noise it had made as it had arrived. Bessie felt nervous as she made her way towards the car that was unfamiliar to her. There was definitely someone in the driver's seat, Bessie realised as she walked across the sand. But who?

Bessie was relieved when she recognised the woman behind the wheel. Joanna didn't seem to notice Bessie as she approached. The newly widowed woman was staring through the windscreen at the sea, a steady stream of tears flowing down her face. When Bessie reached the driver's door, she tapped gently on the window.

Joanna looked at her and then slowly rolled her window down. "I hope you don't mind me sitting here," she said to Bessie in a strained voice.

"You're welcome to sit here as long as you like," Bessie told her. "Or you can get out and sit on the beach, if you'd prefer. You could even come inside and have a cuppa if you'd like."

"Can I?" Joanna asked plaintively.

"Of course you can," Bessie told her. "Sweet milky tea will do wonders for you, and I'm sure I can find a few biscuits to go with it as well."

Joanna nodded and then glanced down. "I'm wearing my pyjamas," she said, sounding surprised.

"I don't mind what you're wearing," Bessie told her. "I once had a new widow at my table in nothing but a skimpy silk nightie."

"I'm a widow," Joanna said slowly. "I hadn't realised."

The tears, which had slowed, began to fall heavily again.

"Come on, now," Bessie said briskly. "It's no good crying out here. Come on inside and have some tea and sympathy."

Joanna nodded and then slowly put the window back up. When it was in place, she opened her car door and climbed out slowly. Bessie was relieved to see that she apparently slept in quite sensible pyjamas, although the woman's fuzzy slippers weren't well suited to crossing the sandy parking area.

"Sit back down and let me go and get you some shoes," Bessie suggested. "You'll ruin those slippers walking on the sand."

"These are my old slippers," Joanna told her. "I use them for taking out the bins and things. They're already in pretty bad shape."

Bessie would have argued further if Joanna hadn't strode away from her, straight towards Bessie's cottage. Bessie only just caught up when Joanna reached the cottage door. After unlocking it, Bessie ushered the other woman inside.

"Sit down and relax," she told Joanna. "I'll just get the kettle on."

Joanna sank into the nearest chair and rested her head in her hands. Bessie switched the kettle on and then found the nearest box of tissues.

"Here now, have some tissues," she offered as she sat down opposite her weeping guest.

"Thanks," Joanna muttered.

Nothing else was said until the two women each had a cup of tea and a plate of biscuits in front of them. Joanna dried her eyes for the tenth time and then gave Bessie a wan smile.

"Thank you," she said, taking a sip of her tea.

"You're welcome," Bessie replied. She picked up a chocolate digestive and took a large bite. Some situations simply required chocolate.

"I'm crazy," Joanna said after a second sip.

"I'm sorry for your loss," Bessie replied, deliberately not reacting to the woman's words.

"Thank you," Joanna said. She shook her head. "It's crazy how upset I am. We were talking about getting a divorce. We weren't happy. I, well, I was going to leave him next month. I had it all planned out. And here I am, carrying on as if I'd just lost the love of my life."

"Grief is an odd emotion," Bessie said. "It rarely affects us the way we think it should."

"When the police came, I didn't really believe them. I'm not sure I believe it now, really. Matthew was, well, not the easiest man to live with. I knew he had his demons, but I never thought he would ever take his own life. I'm not sure that he did."

Bessie patted her arm. "I'm sure the police will investigate thoroughly. They'll work out exactly what happened."

"After the police came and told me what had happened, I rang my mother," Joanna said. "She never liked Matthew, but then she's never liked any of the men in my life. I was just so shocked that I didn't know what else to do."

"Was she not very sympathetic, then?" Bessie asked.

"That's one way of putting it," Joanna said with a bitter laugh. "She said a lot of very hurtful things, but that's not why I'm here."

"Why are you here, then?"

Joanna looked at Bessie intently. "You have friends in the police. You know what's going on with the Kelly girls' case. Have they really found the bodies after all these years?"

"They've certainly found bodies," Bessie told her. "Although I think the word skeletons might be more accurate. As far as I know, they haven't been able to identify any of the remains as yet, though."

"Who else could it be?" Joanna asked. "It isn't as if we have groups of people disappearing from the island every day. If they found three skeletons of teenaged girls, they can't be anyone else."

"I'm sure the police will be sharing their findings very soon," Bessie said, not wanting to speak out of turn about the fourth body.

"Yes, but, I mean, you see, my mother suggested that the reason Matthew committed suicide is because he killed the Kelly girls," Joanna said.

The woman's eyes filled with fresh tears as Bessie struggled to work out how to respond.

"I suppose that's one possibility," Bessie said eventually. "But only one of a number of them."

"I lived with the man for several years," Joanna said. "He wasn't the smartest or nicest or whatever, but there's no way he ever killed anyone."

"Did you know him back when the girls disappeared?" Bessie asked.

"You're as bad as my mother," Joanna snapped. "No, I didn't know him then, but no matter how much people change over time, he wasn't a murderer. I'd have been able to tell."

"I've met more than my fair share of murderers over the past year,"

Bessie replied. "One or two might have raised my suspicions when I met them, but for the most part, they all just seemed like perfectly normal people."

"Matthew wasn't bothered about the divorce," Joanna said. "We had some fun together at first, but it wasn't working out, that's all. If I'm honest, I'm not really sure why we got married in the first place, except my mother kept nagging us about it. Who worries about living in sin these days?"

Bessie pressed her lips together and counted to ten. While she knew she shouldn't judge other people's choices, she personally felt that living with someone was a poor substitute for being married. While she'd never been married herself, she'd also never lived with a member of the opposite sex. Things had been different in her youth, of course, but to her mind some things hadn't improved as the years had passed.

"Yes, well, mothers always want what they think is best for their children," she said eventually.

"Yeah, the key there being what they think is best. Never mind what I thought was best," Joanna replied. "I didn't really mind getting married, I suppose, I mean we didn't have a big wedding or anything, but we got a few presents from friends and family. That's always nice. Anyway, I was talking about Matthew's state of mind. He wasn't unhappy. I can't understand why he'd kill himself."

"When did you see him last?" Bessie asked, feeling nosy.

"He came home after work around five. I had to work the last shift down at the pub, so I made us both some dinner and then I left for work around six. He wasn't home when I got back."

"Was that unusual?"

Joanna shrugged. "It wasn't exactly usual, if you know what I mean, but it wasn't the first time, either. A lot of times, especially if I was out, he'd go back to the garage for a while. He had a couple of his own projects in the extra garage at the back, and sometimes he'd go and tinker for a while. He was usually home not long after midnight, though."

"Were you worried when he didn't come home?"

"I worked from six to half twelve," Joanna told her. "I was exhausted when I got home and went straight to bed. I might have worried, if I'd been awake, but I was fast asleep until the police knocked on my door."

"I'm afraid I don't know anything about what happened," Bessie said. "The only thing I'd heard before you came was that he'd passed away."

"Someone stopped to pick up their car this morning and they couldn't find him anywhere. Apparently, when they walked around the garage, they could hear a car running in that garage at the back where Matthew kept his own things. When they didn't get an answer to their knocks on the garage door, they rang the police."

"How awful," Bessie said.

"The police rang the owner of the garage and he brought the key," Joanna continued. "Matthew was in the garage, sitting on the floor between the two cars he'd been working on. Both engines were running and the entire space was filled with toxic fumes."

"Maybe it was an accident," Bessie said soothingly as the woman began to cry yet again.

"Matthew worked with cars his entire life," Joanna replied. "He knew everything about them, including how dangerous they could be. There was no way he would have shut all of the garage doors and then started both engines. Anyway, the police said there was a cloth or something pushed in all along the bottom of the garage's overhead door, filing in the small gap there. That had to have been put there deliberately and for only one reason."

"So if he didn't kill himself, it was murder," Bessie said, thinking aloud.

Joanna gasped. "Surely not," she protested. "Why would anyone have wanted to kill Matthew? He was hard to live with, but then so are most people. My first husband was much worse and he's still alive, more's the pity."

Bessie shrugged. "I'm probably chasing shadows," she said. "But I'm sure the police will be considering the idea as well."

"No one had any reason to kill Matthew," Joanna said. "But then,

143

he didn't have any reason to kill himself, either." She sighed deeply. "It's all just a big mess," she said sadly.

"You mentioned the missing girls," Bessie said. "It does seem possible that Matthew's death is tied to that somehow."

Joanna sat for a moment, seemingly thinking hard. "Matthew must have known who killed those girls," she said eventually. "Maybe the killer was afraid he'd talk, so he shut him up for good."

"As I said, I'm sure the police are considering every possibility," Bessie said.

"But which is worse?" Joanna asked her. "I hate the thought of him killing himself, but that seems slightly less horrible than thinking he was murdered."

"You should simply mourn the loss of the man you loved," Bessie told her. "Whatever happened to him, that doesn't change."

Joanna nodded. "I suppose I can do that," she said. "I think I'd better get home and, well, I need a shower and some clothes. That would be a good start. Thank you for the tea and the conversation."

"You're welcome any time," Bessie told her. "Do let me know about funeral arrangements and whatnot, won't you?"

"Oh, there will be something formal in a few days, but there's going to be a gathering at the pub tonight for friends and family. You're more than welcome to join us. Peter suggested it. He reckons my friends and family will turn out to support me. We aren't really expecting much from Matthew's family."

"I may try to come by," Bessie said. "Is it okay if I bring a friend?"

"Oh, the more the merrier," Joanna said. She frowned. "That isn't exactly what I meant," she said quietly.

"I know what you meant," Bessie assured her. "And I'll probably see you later."

"Any time after six," Joanna said as she walked to the door. "I'll probably be there until midnight or later. Officially, I have the night off, but I think I might be better off working, really. I need to find ways to keep my mind occupied, you know?"

"I'm sure Peter will do what he can to accommodate you," Bessie said. "I'll see you later."

She let Joanna out and then sat back down at the table and began absentmindedly nibbling her way through another biscuit. When her phone rang, she jumped.

"Bessie? John and Hugh are too busy to do anything, but I thought maybe you and I could have dinner tonight," Doona suggested.

"Yes, let's," Bessie agreed. "How about at the Cat and Longtail?"

"The pub?" Doona asked. "I suppose we could."

"Joanna was just here. They're having a gathering there tonight in memory of Matthew," Bessie explained. "I told her I'd come for a short while."

"Why don't we have dinner somewhere a bit nicer and then just stop in for a drink after?" Doona suggested.

Bessie couldn't argue with that and they quickly agreed on their plans. With less than an hour to go before Doona was due to collect her, Bessie rang Mary.

"I just wanted to make sure our plans for Hugh and Grace are still on track," she told her friend.

"I just talked to Kristen this morning about everything," Mary told her. "It's definitely coming together."

"Let me know what else you need from me," Bessie said, feeling a bit guilty about the work Mary was putting into the surprise. It had been Bessie's idea and she really should have been taking care of all of the details.

"I'm so pleased to have this project to work on," Mary said. "Although I do feel as if I've taken it away from you. If you want me to step back, just say so. It's only because I've so much time on my hands right now, with the house coming along nicely and George across for a fortnight."

"I didn't know George was across," Bessie said.

"Oh, yes, he's visiting some old friends that I never liked," Mary told her with a laugh. "I used having to plan Hugh's honeymoon as my excuse for not going, so now I feel as if I have to do the work."

Bessie laughed. "If you're happy to do it, I won't argue," she said. "I'm quite caught up in Hugh's cold case."

"I hear it's getting quite hot, that case," Mary said. "Do be careful, won't you?"

"That's enough fussing," Bessie said. "And no more ringing the police on me, either."

"I am awfully sorry about that," Mary replied.

"I know, and I won't mention it again," Bessie said. "As long as it never happens again," she added silently.

With that phone call out of the way, Bessie went up the stairs to change. She and Doona were going to her favourite restaurant, and she wanted to look nice. When she went through her wardrobe, though, she hesitated over her choice. After dinner, the gathering at the pub was something roughly akin to a memorial service or funeral. While considerably more informal, it still required a certain standard of dress.

Bessie sighed as she pulled a plain black dress out of her wardrobe. No matter what anyone else was wearing, she wouldn't feel appropriately dressed for the gathering at the Cat and Longtail in anything else.

Once she was ready, Bessie found her place in her book and settled in, hoping to get through a chapter before Doona arrived. She laughed at herself when she jumped a short time later. Knowing that Doona was coming hadn't prepared her for the sudden knock on the door, at least not during the particularly intense scene she was reading.

"Come in," she invited her friend. "I hope we can spare two minutes so I can finish this chapter? I know they'll get out alive, but I'd really like to know how they manage it."

Doona laughed and followed Bessie into the sitting room. Bessie grabbed her book and quickly found her place again while Doona plopped herself down on the couch. Two minutes later Bessie shook her head and slid her bookmark into place.

"Not happy with it?" Doona asked.

"I hate when authors pull rabbits from hats," Bessie grumbled. "Or in this case, suddenly have one of the characters reveal a hidden talent for lock picking and the ability to hold his breath for several minutes on end." She sighed. "It is called fiction for a reason," she conceded.

"As I get older, I have less and less patience with books I don't like," Doona said. "I actually stopped reading a book after one chapter the other day. I used to force myself to read the entire book, no matter what. Then I decided that if I wasn't interested once I reached the halfway point, I could stop. Now, I stop whenever I decide I'm bored. I should get through a lot more books that way."

Bessie laughed. "I'll finish this one," she said. "The big escape was the climax. It's all just tying up loose ends now and I do want to find out what happens to a few of the characters. Some of them I quite liked, although I must admit that I wasn't fond of the man who turned out to be half magician and half fish, even before he saved the day."

"We really don't have time for you to finish it now, though," Doona pointed out, glancing at her watch.

"Oh, no, it will be exactly what I need when I get home tonight," Bessie told her as the pair walked back into the kitchen. "Whatever happens at the pub later, I'll need a nice happy ending to fall asleep with."

"Let's just hope the author didn't leave a cliffhanger, then," Doona said.

"If she did, I won't buy the next book," Bessie said stoutly.

"You could just wait and get it from the library," Doona suggested.

"That's a wonderful idea," Bessie laughed. "I really should spend more time in our local library. When I was younger and I had to be more careful with my money, I used to get nearly all of my reading material from the library. Just because I can afford to buy books now doesn't mean I should."

Bessie found her sensible black flats and slipped them on. She'd already switched her essentials into the matching black handbag. Now she dropped her mobile phone into the bag and smiled at Doona.

"I'm ready and I'm starving," she said.

"Me, too," Doona replied.

The drive was a short one and Bessie was happy that they'd made a booking when she saw how full the car park was. "Are they ever not busy?" she asked as Doona squeezed her car into one of the last spaces available.

"I don't think so," Doona replied. "But they do have the best food in Laxey, so it's hardly surprising."

"It's certainly one of the best restaurants on the whole island," Bessie said. "Although I do think it was even better when Andy was doing the puddings."

Andy Caine had grown up on the island and spent a great deal of his childhood at Bessie's as he tried to avoid his difficult family life. Once he'd turned eighteen, he'd moved across, only returning to the island during a recent family crisis. When everything was resolved, he'd found himself heir to a great deal of money, which was now allowing him to pursue his dream of attending culinary school. When he finished, he was hoping to open his own restaurant on the island.

"Ah, Miss Cubbon and Mrs. Moore," the host greeted them. "We have your table ready for you in a quiet corner."

The pair followed the man across the room and settled into their chairs.

"We have a new menu," the man told them both. "Many of the old favourites are there, but we've add a few new things and made small changes to some of the other menu items as well."

Bessie opened her menu and glanced appreciatively at the selection. It was a good thing she was hungry, she thought as she almost immediately spotted several things that sounded good.

"We also have a new pastry and pudding chef," the man continued. He glanced around the room and then leaned closer to Bessie. "He isn't quite in Andy Caine's league," he admitted softly. "But he's quite talented in his own way and he's done a few clever things with some of our standard offerings."

"Maybe I should look at the puddings menu first," Doona said. "Then I'll know how much else I want to eat."

"I'm happy to share that menu with you now, if you'd like," the man replied.

"Oh, no," Doona said. "I'd be far too tempted to simply get two or three puddings and skip the main course altogether."

"I wouldn't recommend that," the man told her. "But I know exactly what you mean. I think we should petition the House of Keys to declare one day a year 'eat pudding first' day, where you're allowed to do all those things that aren't really good for you, but won't do you any harm once a year."

"If you want to run for office on that platform, you'll get my vote," Doona told him.

"I'll keep that in mind," he said, winking at her.

"What a lovely idea," Doona remarked as she opened her menu.

"Hm," was all that Bessie said in reply. Perhaps she was just a touch too old-fashioned, but the very idea of eating pudding before you'd had a nice healthy meal made her uncomfortable.

"Should we get wine?" Doona asked as the waiter approached.

"I think I'll stick to tea for now," Bessie said. "As we're heading to the pub later."

"Oh, yes, I suppose you're right," Doona said, sounding disappointed.

They placed their orders for drinks and food and then sat back in their chairs.

"It's really busy tonight," Bessie remarked as she looked around the full dining room.

"As you say, it always is," Doona replied.

Bessie nodded and smiled at a few people she recognised around the room.

"So why are we going to the pub later?" Doona asked. "It seems a strange place for a memorial service."

"It's more of an informal gathering," Bessie explained. "Mostly to support Joanna more than anything else. She's pretty upset."

"From what I'd heard, the pair of them didn't get along very well," Doona said. "I wouldn't expect her to be happy, but I'm surprised she's upset."

"Sudden loss is always upsetting," Bessie replied. "And she must have loved him once or she wouldn't have married him."

"I'm hardly one to talk," Doona admitted. "I was devastated when Charles died, even though we'd been apart for two years and I'd filed for divorce. I think I was more upset about missing out on what might have been than what really was, but whatever, I was definitely upset."

"I'll be curious to see who else turns up tonight," Bessie admitted as the waiter delivered their drinks.

"Who are you expecting?" Doona asked.

"That's just it," Bessie explained. "I'm not sure who to expect. It might be just you and me and Joanna, or nearly everyone involved in the Kelly girls' cold case could show up. I imagine the reality will be somewhere between those two extremes."

"You're not to question suspects," Doona said quickly.

"I wouldn't dream of it," Bessie said airily.

Doona frowned. "Maybe I should ring John and have him meet us there," she said thoughtfully.

"Didn't you say he was busy tonight?"

"I did. There's a lot going on at the old Grantham place still, and now there's a new crime scene to investigate."

Bessie opened her mouth to ask a question, but Doona held up a hand.

"I should say potential crime scene," she said quickly. "Under the circumstances, no one is rushing to any conclusions on what happened to Matthew Kelly just yet."

"Perhaps we should let John know about the gathering at the pub," Bessie said as the waiter presented their dinner plates. "If half the people I'm thinking might be there actually do show up, it could turn into an interesting evening."

Doona nodded and then took a bite of her entrée. "This is delicious," she told Bessie as she picked up her handbag. She rummaged around in the bag for a moment before pulling out her mobile. Before using it, she took a second bite.

Bessie concentrated on her own meal as Doona spoke to John. The conversation was short and Doona was quickly eating again.

"He's going to try to get there," she told Bessie between bites. "Or he might send Inspector Lambert."

Bessie frowned and took another bite to prevent herself from speaking. She didn't like Anna Lambert and she wasn't convinced that the woman was good at her job, but Doona already knew all of that. As Doona worked with the woman every day, she had her own reasons to dislike the disagreeable woman.

"I told John I thought it would be best if he was there," Doona added. "Or Hugh, as it is still technically his case."

The women ate every bite of their meals and then turned their attention to the new sweets menu. Bessie debated for a moment between two choices, but in the end chose the selection with the most chocolate.

"Two triple chocolate sponge cakes," the waiter said. "Excellent."

When they were finished, both Bessie and Doona agreed that they'd made the right choice.

"Andy may be slightly better, but I can't possibly complain about your new pastry chef," Bessie told their waiter. "That was delicious."

Dinner had been thoroughly enjoyable, but now, as Bessie slipped on her jacket, she felt apprehensive. She was suddenly grateful that Doona had rung John. Knowing a senior police official was going to be there made her feel slightly better about the evening ahead, even if it did turn out to be Anna Lambert at the pub.

CHAPTER 11

*T*he pub was busy when Doona reached the car park. She pulled into one of the only spaces left and glanced at Bessie. "It looks as if Matthew was a popular man," she said.

"I suspect people are here for Joanna's sake, rather than because they were fond of Matthew," Bessie replied.

"I didn't think it would be this busy," Doona remarked as she opened her car door. "Maybe no one will notice us and we'll manage to hear something interesting."

"No doubt we'll hear a lot of skeet," Bessie answered. "Whether any of it will be relevant to Hugh's cold case is another matter."

Bessie was disappointed when they got inside. While the pub was crowded, she couldn't see anyone that was in any way involved in the investigation into the Kelly girls' disappearances. Joanna was sitting on a bar stool in the centre of a large group. She'd clearly been crying recently, but the man next to her said something that made her laugh just as Bessie caught her eye.

"Ah, Bessie, you came," Joanna shouted across the room. "Come and get a drink. Peter is buying for everyone tonight."

"That explains the crowd," Doona murmured as she and Bessie crossed the room.

"I'm so sorry for your loss," Bessie told the woman as Joanna hugged her tightly. "It's so nice to see so many people have come out to pay their respects."

Joanna laughed. "They're here because the drinks are free," she told Bessie in a confiding tone. "But I don't mind. I need to keep my mind off my troubles and getting drunk with friends is the perfect way to do that."

Bessie didn't agree with the sentiment, but she wasn't about to argue with Joanna right now. "Meet my friend Doona," Bessie said, gesturing.

"Nice to meet you, I'm sure," Joanna replied, nodding in Doona's direction. "Get yourselves some drinks and then come back and talk to me, won't you? Doona, you can tell me your life story. You look as if you've had an interesting life."

Doona shrugged and then she and Bessie took the handful of steps needed to reach the bar.

"Ah, Bessie, I'm ever so glad to see you," Peter said from behind the bar. "I know you're here to support Joanna and pay your respects. You didn't just come in for a free drink."

Bessie shook her head. "I'll happily pay for my drink, even," she told the man. "I do what I can to support our local businesses."

Peter laughed. "That's kind of you, but unnecessary. I can afford to pour a few free drinks tonight for Joanna. What would you and your friend like?"

With glasses of wine in hand, Doona and Bessie turned back around to survey the room. "Is there anyone here you'd like to talk to?" Doona asked curiously.

Bessie let her eyes wander around the space. She knew nearly everyone there, at least in passing, but she didn't really want to talk to anyone she saw. Maybe coming wasn't such a good idea, she thought as she looked back at Joanna, who had a small crowd around her now. A couple sitting in the corner of the room caught her eye.

"My goodness," she exclaimed. "It's James and Sarah Kelly. I wasn't expecting to see them here."

"Which ones are they?" Doona asked.

"Susan's parents," Bessie told her. "I haven't spoken to them in years. Time to remedy that."

She crossed the room with Doona on her heels. As she approached the table where the couple was sitting, James was just getting to his feet. Bessie walked a bit faster, but she needn't have bothered, as James struggled to get upright. He'd just dropped back into his seat when Bessie arrived.

"James and Sarah, how wonderful to see you both," she gushed as she reached the table. "Neither of you seems to have aged a bit since I saw you last."

Bessie wasn't lying. The hard-working farmers had both always looked somewhat older than their years. Now, as time had passed, their appearances seemed to have stayed the same while the calendar caught up with them.

"Ah, Bessie, I wasn't expecting to see you here," James told her. "Mind you, I wasn't sure who might turn up. I suppose you're less of a surprise than most of the people here."

"I'm sure I don't know any of them," Sarah said. "And I doubt many of them had any connection to Matthew, either."

Bessie sat down next to Sarah and introduced Doona before she replied. "With free drinks on offer, I'm sure all of Laxey will turn up at some point tonight," she said. "But I wasn't really expecting to see you two, either."

"Oh, I always had a soft spot for Matthew," Sarah told her. "He spent a lot of time at our house when he was young. His mother had the twins only eighteen months after he was born, so she was a bit overwhelmed. We weren't far away, just across the fields. He used to come to ours after school every day when he was in primary school."

"I'm sorry. This must be difficult for you," Bessie said.

"We've lost so many people over the years," James replied. "Family and friends. No idea why we're both still plodding along, but here we are."

"All sorts of ugly rumours are going around," Sarah said. "We needed to come and make sure that people knew we didn't believe them."

"Rumours?" Bessie asked.

Sarah glanced around and then leaned in closer to Bessie. "You know they've found some bodies out at the old Grantham place, right?" Bessie nodded.

"They think they might have found Susan," James said. "After all these years, it hardly seems worth the bother."

"We've known she was dead for years," Sarah told Bessie. "At least, that was what we hoped. If she was alive, someone was keeping her from contacting us, which was horrible to think about. Otherwise, she'd have rung or sent us a letter or something. She was a good girl, our Susan."

"She was," Bessie agreed. "But what does that have to do with Matthew?"

"Someone said he killed himself because he'd been found out," Sarah replied. "That he'd buried the bodies out at the Grantham place and when they were found, he, well, ended his life rather than go to prison."

"He was always one of the suspects in the disappearances, wasn't he?" Bessie asked.

Sarah shrugged. "The police never told us anything," she replied. "He probably was, though. He was a little bit wild in those days. Hung out with the wrong crowd, really. But we knew he'd never have done anything to hurt Susan. No one would have."

"So what do you think did happen?" Doona asked.

Bessie glanced at her and Doona flushed. Neither one of them was meant to be questioning suspects, but Doona worked for the police. Bessie didn't want her friend to get in trouble.

"Maybe there was an accident," James suggested. "Or maybe the bodies don't have anything to do with us. Or maybe some visitor came over and killed them and then left the island. I'll bet the police aren't even considering that."

"They are, actually," Doona told him. "There are two officers going through ferry and airline records, trying to find out exactly who was on the island at the time."

"We should be going," Sarah said. "We were just getting up when you came over. We need to be away before Harold gets here, anyway."

James pushed back his chair and struggled to his feet. "Bad knees," he told Bessie after his third attempt at standing finally succeeded. "Too many years in the fields, I suppose. Doctor wants to replace them with something fancy, but I'm not sure it's worth the effort."

"Of course it is," Sarah scolded him. "We just have to find the time to get it done, that's all. One of these days."

James shrugged and then took Sarah's arm. The pair made their way slowly towards the door while Bessie and Doona watched.

"Who's Harold?" Doona asked as the door shut behind the couple.

"James's brother and Helen's father," Bessie told her. "I understand they haven't spoken since the girls disappeared."

"Why?"

"Something to do with James blaming Karen for Helen's running away."

"Maybe they'll make up now that the bodies have been found," Doona suggested.

"I hope so," Bessie said. She sat back and looked around the room. "Ah, someone else I was hoping to see," she told Doona.

"Who is it?" Doona asked as they both stood up.

"Claire Kelly," Bessie replied. "The woman I had coffee with the other morning. I'm hoping that's her husband with her."

The couple was sitting at a small table together, and as they approached, Bessie could see that Claire had been crying.

"Good evening," Bessie said as she reached the table.

Claire blinked at her and then gave her what looked to be a forced smile. "Miss Cubbon, isn't it?" she asked.

"Yes, and this must be Todd. My goodness, you've grown a lot since the last time I saw you," Bessie told the man who looked older than his years. He was almost completely bald and what hair he did have was very short and grey. His eyes looked tired as he studied Bessie.

"Of course, I remember you from my childhood," he said eventually. "You used to shop at the market in Laxey and everyone knew you. You're looking well."

"Thank you," Bessie replied. "I'm sorry to see you at such a sad occasion."

"Matthew was, well, he was difficult in adulthood, but we both have fond memories of him in his youth," Todd told her.

"As do I," Bessie said. She introduced Doona and then sat down next to Claire. "But who's watching the children?" she asked.

"Oh, we've left Uncle Timothy in charge," Claire said, smiling. "The older two are out with friends, so it's only the little one for him to manage."

"And he does an excellent job with her," Todd added. "She adores him."

"But we can't stay out for too long," Claire said, looking at her watch. "If nothing else, Timothy wanted to stop in here to pay his respects."

"He and Matthew were good friends when they were younger," Todd said. "Until Matt started spending all of his time with Jonas, at least."

"I might have to stay a while longer, then, if Timothy is coming," Bessie said. "I haven't seen him in many years, either."

"You won't have any trouble recognising him," Todd laughed. "While the rest of us have been getting older, he looks exactly the same."

"Lucky him," Bessie said.

"Bessie, you know people in the police," Claire said. "Is there any truth to the rumour that they think that Matthew killed himself because he'd killed the Kelly girls?"

"I know some police officers," Bessie replied. "But I'm certainly not privy to that sort of information. I take it you don't think that's what happened?"

Claire looked at her husband and didn't reply. After a minute, Todd spoke.

"We don't know what to think any more," he said. "I'd always thought Susan just ran away. Everyone always talked about what a sweet girl she was, but she had a new boyfriend and she was starting to behave differently, trying to sneak out and things. I suspected she got herself pregnant and went across to take care of it. When she didn't come back, I thought maybe she'd decided to have the baby and stay there. I never once imagined that anything bad had happened to her."

"They haven't identified the bodies yet," Bessie pointed out.

"No, but who else could they have found?" Todd asked. "It isn't like dozens of young women go missing from the island every day. This isn't London. I'm sure one of the bodies they've found is my baby sister. I just wish I knew what happened to her."

"I'm not sure we really want to know," Claire said, shuddering. "I just can't believe that Matthew was involved."

"If he was, Jonas was, too," Todd said stoutly. "There's no way Matthew would have done something like that on his own."

"I'm surprised Jonas isn't here," Bessie remarked.

"No doubt he will be," Todd told her. "That man has never once passed up a free drink in his life."

"I thought Peter Clucas might be here as well," Bessie said.

"Peter tries to avoid the pub," Todd said. "Too much temptation, I think. Besides which, he doesn't want to run into his clients. That would be awkward, to say the least."

"It's good to see that he's turned his life around," Bessie said.

"Yes, he was really wild for a little while there," Todd replied. "And then, overnight, he just stopped."

"Overnight?" Bessie echoed.

"It really was, wasn't it?" Claire asked. "His parents split up and his mum moved to Port Erin. One day Peter was out drinking and carrying on and the next thing I knew, he'd moved to Port Erin and gone back to school."

"And this was around the same time Susan disappeared?" Bessie asked.

Claire frowned. "It wasn't long after," she said after a moment. "Maybe a month or so after the disappearances."

"There's no way Peter had anything to do with that," Todd said firmly. "The timing was just a coincidence. Or maybe the disappearances made him realise that life is too short to be wasted. Whatever, he would never have done anything to hurt the girls."

"Todd? My goodness, it's been years," a voice said at Bessie's elbow. She turned and smiled at Amy Kelly, who was staring at Todd.

"Mrs. Kelly, it's a pleasure to see you again," Todd said, rising to his feet. "This is my wife, Claire," he added.

"Nice to meet you," Claire said.

"I can't believe you're old enough to have a wife," Amy laughed. "I mean, I know my Henry is all grown up, but the rest of you didn't have to go and grow up as well, did you?"

Todd grinned. "Growing up wasn't so bad. It's this growing old I could do without."

A ringing mobile interrupted everyone's laughter. Claire pulled her phone from her bag. After a short conversation, she frowned at Todd.

"Your brother is eager to get over here and have a drink," she said. "And it seems our little darling doesn't want to go to bed, either."

"Timothy will have her all wound up and excited," Todd said with a sigh. "We'd better get home and calm her down."

The pair got up and said their good-byes. Todd gave Amy a hug before they headed for the door.

"It was lovely to see you again," he told her. "Even if the circumstances are quite sad."

As they walked away, Amy sank down into one of the now vacated chairs.

"It is sad," she said to Bessie. "Especially if it was suicide. Matthew didn't have any reason to kill himself."

"Presumably he didn't see it that way," Bessie suggested.

Amy shrugged. "The police think they've found Helen," she said. "I can't quite get my head around it, though."

"I'm sorry," Bessie told her.

"I said I didn't want to know," Amy said. "But now, when the answer seems so tantalizingly close, I want to know more than anything. If it is Helen, well, I suppose I didn't realise how it would feel to finally have an answer."

"I hope they can identify the bodies quickly," Bessie said.

Amy nodded. "But, really, who else is it going to be? I'm starting to come to terms with it all, at least I think I am."

Bessie patted her arm. "I can't imagine how you're feeling," she said.

"I'm not sure I know how I'm feeling," Amy said, shaking her head. "So many years of uncertainty. So many years of looking for a face that wasn't there in every crowd. So many years of answering every telephone call with just a smidgen of hope, every single time. And now, to have to consider burying my baby girl." She took a shaky breath.

Doona pulled a packet of tissues out of her handbag and passed them to the woman. Amy took one and wiped her eyes. "I'm sorry," she said. "I'm trying to be strong. I felt like I had to come tonight. I don't want people thinking that I blame Matthew for anything."

"That was good of you," Bessie said.

"I knew him," Amy said. "Not well, and I didn't really like him, but I knew him. The man wasn't a murderer."

"Let's just hope the police can work out exactly what did happen to the girls," Bessie said.

"Yes," Amy replied. "Although here I go again. I'm not sure I want to know. Maybe, once we have all of the answers, I'll feel differently, but right now, after all this time, I just want to bury my baby and move on."

"Surely you don't want to see someone get away with murder?" Doona asked.

"Someone already has," Amy told her. "Whoever did it has had thirty or so years of getting away with it. My Helen never got to grow up, get married, have children of her own. Whoever killed her has probably done all those things. Throwing him or her into prison won't change that."

"It might stop him or her from killing again," Bessie suggested.

Amy looked surprised. "Killing again? But, that is, I mean," she took a deep breath. "I hadn't even considered that as a possibility," she said. "I suppose I just assumed that, well, that something happened, more of an accident than murder. You don't think the killer has killed more than just the three girls?"

"I think the police need to investigate thoroughly, find the responsible party and make sure that he or she is locked away," Bessie told her. "And I would feel that way even if there was only one victim."

Amy sighed. "I'm not thinking clearly," she told Bessie. "I haven't been since nineteen-seventy."

Bessie patted her arm again. "I can't begin to understand," she said. "But I'm sorry."

Amy drew a sharp breath. "I think that's my cue to leave," she said, getting to her feet. "It was nice to see you again." Before Bessie or Doona could speak, the woman was on her way to the door. Doona looked at Bessie with a questioning look in her eyes. Bessie scanned the room.

"Ah, that must be Harold," she said. "I'm not sure I would have recognised him if Amy hadn't reacted that way."

Doona glanced at the man who was standing at the bar next to Joanna. "All little old men look very similar," she said as Bessie got to her feet.

"He and James look a lot alike, but they are brothers," Bessie replied. She took a few steps towards the man, but stopped when someone touched her arm.

"Bessie Cubbon?" a voice said. "After not seeing you for thirty years, this makes twice in a week."

"Peter Clucas," she said. "It's lovely to see you again." Bessie introduced Doona. "If I hadn't just seen you the other day, I don't know if I would have recognised you," she told him. "You've changed a lot over the years."

The man frowned down at the glass in his hand. It was half full of an amber liquid. "Maybe not as much as I should have done," he muttered.

"I understand you're doing great things for the island's youth," Doona said.

"I try hard," Peter told her. "I have a lot of my own mistakes to try to make up for, after all." He took a sip of his drink and then put the glass on the table. After a deep breath, he pushed the glass a few inches away from himself.

"You and Matthew were good friends," Bessie said. "I'm sorry for your loss."

"We were friends many years ago," Peter said. "But we hadn't spoken for quite some time. We had a bit of a falling-out at one point and we never really sorted it out."

"That's a shame," Bessie said.

"It happens," Peter shrugged. "We really only had drink in common, so once I quit drinking, we would have drifted apart anyway."

"It was nice of you to come and pay your respects," Doona said.

Peter smiled at her. "I don't remember you from my childhood in Laxey. Of course, you're much younger, but you don't look familiar."

"I grew up in the south of the island," Doona told him. "It's only in the last three years that I've come to appreciate what Laxey has to offer."

"I'm in Douglas now, but I do miss it up here," he replied.

"I really need to have a word with Harold," Bessie told the other two. "It looks as if he might be leaving. I'll be right back."

She didn't wait to see if Doona would protest. Harold had been talking to Joanna, but while Bessie had been watching, he'd turned and begun to head for the door. It only took Bessie a few steps to catch up with him.

"Harold?" she asked. "How are you?"

The man looked at her and blinked slowly. "Can't hear a bleeding thing in here with all this noise," he shouted. "I'm going outside for some peace and quiet."

Bessie nodded and then followed the man to the door. When she walked outside with him, he looked surprised. "Didn't know you were coming, too," he said loudly. "What did you want?"

"I just wanted to say hello," Bessie replied.

"Pardon?" he said, cupping his ear.

Bessie repeated herself, more loudly. "It's been a long time," she added.

"Oh, aye, a long time," he replied. "It's Bessie Cubbon, right? I remember you from Laxey in the old days."

"Harold, turn up your hearing aids. You're shouting." The woman who'd just joined them was another who looked only slightly familiar. Bessie placed her as much from context as appearance.

"Brandy?" she asked.

"Yeah, it sounded a lot sexier when I was twenty-two," Brandy laughed.

Bessie couldn't help but agree. The name didn't really seem to suit the woman, who was plump with grey hair and thick glasses. "How are you?" she asked.

"Oh, we're getting by," Brandy replied. "He's deaf as a post, really, but he doesn't think he is."

"Pardon?" Harold asked. "You should speak up," he told Brandy.

"I was talking to Bessie," Brandy shouted at him. "Don't you worry."

Harold nodded and then shuffled a few steps away from the women.

"He's getting a bit senile as well," Brandy confided. "He doesn't know about the bodies. I'd appreciate it if you didn't tell him."

"It isn't my place to tell anyone anything," Bessie told her. "Will you tell him if they identify Helen?"

Brandy sighed. "I don't know," she said after a moment. "I think he ought to know, but I'm not sure that he'll understand. I might leave that decision up to his son. I'd leave a lot more of his care up to Henry as well, if the man would step up."

Bessie knew better than to get involved in that particular argument. "Have you told him about Matthew, then?" she asked.

"Someone else did," Brandy replied. "And then he insisted on coming to see Joanna. He was quite lucid today, actually. He talked a lot about Matthew and how sorry he was that he's passed. I don't know if he'll remember any of it tomorrow, but at least he was able to share some memories with Joanna tonight."

"I'm sure this is difficult for all of you," Bessie said.

"I thought I knew what I was getting into, marrying a man with children," Brandy replied. "I never once imagined that one of my stepchildren would vanish. Harold has never really recovered from that, you know."

"It must be awful for you," Bessie said.

"It's awful for me," Harold boomed. "It was my daughter, not hers. She doesn't understand."

Bessie gave Brandy a sympathetic look before turning to Harold. "I'm sorry," she said. "About Helen and about Matthew."

"I always thought Matthew knew what happened to Helen," Harold said. "And now he's dead and we might never know. That's what makes me sad about his passing, you know."

Bessie patted his arm and murmured something, wondering at his words.

"We should go," Brandy said, taking Harold's arm. "We'll have a cuppa and a digestive when we get home."

"Or whiskey," Harold replied. The pair walked away, arm in arm, while Bessie watched thoughtfully. When they were out of sight, she turned and went back into the pub.

Doona was still sitting with Peter where she'd left them. "Is everything okay?" Doona asked as Bessie slid back into her seat.

"It's fine," Bessie assured her. Before she could speak again, the pub door swung open and the room fell strangely silent.

"That's my cue to get out of here," Peter muttered, sliding down in his seat.

Bessie watched as Jonas and his wife crossed the room to Joanna. The conversation looked tense as everyone around the room seemed to be watching the interchange.

"Let me get the next round," Jonas said loudly as he turned away from Joanna.

"Not necessary," Peter Yates called from behind the bar. "But what will you and your lovely wife have?"

Jonas steered Tara to the bar.

"Maybe he won't notice if I sneak away," Peter said from his seat

164

beside Doona. "If he looks my way, create a distraction," he said to Doona. His tone was joking, but his face was serious.

"Why don't you want to speak to him?" Bessie asked.

"He's another one that I had a bit of a falling-out with," Peter explained. "Although ours was rather more serious."

While Bessie watched, the man headed towards the door, seemingly deliberately keeping to the darkest edges of the room as he went. Both Doona and Bessie blew out breaths as he escaped from the pub.

"That was odd," Bessie said.

"He was trying to get my phone number before you came back," Doona reported.

"Was he? He has a son," Bessie told her.

"I know," Doona replied. "His wife passed away some years ago and he's been single ever since. He seems really nice, but, well, I'm not looking for a man just now."

Bessie couldn't help but wonder how much John Rockwell played into Doona's reluctance to get involved with anyone, but she didn't voice the question. Instead, she turned her attention back to Jonas and Tara, who were making their way around the room. Jonas was greeting everyone as if they were long-lost friends, while Tara sipped her drink and looked bored.

"Ah, Bessie Cubbon," he said when he reached their table. "It's delightful to see you after all these years."

"You're looking well," Bessie told the man.

"Life's been good to me," Jonas replied. "But have you met my wife?"

"I don't believe I have," Bessie replied.

Jonas introduced her, and Bessie did the same for Doona.

"I'm sorry for your loss," Bessie said once the introductions were out of the way. "I know you and Matthew were good friends once."

"He and I had a lot of fun together," Jonas replied. "I haven't had a friend quite like him since, if I'm honest. We always pushed one another to try increasingly outrageous things." The man laughed. "I suppose I should be embarrassed, really, by some of the things we got up to, but it was all just youthful hijinks, really."

Bessie thought about the stories she'd heard about the young men. Much of what they'd done had been criminal and not at all what she would classify as "youthful hijinks," but she bit her tongue.

"The police are being awfully quiet about what happened to Matthew, aren't they?" Jonas asked. "I mean, I heard he committed suicide, but no one will confirm that."

"I'm sure I haven't heard anything," Bessie replied.

Jonas looked around furtively and then leaned in close to Bessie. "I've even heard a rumour that he topped himself because he was going to get charged with murder. They've found the bodies, as I understand it."

"I've heard that the police have found some bodies," Bessie said. "But I don't know anything beyond that."

"You don't know much, do you?" Jonas snapped. He took a long swallow of his drink and then spoke again. "Sorry, but this whole thing has me feeling unbelievably stressed. The thought that Matthew might have killed those girls? They were my friends, I was even seeing one of them. I have to imagine that they turned down his advances or something." Jonas shook his head. "I knew Matthew for most of his life and I would never have imagined that he was capable of murder."

"I don't think anyone is suggesting anything of the kind," Bessie said coolly.

"I have my sources," Jonas told her. He glanced at Doona and then looked back at Bessie. "I can tell you that he was quite jealous of my success with women. Maybe that was behind some of it, maybe why he targeted Helen. I'm not sure we'll ever know."

With that he turned on his heel and strode away. Tara was gazing vacantly into the middle distance and didn't seem to notice. Jonas had taken four or five steps before he looked back.

"Tara," he snapped. The woman glanced over at him, a terrified look on her face. She nearly ran the short distance between them, and Bessie could hear the apologies spilling from her lips when she reached Jonas's side. Grabbing her arm, Jonas dragged her across the room.

"I don't like him," Doona said.

"I don't either," Bessie replied. But that doesn't make him a murderer, she added to herself.

Half an hour later the pub was clearing out. Bessie and Doona decided that they'd had enough excitement for the evening and headed for the door themselves. Bessie stopped to give Joanna another quick hug on their way.

"I'm rather very drunk," Joanna told her, enunciating carefully. "It's what Matthew would have wanted."

Bessie wasn't able to argue with that. She and Doona made their way to the door, where a man who'd been sitting on his own in a dark corner all evening joined them.

"I hope you have some interesting things to tell me," John Rockwell murmured to Bessie as the trio left the building.

"Come back to mine for tea," Bessie invited him. "We can talk there."

CHAPTER 12

*D*oona drove Bessie home with John following close behind. At the cottage, the women sat in the kitchen while John did a quick inspection.

"No one hiding under my bed?" Bessie asked when he joined them.

"Just a few dust bunnies," John replied.

"There aren't," Bessie retorted. She worked hard to keep her small cottage neat and tidy. The idea that there might be dust under her bed wasn't worth thinking about.

"Actually, there aren't," John agreed. "How do you keep the cottage so clean?"

"I'm only one person," Bessie said. "I don't make much mess."

John looked around the compact kitchen and nodded. "I suppose, if I made more effort to tidy after myself every day, I wouldn't have as much cleaning to do when I do clean."

"But you work very hard," Bessie pointed out. "You don't have much time at home. Maybe you should hire a cleaning service."

John shrugged. "I'm not happy with the idea of having strangers in my house," he told her.

"I'll just put the kettle on," Doona said. "Maybe a few biscuits as well?"

Bessie chuckled as she sat down. "Of course my guests also look after themselves," she told John. "And of course we'll have biscuits," she told Doona.

Doona found a box of expensive chocolate ones at the back of Bessie's cupboard. "Oh, I don't suppose we should open these," she said.

"I think that's all I have in at the moment," Bessie replied. "I haven't been shopping or baking. Open them up and let's see if they are good as they should be."

Doona made a pretty arrangement with the sugary treats while Bessie worked on the tea. They all sat down together a few minutes later.

"So, what did you learn tonight?" John asked after they'd all had their first biscuit.

"That these were worth every penny," Bessie said, gesturing towards the plate in the centre of the table. "And nothing much else."

"You seemed to talk to a lot of people," John said.

"I did," Bessie agreed. "And I don't think any of them like Jonas Clucas, but I'm not sure that's news."

"Not really," John said. "But it's still a long way from there to seeing him as a murderer."

"Some people seem to think he was involved," Bessie said. She took another biscuit and then walked John back through her evening, recounting each conversation as well as she could remember.

"There are lots of rumours flying around, then," John remarked when she was finished.

"That's hardly surprising, under the circumstances," Bessie said.

"We've just sent a press release to the local paper," John told her. "If you're interested in an update, I'll tell you now what's being released."

"Of course I'm interested," Bessie told him.

"We're still digging on the site, but we know for a fact that we have the remains of at least five individuals," John said.

"Five?" Bessie repeated.

"Yes, all young women, somewhere between thirteen and twenty as an approximation."

Bessie shook her head. "But how is that possible?" she asked.

"We won't know for certain until we identify them all," John replied. "We're reasonably certain that we've found Karen Kelly, though."

"I thought DNA testing took a week or more," Bessie said.

"It does," John told her. "But Karen suffered from several broken bones in her short life, including a bad break in her right arm that left the bone broken in three places. One of the skeletons shows evidence of the same injury."

"She was hit by a car," Bessie remembered. "She was about ten, I think, and already a little bit wild. She and her family were at the beach in Port Erin and she wanted ice cream. It was something like that."

"As I heard the story, she ran off with some of her mother's money to get herself an ice cream and ran straight into oncoming traffic. She was lucky to get away with a badly broken arm, really," John told her.

"If Karen is there, that suggests the other two are as well," Bessie said, sadly.

"It does," John agreed. "We've also made a tentative identification on one of the other bodies."

"Really?" Bessie asked. "Who was she?"

"A young runaway from Liverpool," John said. "She disappeared in nineteen seventy-one."

"So after the Kelly girls," Bessie mused.

"Yes. We were able to identify her in a similar way, from broken bones she'd suffered in childhood," John said.

"Did she run away to the island?" Bessie asked.

"That's one of the things we're hoping to find out," John said. "That's a possibility, certainly."

"If she didn't, then someone brought her here," Bessie said thoughtfully. "Did they bring her here just to kill her?"

John shrugged. "We could speculate all night about that," he said. "Or even about whether she was still alive when she arrived, but I don't know that we'll be able to find answers to any of those questions until we find the killer."

"You're sure they were murdered?" Bessie asked. She shook her head. "That was a dumb question," she said quickly.

"We are considering other options," John told her. "After all this time, there's no way for the coroner to determine a cause of death for any of the victims, so at least one or more of them could have died accidently. That doesn't explain why we found the bodies all dumped together at an abandoned property, of course."

"No one I spoke to tonight thought Matthew was capable of murder," Bessie said.

"He's certainly still on my list of suspects," John replied. "People do change. When people were questioned at the time of the disappearances, quite a few people suggested that he was involved."

"His suicide seems to suggest that he was," Bessie said.

"If it was suicide," John said.

"You don't think he was murdered, too?" Bessie asked.

John shrugged. "We aren't ruling out anything at this point."

"Joanna said he was found in a shut garage with multiple car engines running," Bessie said.

"We were hoping to keep the details quiet, but yes, that is what happened," John admitted.

"What a horrible way to die," Bessie said, shuddering.

"Are there good ways to die?" Doona asked.

"I'd like to die peacefully in my bed when I'm a hundred and fifty-seven," Bessie said.

"Why that age?" Doona asked.

"I chose it at random," Bessie told her. "But it seems a nice long way from now, anyway. I'll probably change it when I get closer to it."

"You saw Matthew Kelly not long before he died," John said. "Did he seem unhappy or upset about anything?"

"He was unhappy," Bessie replied. "But I got the impression that was just his personality. I've told you what happened when he saw me in the truck. He was upset about that for some reason." She shrugged. "I wouldn't have thought for one minute that he was considering taking his own life, but maybe he wasn't at that point."

"If he didn't kill himself, who could have done it, and why?" Doona asked.

"The motive has to be something to do with the Kelly girls," Bessie said. "Maybe he was the anonymous caller who rang with the suggestion to dig up the Grantham farm."

"That's one possibility," John said.

"But that would mean that he knew about the bodies for all these years," Doona protested. "Surely he would have said something before now?"

"Someone knew," Bessie pointed out. "Someone knew and rang the police with the tip. I'd love to know why he or she kept quiet for so long, and why the caller decided to tell someone now."

"Maybe the killer is dead, so the caller felt it was the right time to talk." Doona said.

"None of the main suspects is dead, though, aside from Matthew, who died after the bodies were found," Bessie argued.

"So maybe the police are investigating the wrong people," Doona said.

"Maybe the caller's conscience just got the better of him or her after all these years," Bessie suggested. "I can't imagine keeping a secret like that for such a long time."

"And maybe it was Matthew and it got him killed," Doona said.

"The caller should have told us everything he or she knew," John said. "Knowing about the location of the bodies suggests that he or she also knows who put them there in the first place. It's frustrating to think that someone knows that and won't tell us."

"Unless it was Matthew and now he can't tell you," Doona reminded him.

"What about Jonas?" Bessie asked. "Everyone I spoke to tonight seemed quite happy to cast him in the role of killer."

"Again, we're considering all possibilities," John said. "He was one of the chief suspects in the original investigation, but he had something of an alibi for at least one of the disappearances. That's one of the reasons why Inspector Harris focussed on Matthew Kelly and Peter Clucas rather than Jonas."

"How good of an alibi?" Bessie asked.

"Good, but probably not unbreakable," John replied. "Like most people most of the time, he couldn't prove exactly where he was the entire time in question, but the night one of the girls disappeared, he was at a family party. No one could say for sure that he was there continually, but no one missed him, either."

"I was hoping he'd done it," Doona said. "He's the least likable of the three suspects."

"Unfortunately, being a horrible person isn't actually proof of guilt," John said.

"Peter has really turned his life around," Bessie said. "I'd hate to think he was involved."

"He seemed really nice when I met him," Doona added, blushing slightly.

John gave her a quizzical look. "Did he?"

"We only talked for a few minutes, while Bessie was speaking to Harold and Brandy," Doona said quickly. "But he told me about his work. He's doing some wonderful things with troubled youngsters."

"He is, yes," John agreed. "But he was in plenty of trouble himself when he was younger. I have to keep him on the short list, at least for now."

"This would have been easier if Matthew had left a nice neat confession," Bessie said.

"Not really," John replied.

Bessie gave him a quick look. "He left a confession?" she asked.

"No comment," John said steadily.

"So he did," Bessie said, jumping to conclusions. "But there must be something suspicious or off about it or you'd have closed the investigation by now. How interesting."

"I didn't say any of that," John said.

"You didn't have to," Bessie replied, certain she was correct. "So if Matthew confessed, but you aren't sure that it's legitimate, he must have been murdered."

"You're getting way ahead of the evidence," John said.

"But I'm right," Bessie shot back. "Which means Matthew didn't kill the girls. Which means the killer is still out there and probably killed poor Matthew."

"So what about means and opportunity for Jonas and Peter when Matthew was killed?" Doona asked.

"Everyone knows that running a car in a garage is dangerous," Bessie said. "And Matthew would know that better than most. He worked with cars his entire life."

"So if it was murder, all someone had to do was get Matthew into the garage and start the cars," Doona mused.

"They must have drugged Matthew first," Bessie said. "Otherwise, he would have simply switched the cars off, wouldn't he?"

"Drugged him or hit him over the head," Doona suggested. "Or maybe just got him drunk."

"He would have been happy to have a drink with anyone," Bessie said. "Then, once he was too drunk to realise, the killer just had to shut the doors and start the engines."

"I'll just remind you both that this is just speculation," John said sternly. "We're still trying to work out exactly what happened in that garage."

"But our scenario would work, wouldn't it?" Bessie asked.

"Possibly," John said hesitantly. "But it certainly isn't the only possible answer."

"Where were Jonas and Peter when Matthew died?" Bessie asked him.

"I can't tell you that," John said.

Bessie sighed with disappointment. "So we don't know if either has an alibi."

"Is there any other reason anyone might have had for wanting Matthew dead?" Doona asked. "I mean, we're assuming it had to do with the Kelly girls, but maybe it didn't."

"He and his wife were having problems," Bessie said. "But I can't see Joanna killing him. She was ready to file for divorce, that's all."

"What about problems at work?" was Doona's next question.

"Not that I know of," Bessie said. "Apparently he was a good mechanic, even if he wasn't the nicest of people. He sometimes turned up late or drunk, but as I understand it, the owner of the shop was used to him and they got along fine."

"If he wasn't killed because of the Kelly girls' case, it's a strange coincidence," Doona said.

"Too much of one," Bessie replied. "There has to be a connection."

"So the man or woman who killed the Kelly girls killed Matthew, presumably because Matthew was the one who rang the police and told them where to find the bodies," Doona summarised.

"You said 'man or woman,' but I don't think there are any female suspects, are there?" Bessie asked. "The only two serious suspects I know of are Peter and Jonas Clucas."

Both women looked at John. "Those two and Matthew were the main focus of the original investigation," he said. "But that doesn't mean they're the only possible suspects. When we reopened the case, we started back at the beginning. That means that everyone who was in the area is a suspect."

"But Inspector Harris knew what he was doing," Doona said. "If he'd narrowed it down to those three, he was on to something. What we have to determine is whether Matthew was the guilty party and the case can be closed, or whether the killer went after Matthew to shut him up."

"What does Hugh think of all of this?" Bessie asked. "It seems strange even talking about it without him here, as it was his cold case to start with."

"Hugh's a bit overwhelmed with wedding planning," John told her. "And I think he's a bit overwhelmed by everything that's happened with the case as well. Reopening cold cases is usually about as exciting as watching paint dry. Typically, you go around and talk to everyone who was interviewed the first time around, and then you bemoan the fact that no one remembers anything before you type up a neat report to add to the file that goes back into the back of the filing cabinet."

"That certainly hasn't happened this time," Bessie said. "Not only have you turned up bodies, you've had a new murder."

"We don't know for certain what happened to Matthew," John said.

175

"But a suicide is just as shocking of a consequence. In some ways I'm afraid Hugh feels guilty about reopening the case."

"If he can find the killer, it will all have been worth it," Doona said.

"It's already been worth it, because he's found the bodies," Bessie insisted. "He's given the families an answer as to what happened to their loved ones. It may not be the answer they wanted, but at least they know."

"So where does all of this leave us?" Doona asked as she started the washing-up.

"I don't know," Bessie said. "It seems as if we've narrowed the field down to two suspects, but how do we work out which one is guilty?"

"What if they both are?" Doona asked. "Maybe all three of them were in on it together, even."

"That would be horrible," Bessie said. "I don't know what happened to those poor girls, but all three of the men were men they knew well. I can't imagine how awful it would have been for them if all three were involved."

"I think you've done enough speculating for today," John said. "We're still clearing the site at the Grantham property. There might be more bodies still to be discovered. Identifying them all is the next big job."

"I still think it was Jonas," Bessie said as she walked Doona and John to the door. "He's always had a high opinion of himself. I can see him getting angry if one of the girls turned him down or something."

"I wouldn't go repeating that outside of your cottage," John warned her. "He still has very powerful friends. Even if he didn't, accusing someone of murder is serious business."

Bessie nodded. "If you think of anything I can do to help, just let me know," she told John. "Otherwise, I'll just keep listening to the skeet and see if I hear anything interesting."

"That's probably all you can do for now," John said. "Just stay away from the suspects and keep yourself out of trouble."

Bessie laughed. "I think I can manage that," she said.

"Speaking of managing," Doona said. "How are the plans going for Hugh's honeymoon?"

"I spoke to Mary today, and everything is going well," Bessie replied. "The travel agent is going to get in touch with both of you to coordinate your parts of the surprise."

"She rang me today, actually," John said. "She seemed very efficient and it all seems to be coming together well."

"I just hope they like it," Bessie fretted.

"An all-expenses-paid trip to Paris? What's not to like?" Doona demanded. "They'll love it and it will be the perfect start to their married life together."

"I certainly hope so," Bessie said.

Doona had Bessie give her Kristen's phone number so she could contact the woman herself. "She probably rang me a dozen times so far and never got an answer," Doona said. "I've been ignoring my phone lately. Too many double-glazing and insurance salesmen ringing."

"If you had an answering machine, you wouldn't have that problem," Bessie said.

"And I keep meaning to replace the one that broke, but the people that I really want to talk to ring my mobile these days. Really, the only ones who ring my home phone are trying to sell me something."

Bessie shook her head. "I ring your home phone," she said.

"Yes, but when I don't answer, you hang up and ring my mobile," Doona replied.

Bessie opened her mouth to argue, but Doona was right. If she couldn't reach Doona at the police station, she often rang the woman's mobile, sometimes without even trying the home number first.

"Okay, time for all of us to get some sleep," John said. "I'll stop back or ring tomorrow if there are any new developments."

"I hope you don't find any more bodies," Bessie replied. "I think five is quite enough."

With those as yet unidentified bodies on her mind, Bessie slept restlessly that night. It was hard for her to imagine why anyone would kill several young women, and even harder to believe that it had happened on the island she loved so much. She tossed and turned until half five and then gave up on sleep and took a long shower instead. She set a pot of coffee brewing before she went out for her walk.

A light rain was falling when Bessie started out, but it wasn't enough to send her back inside for her waterproofs. She'd just have to make it a short walk, she decided. Once she was moving, though, she found that she was happy to march down the beach, letting the cool breeze and brisk morning air wake her up. She'd gone as far as Thie yn Traie before she'd realised. The drizzle had tapered off to more of a general dampness, so Bessie pressed on for a while longer. By the time she turned around, the sun was doing its best to make an appearance.

She'd only turned around because she'd suddenly remembered her coffee pot, no doubt busily brewing away while she'd wandered. If she left it too long, the coffee would start to get bitter and unpleasant, so she hurried back past Thie yn Traie for home. The two figures huddled on the beach in front of the holiday cottages startled her. In autumn and winter she nearly always had the beach to herself. She slowed her steps and walked cautiously towards them, hoping she'd recognise them before too much longer.

"Ah, good morning," the man, who was wrapped in a warm overcoat, called as Bessie approached.

"Yes, good morning," the woman by his side said. She too was dressed in a heavy coat, well insulated against the cool sea air.

"Good morning," Bessie said, trying to sound courteous, rather than curious.

"I hope this isn't a private beach," the man said as Bessie reached them. "We didn't see a sign."

"Oh, no, not at all," Bessie assured them. "It's usually quite quiet this time of year, though."

"It's the cold," the woman said. "It's far too cold to be sitting on a windswept beach in the rain."

"It isn't raining," the man replied.

"At the moment," the woman shot back.

"Winters are quite damp," Bessie said almost apologetically. "But the beach is beautiful in the summer."

"It's lovely now," the man told her. "I hope, I mean, how long have you lived here?"

"Since I was eighteen," Bessie replied. "That's my cottage," she added, gesturing towards Treoghe Bwaane.

"Do you live alone?" the woman asked.

"I do," Bessie replied.

"Oh, I'd hate that," the woman said. "I'd be ever so lonely, and too afraid to sleep at night."

"The island is very safe, and I'm never lonely as long as I have books," Bessie said.

"I don't know how safe the island is," the woman snapped. "It wasn't safe for our Jessica, was it?"

"Jessica? I'm sorry," Bessie replied, feeling confused.

"Oh, you mustn't mind us," the man said, shaking his head. "We've only just found out that our lost daughter has been found, and, well, we were hoping for better news, that's all."

"Your lost daughter?" Bessie echoed. "Oh, dear, she wasn't one of the girls found at the Grantham farm, was she?"

"I believe that's what the policeman said," the man replied. "Apparently there were lots of girls buried there, at least five or six or something. Our little Jessica was one of them."

"She wasn't little anymore," the woman said bitterly. "She was all grown up, or she thought she was. Wouldn't listen to us anymore. Always off with her friends, out too late, skipping school. When we finally told her she had to start behaving better, she went and ran away."

"I am sorry," Bessie said.

"We've been hoping all these years that she'd turn up safe and sound," the man said. "We'd been hoping maybe she'd found someone nice and settled down. We never wanted the phone call we got yesterday."

Bessie shook her head. "I can't imagine."

"Do you have children?" the woman asked.

"No, I don't," Bessie replied.

"There's no one in the world that can make you angrier," the woman told her. "Jessica was brought up well, but she decided she knew more than we did, and I'll admit it, I was angry with her. But that doesn't mean I ever stopped loving her or wanting her back."

The woman's eyes filled with tears and she turned away from Bessie to stare at the sea.

"We're having trouble accepting what we've heard," the man told Bessie. "We didn't know she'd ever left Liverpool, and we never imagined that she'd come over here. We've never been to the island before ourselves."

"It really is a lovely place," Bessie said. "But I understand you might not see it that way."

"I want to," the man told her. "We came down here to see the sea and the beach. I want to believe that Jessica saw this before, well, before whatever happened to her. I want to picture her sitting on this beach with friends, enjoying life."

"It's a very busy beach in the summer months," Bessie said.

"She disappeared in June," the man told her. "The tenth of June, nineteen seventy-one."

"The police can't tell us when she died," the woman interjected. "There isn't anything left but bones. They don't know when she died, and they don't know how she died. I'd almost rather they hadn't found her. We have an answer to one question and now we have a thousand more questions."

"I'm very sorry," Bessie said, not knowing what else to say.

"She might have been here," the man said. "She might have stood right on this spot. She might even have spoken to you."

"I speak to many people in the summer months every year," Bessie said.

The man reached into his pocket and pulled out his wallet. He opened it to an old photo that had clearly been in the wallet for many years. "This is Jessica," he said softly. "I know you won't recognise her, but I wanted you to see her."

Bessie studied the photo. The girl had been blonde and blandly pretty. Another glance at her parents had Bessie marveling at genetics. Neither of them looked anything like the girl.

"Her mother looked just the same when she was a teenager," the man said, gesturing towards the woman. "I fell in love with her when she was just sixteen, but her parents wouldn't let us see each other until she was finished with school."

"Except we just lied and sneaked around behind their backs," the woman said. "Jessica always loved hearing stories about our unconventional courtship. When she first ran away, we assumed she was trying to recreate our story with her own disreputable boyfriend, or something like that. We never imagined…"

"He always insisted that he didn't have anything to do with her disappearance," the man said. "He told us that they'd had a fight and she'd started seeing someone else. Maybe he was telling the truth."

"She was lovely," Bessie said.

"She was," the man agreed. "We never had any more after her, although we never knew why. It just never happened, I suppose. I didn't mind. Jessica was enough of a handful."

"She was at that," the woman agreed. "And she was so sure of herself. She thought she knew everything and that her father and I were stuck in the past. We should have warned her more about the dangerous things in life, I suppose. We were afraid she might get herself into trouble and end up on her own with a baby to look after. We never thought she'd end up far from home like this."

"I hope the police can find more answers for you," Bessie said.

"I don't know if I want to know more," the man replied. "I'd like to think that she was happy here and then, maybe, I don't know, slipped and fell and hit her head and died in a tragic accident. Maybe the people she was with didn't know what to do, so they hid the body. That's possible, isn't it?"

"Of course it is," Bessie said soothingly.

"Stanley, we should stop bothering this poor woman," the woman said suddenly. "I'm sure she has things to do."

"I hope you can find some things to like about the island," Bessie said. "In spite of the tragedy that brought you here."

"Everyone has been very kind," the man told her. "The police have been especially good to us. We met the nicest inspector who spent hours talking with us."

"Inspector Rockwell?" Bessie asked.

"No, that wasn't it," he replied. "What was her name?" he asked the woman.

"Anna something," the woman replied. "She told me that she'd lost her own daughter a long time ago, so she understood our loss. She couldn't have been any nicer to us."

"Anna Lambert?" Bessie said, knowing she sounded shocked.

"Yes, that was it," the man said. "And you've been very kind as well. Thank you for talking with us. I think we're both a little crazy at the moment."

"Again, I'm very sorry for your loss," Bessie said.

She walked away from the couple, back towards her cottage. As she reached it, she turned around and saw that they were both silently staring at the sea. Bessie let herself into the cottage and poured herself a cup of coffee. When she looked back down the beach a few minutes later, the couple was gone. She sat at her kitchen table, her mind turning over what she'd learned about poor Jessica, but more so the surprising revelation about Anna Lambert.

CHAPTER 13

The longer Bessie sat in her kitchen, the more she wanted to talk to John Rockwell. He'd told her he would ring her later, but she decided she didn't want to wait.

"Ah, Bessie, John's not in at the moment," Doona told her when Bessie rang the station. "I can have him ring you back."

"Is Hugh in?" Bessie asked. "I'd like a word with him anyway."

"He is," Doona replied. "He's working on a pile of paperwork and I'm sure he'd love to be interrupted."

Bessie laughed and waited while Doona connected the call.

"Bessie? What can I do for you?" Hugh's voice came down the line a moment later.

"Two things," Bessie told him. "First, I met a couple on the beach this morning and I wanted to tell someone involved in the investigation about it."

"Go ahead," Hugh told her.

Bessie told him everything she could remember about her encounter on the beach. Hugh was silent throughout. When she finished, he cleared his throat before he spoke.

"Yes, I met them when they came to the station," he said. "They, um, they told me they were quite grateful that I'd found their daughter, even under the circumstances. They seemed like very nice people. I was quite relieved when Inspector Lambert stepped in and took them to her office. You wouldn't think it, but she can be quite good with crying mothers."

Bessie had told Hugh that the couple had mentioned the inspector, but she hadn't told him exactly what was said. She simply didn't feel that it was her place to share such a personal piece of information with anyone. "You're right, I wouldn't think it," Bessie said.

"Anyway, they were here for about an hour, talking with me and then with the inspector. John is back out at the Grantham farm. It looks as if they might have found another body, but you didn't hear that from me."

"How dreadful," Bessie said. "And we still don't know the identities of the others yet."

"We're hoping the DNA results will start coming in soon. I'd really like some answers before the wedding. I know we're only honey-mooning in Ramsey, but I'd rather not have any contact with the office while we're there. I'm not sure I can wait until I'm back to hear what the DNA results show, though."

"You will go on your honeymoon and focus on your wife," Bessie said firmly. "You can find out about the DNA when you get back."

"I'm sure it will all be in the local papers, anyway," Hugh said. "We won't be able to avoid those."

You will in Paris, Bessie thought. "Yes, well, I hope you don't find time to look at newspapers," she said instead. "This will be a very special week for you and Grace. You must make sure to put her first."

"I know. Because once we're back, the job will get in the way of everything for the rest of our lives," Hugh said. "John has already talked to me and Grace about that, at length. I know his marriage didn't work out, so I'm grateful for his advice."

"His wife wasn't suited to being married to a policeman," Bessie said. "I hope Grace will do a better job of it."

"Me, too," Hugh said with alacrity.

"I'm sure you have a lot to do; I shouldn't keep you."

"You said there were two things," Hugh reminded her.

"Oh, the other one was simple," Bessie replied. "I just wanted to know how you're doing, with the wedding only a week away. It sounds as if you're ready, though."

"I'm really ready for it to be over," Hugh said fervently. "All this planning and fuss is starting to make me crazy. I'm so glad we agreed to have a short engagement. How some people spend a year or more planning a wedding is beyond me. It's only one day, as well. I can't imagine going into debt and all that for just one day. Grace and I have our whole lives ahead of us, after all."

"And you're both very sensible," Bessie said. "The day will be special because you'll be surrounded by people who love you, but even more importantly, at the end of it you'll be married to the woman you love. Everything else is just window dressing."

"I'm not sure Grace's mum sees it that way," Hugh said with a sigh. "She's been making Grace crazy worrying about the flowers for some reason. Grace told them that she's happy with whatever is affordable, but her mum seems to think that Grace has to have roses and some other thingy I can't even pronounce. Grace is nearly pulling her hair out, which is another problem, actually. Her mum wants her to have her hair done up all fancy and Grace was just going to wear it down. I suppose I should be grateful that all I have to do is turn up looking presentable."

Bessie laughed. "I think a lot of weddings end up being more about what the mother of the bride wants than the bride," she said. "But it is a special day for her as well. Her baby girl is getting married, after all."

"Yes, I know," Hugh sighed. "And Grace keeps reminding me of that whenever I forget."

"Only a few more days," Bessie said soothingly. "And then it will be all over and you and Grace can relax and enjoy some time alone."

"If I can get all my paperwork done," Hugh said. "Inspector Lambert wants a dozen different reports written before I go, including everything to do with the Kelly investigation, so that the investigation can carry on while I'm gone. I know she's right, but I'm not very good at writing reports and I'm terrible at typing. If I'm late for the wedding, it will be because I'm still working on getting them all done."

"I'm sure you'll manage," Bessie said. "But I'm not helping, chatting away, am I? You get back to work. Can you put me back through to Doona?"

"Sure," Hugh said. "I'll see you soon."

"Sunday, if not before," Bessie said.

"What else can I do for you?" Doona asked when Bessie was reconnected to her.

"I just realised that we've booked Hugh's honeymoon in Paris but haven't cancelled his booking in Ramsey," Bessie said. "I don't want to ring and cancel. It's really the sort of thing that should be done in person."

"I can run you over there during my lunch break, if you'd like," Doona said. "I'm looking for an excuse to get out of the office and I could do with a quick trip to Ramsey. I need a new toaster."

"If you're sure you can spare the time," Bessie said.

"I have a long lunch today," Doona replied. "The schedules are all over the place at the moment because there's so much going on."

Doona arranged to collect Bessie only a short time later. Knowing that Doona was missing her lunch for the trip, Bessie quickly put together a selection of sandwiches for the journey. While she would have preferred something hot to drink, she added some cans of fizzy drink to the small bag she'd packed with the sandwiches. Cans would be easier to manage on their way to Ramsey.

Doona was right on time and Bessie was quick to climb into the car's passenger seat. "I brought sandwiches," she said to Doona, "and cold drinks. I didn't want you to miss lunch."

"What a wonderful idea," Doona said. "I was trying to work out how I was going to grab something later."

Ramsey wasn't far away, so there was no time for conversation as they ate their impromptu lunch. Doona pulled up in front of the Seaview as Bessie was wiping crumbs from her mouth.

"I'll be back in fifteen minutes or so," Doona told Bessie. "I'll look for you in the lobby."

Bessie nodded and climbed out of the car. As she crossed to the large sliding doors at the front of the glorious old hotel, she suddenly thought that she should have rung first. The manager might well be having his own lunch at the moment.

She needn't have worried, though. The young man behind the reception desk rang someone, and only a moment later a door opened at the back of the room.

"Elizabeth Cubbon, this is a pleasant surprise," the man who rushed through the doors said in a booming voice. He was a short and plump man in his forties. Immaculately dressed, his dark hair was beautiful styled and his eyes sparkled as he greeted Bessie.

"Jasper Coventry," she replied. "It's lovely to see you again."

The man grinned and then offered Bessie his arm. She took it and let him lead her through the hotel's grand foyer and through a door marked "staff only." Things were considerably less sumptuous on the other side of the door and Bessie hid a smile at the bare concrete floors and badly scuffed walls.

"I know," Jasper said with a grin. "Everything back here needs a facelift. But the public areas are divine, aren't they?"

"What I saw, which was just the lobby, was gorgeous," Bessie said.

"You must let me give you a grand tour," the man said.

"Another time," Bessie told him. "My friend is coming back for me in a very short while."

Bessie had known Jasper in his youth, as he'd grown up in Laxey. He'd gone to London for university and then spent many years working his way up in the hotel industry. Some time back, Jasper and his partner, Stuart, had purchased the crumbling hotel and had spent an incredible amount of time, effort, and money restoring it to its former glory. They'd been open again for less than a year, but Bessie had heard nothing but good things about the place.

Jasper escorted Bessie into a small room that was clearly an office. Photos of a dog nearly covered one wall. Jasper sat down behind the desk and gestured towards the chair opposite him. "Please sit down," he said. "I promise the chair is more comfortable than it looks."

Bessie gave him a doubtful smile, but sat anyway. Jasper was right. The oddly shaped plastic chair was quite comfortable.

"It's one of several that we found when we bought the hotel," Jasper explained. "At some point, the entire dining room was furnished with those chairs. They're meant to be modern and cool, I think, but they're pretty awful looking, to my mind. The only good thing about them is that they are surprisingly comfy."

"I wouldn't want them in my house," Bessie replied. "But now that you mention it, I do remember them in the dining room here. I can't remember why I was here, but these chairs were at every table. I'm sure they came in different colours as well."

"We found several blue ones, a handful of red and just one or two white," Jasper told her. "There was one badly broken yellow one in one of the guest rooms as well."

Bessie shook her head. "They are rather ugly," she said. "But I'm sure they were expensive."

"They were, and weirdly they're still valuable," Jasper replied. "We sold several of them for a ridiculous amount of money, really. But neither Stuart nor I liked them enough to want to keep them. I have this one in my office and there are a few more being kept in storage in case we need a quick influx of money. The rest we sold."

"And I'm sure you don't miss them," Bessie said.

"But you didn't come to talk about chairs," Jasper said. "What can I do for you?"

"I need to change someone's booking," Bessie said.

Jasper raised an eyebrow. "Bessie, you know I love you dearly, but I can't let you change someone else's booking."

Bessie nodded. "Let me explain," she said. "It's for Hugh Watterson."

"You can't possibly change his booking," Jasper said quickly. "He's honeymooning here with the lovely Grace. I've given him a very special rate on one of our nicest rooms. He was a big help when we found ourselves having some issues with one of our staff recently."

"Yes, I know, but some of Hugh's other friends and I are all pooling our resources," Bessie explained. "We're sending Hugh and Grace to

Paris for the week. They'll still need to stay here the night of the wedding, but then they're being whisked away for a glorious week in France."

Jasper grinned. "What a lovely idea," he said. "They'll have a wonderful time. It's such a romantic city. It's perfect for a honeymoon."

"I am sorry about the short notice," Bessie said. "I hope it isn't too much bother. If you need to charge a penalty or anything, I'll pay it, of course."

"Oh, goodness, no," Jasper waved a hand. "We only require twenty-four hours notice for cancellations, and for you even that doesn't apply."

"Thank you," Bessie said. "I hope you won't have any trouble filling their room for the rest of that week."

"It's February," Jasper said. "We're lucky to fill any rooms at all, really."

"Oh, dear, I am sorry," Bessie said.

"I'm exaggerating slightly," the man admitted. "But it is a slow time for tourists. We do get a handful of business travellers during the week, but most of them stay in Douglas. Things are looking up, though. I just took a booking for a large party for next month. Some billionaire has just married his fifth wife and they're going to celebrate here with all of his children from all of his other marriages."

"How awful," Bessie exclaimed.

Jasper laughed. "I'm sure it will be perfectly dreadful," he agreed. "But they've booked a dozen rooms and his secretary is working with our events manager on planning a huge dinner party for everyone. It's going to be profitable for us, anyway."

"Does he have ties to the island?" Bessie asked.

"I think she does," Jasper replied. "I didn't really ask, although now that you mention it, I should have."

"It probably doesn't do to look too nosy," Bessie said. "But you'll have to tell me all about it once it's over."

"You should come for lunch one day," Jasper suggested. "I'll give you a tour and then treat you to some of the specialties of the house."

"I'd like that," Bessie told him.

"I'll ring you once I've checked my diary," he told her. "Stuart has it at the moment, as he's trying to plan our schedules for spring and summer. Once tourist season started last year neither one of us got a day off until autumn. He's hoping to plan things better this year, although I can't see it working."

"It's worth trying," Bessie said.

Jasper walked Bessie back out to the reception desk. "Tell young Hugh we're happy to have them on his wedding night and that the discount offer is good for whenever he and Grace want a week away," he told her at the door. "Even in the height of our summer season."

"Thank you," Bessie said. She walked outside just as Doona pulled up.

"Honestly, how difficult is it to buy a toaster?" Doona demanded as Bessie fastened her seatbelt.

"I'm assuming it was more difficult than you'd anticipated," Bessie laughed.

"All I wanted was something to put bread in," Doona told her. "I quite liked the little wire rack that popped up on my old one so that I could heat pastries as well, but that was about as sophisticated as I ever got. I wasn't expecting to have so many choices this time around."

"What sort of choices?" Bessie asked curiously. She'd purchased her current toaster at least ten years earlier and hadn't given the small appliance a single thought since. Every day it made her a slice of toast just the way she liked it. What else could she possibly need?

"They come with all sorts of special settings now," Doona told her. "You can adjust things for how thick your bread is or use a special setting for those toaster pastry things. There are even some that defrost your frozen bread before it toasts it."

"My goodness, how fancy," Bessie said.

"I just wanted the exact same toaster I already have," Doona said. "I loved my toaster right up until I accidently spilled water inside of it while it was toasting."

"Should I ask how you did that?"

Doona shook her head. "It's such a stupid story, I'd rather not repeat it."

Bessie laughed. "Should I take it that they didn't have the exact same toaster, then?"

"Oh, no," Doona retorted. "That would have been too easy. What they did have was a bunch of salesmen on commission who were determined that I shouldn't leave without the most expensive toaster in the shop and a food processor, as well."

"Do you need a food processor?"

"I made the mistake of telling one of the salesmen that I don't have one," Doona explained. "He wanted to spend the rest of the day telling me why I can't possibly live without one any longer."

"I don't have one either," Bessie told her. "I'm not even sure what they do."

Doona laughed. "I can tell you at great length what they do," she said. "And when I was done, you still wouldn't want one."

They were back at Bessie's cottage and Doona parked the car.

"Do you have time to come in for a cuppa?" Bessie asked.

"Yes, please," Doona replied. "I'm feeling frazzled from my shopping expedition."

"Did you end up getting a toaster, though?"

Doona nodded. She climbed out of the car and opened the boot. Bessie joined her.

"See, isn't it lovely?" Doona asked, holding up the cardboard box that held her new toaster.

"It's very blue," Bessie said.

"One of the hottest new designer colours for small appliances," Doona replied with a shrug. "It was two pounds cheaper than black, so I thought I'd give it a try."

"Designer colours for toasters?" Bessie asked as she led Doona into her kitchen. "What will they think of next?"

"I don't know about them, but I can tell you what I've been thinking," Doona said as Bessie filled the kettle.

"What have you been thinking?"

"I've been thinking about moving," Doona told her.

191

Bessie nearly dropped the kettle. "Moving? Not off the island?"

"Oh, goodness, no," Doona laughed. "Not even very far away."

"Oh, thank goodness for that," Bessie said. She switched the kettle on and found some chocolate biscuits for the pair to share. "But what's brought this on?" she asked as she handed Doona a plate and offered her the biscuits.

"I don't know," Doona said. "You know I'd love to redo my kitchen and my bathroom. Sometimes I think I'd like a bit more space, really. I know I'm on my own, but I'd love an extra bedroom. I'd fill it with books, of course."

" I can certainly understand that," Bessie said emphatically.

"Anyway, now that I have a little bit of money in the bank, I've been thinking about having the kitchen done up and maybe seeing what an extension might cost. It all seems like so much hard work, though."

"It is hard work," Bessie told her. "I've had the cottage extended twice and it was pretty awful both times."

Doona nodded. "When I was talking with Peter Clucas the other night, he mentioned that his son builds houses, and that he'd just finished a row of properties right on the water, down the beach from here."

"I've seen them," Bessie said. "They're ever so modern and nice."

"That's what Peter said," Doona replied. "Anyway, he suggested that I might want to take a look at one. They aren't officially on the market yet, but he offered to arrange it for me. I don't know that buying one of them would cost all that much more than having all of the work done on my current home would, really. And this way I'd have something brand new and trouble-free."

"It does sound tempting," Bessie said. "Are you going to have a look?"

"Yes, after work tonight," Doona replied. "Peter is collecting me at my house so he can have a quick look at it. He reckons he can give me a rough idea of what the sort of remodeling I'm interested in would cost so that I have something to compare the new house price with."

"Just remember that he's interested in selling you the new house," Bessie cautioned.

"Oh, I know," Doona assured her. "I also think he might be interested in getting to know me better, but I'm going to make sure he understands that isn't on the cards."

"Did you say his wife died?" Bessie asked, trying to remember what she could about the man.

"Yes, some years ago now. I gather they were on holiday. He said something about saving up to go away without the kids for the first time, and then she had some sort of accident. I didn't want to pry."

"No, I can see that," Bessie said.

"Anyway, I'll ring you when I get home and tell you all about it."

"Have you mentioned it to John?" Bessie asked as she handed Doona a cup of tea.

"Why would I do that?"

"Peter is a suspect in a murder investigation," Bessie reminded her. "John won't be happy that you're going to be spending time alone with him."

"I hadn't really thought about that. I mean, he seemed so nice and he does such good work, even working with the police. It's hard for me to see him as a suspect."

"You should still tell John," Bessie said firmly.

"Maybe I'll tell Hugh or one of the other constables," Doona said thoughtfully. "They'll put it in a report that John won't see until tomorrow, by which time it will be too late for him to tell me I can't go."

Bessie bit her tongue. She wasn't thrilled with the idea of Doona spending time alone with Peter, even though she couldn't imagine him being involved in the murders.

"I'd better get back to work," Doona said, washing down a second biscuit with her tea. "I only have to go back in for an hour because of the very strange schedule, but at least that means I'll be out in time to see the house in daylight. If I see John, I'll mention my plans for later," she added. "Otherwise, I'll tell Hugh."

Bessie locked the door behind her friend and reached for the phone. She needed to ring the station before Doona got back or else her friend would know she'd rung.

"I'm sorry, but Inspector Rockwell isn't in the office at the moment," the woman who'd answered the phone told her. "I can have him ring you back."

"No, that's okay," Bessie replied. "I can ring him on his mobile."

She was searching through the small pile of papers next to the phone, looking for John's mobile number, when someone knocked on the door. "Got it," she exclaimed as she found the right slip of paper. With the number still in her hand, Bessie opened the door.

"Ah, Aunt Bessie, may I have a minute of your time?" the woman at the door asked.

Bessie studied her for a moment and then smiled. "Julie Landers? But what brings you here?"

Julie smiled back, but the expression looked forced. "I wasn't sure you'd even remember me."

"My memory is still good," Bessie told her as she ushered the woman into the house. "Even if you have changed a great deal since the last time I saw you."

The woman sat at the kitchen table and put her head in her hands. Bessie quickly switched the kettle back on before she joined Julie, trying to recall all that she could about her unexpected guest. The woman was probably in her mid-forties. Her parents had owned a farm that stretched along the border between Laxey and Lonan. Julie had been a pretty and popular child with friends from both villages, even though she'd attended Laxey's primary school.

Julie's hair was cut in a short bob. It was dark brown with streaks of grey that ran through it. The hairstyle was the main thing that had helped Bessie recognise the woman. As far as Bessie could remember, Julie had always worn her hair in that exact same way. Otherwise, the woman at the kitchen table bore little resemblance to the teenager Bessie had once known.

"It's Julie Mortimer now," the woman said when she lifted her head. "Jack and I have been married for more than twenty years."

"I rather lost track of your family when you all moved to Peel,"

Bessie said. "I never thought your father would sell his farm. It was a huge surprise when you went."

"Dad had cancer," Julie told her. "The doctors said they couldn't do anything for him. Mum couldn't look after the farm on her own, so they sold up and moved to Peel, expecting to live off the proceeds of the sale until dad passed. He had enough life insurance that mum would have been okay after that."

"I never heard any of that," Bessie said. "And I didn't realise that your father had passed, either."

"Oh, he hasn't," Julie laughed. "Maybe it was the air in Peel, no one knows, but the cancer suddenly started getting smaller, and then one day it was gone. The doctors still can't explain it, but he and mum are doing great and loving life in Peel. They both had to find jobs, of course, once it became obvious that dad wasn't going to die any time soon."

"Doctors don't always know everything," Bessie said.

"No, they really don't," Julie agreed. "But I think mum and dad will tell you that selling the farm was the best thing that ever happened. Dad worked nearly all the time when he was farming, and it was hard and physical work. Maybe his body just needed a break from that. In Peel he works as a handyman and he really enjoys it, especially because he can set his own hours and only work when he feels like it. Mum works in one of the shops on the promenade, but she's going to retire early next year."

"Give them both my very best," Bessie said. "It's a small island, but it seems as if once someone leaves Laxey I never hear from them again."

Julie nodded. "All the small communities are quite self-contained, aren't they? But they're all equally wonderful."

"Ah, well, I'd have to say Laxey is the best," Bessie teased.

"I won't argue. But I do enjoy Peel, anyway."

The kettle boiled and Bessie made them each a cup of tea. She hadn't put the plate of biscuits away, so now she offered Julie a small plate and then sat back down and helped herself to another sugary treat.

"But what can I do for you?" Bessie asked. "I'd be more than happy to hear that you just stopped by for a chat, but that isn't it, is it?"

"How have you been?" Julie asked, clearly not ready to talk about whatever had brought her to Bessie's door.

She and Bessie chatted for more than half an hour about nearly everyone that Julie could remember from her childhood. While Bessie enjoyed the walk down memory lane, she was starting to get impatient with the woman after she'd handed her a third cup of tea.

"Can we take a walk on the beach?" Julie asked a moment later.

"Of course," Bessie said. She was grateful for the opportunity to get up and move around. It felt as if she'd been sitting at her kitchen table all day. Clearly the woman had something serious on her mind, but it was equally obvious that she wasn't ready to talk about it yet.

The pair walked as far at Thie yn Traie, where Julie stopped. "Those steps look lethal," she remarked, looking at the wooden steps that wound their way up the cliff from the beach to the mansion above.

"They are," Bessie told her.

"Oh, that's right, you fell down them, didn't you?" Julie asked. "It was in the local paper," she explained when Bessie gave her a surprised look. "And then someone else fell down them recently, didn't they?"

"Not exactly," Bessie replied. "I'm hoping the new owners might replace them with something a bit safer."

"Yes, George and Mary Quayle have bought Thie yn Traie, haven't they? That was in the local paper, too," Julie laughed as Bessie stared at her. "I always read all of the news from Laxey," she added. "In a strange way it will always be home to me."

"It's not strange," Bessie told her. "You spent your childhood here, after all."

"You spent your childhood in America, didn't you?" Julie asked. "Do you miss it? Does it feel like home to you?"

Bessie frowned as she thought about the questions. "I'm not sure," she said eventually. "I was born on the island, but we moved when I was two, so well before I remember. I suppose Cleveland was home to me in a way, but for much of my childhood my parents talked about moving back here. I don't think they ever felt settled in the US and that meant that I don't think I did, either. Anyway, I chose to make Laxey my home and I can't imagine anywhere else in the world ever feeling as perfect for me as my little cottage."

Julie nodded. "I'm sorry if I'm prying," she said as they turned and began to walk back towards Bessie's cottage. "And I'm sorry that I'm prevaricating so much. I need to tell someone about something that happened to me a long time ago, but, well, it's something I've tried not think about for many many years."

Bessie stopped at the large rock behind her house. "Sit down," she suggested. "We can talk here with only the gulls to listen in. If you're sure you're ready to talk about whatever it is, I'm ready to listen."

"I'm not ready," Julie said shakily. "But I think I have to do it anyway. I have to tell you, and then once I've gone through it once, I have to tell the police."

"The police?"

"Yes, because I think I know who killed the Kelly girls."

CHAPTER 14

*B*essie took a deep breath and then sat down next to the woman on the rock. "In that case, you'd better tell me everything," she said.

Julie nodded. "I'd rather my parents not know," she began. "Oh, listen to me. I'm forty-six years old, married with three children, and I'm still worried about what my parents will think when they find out I broke their rules thirty years ago." She shook her head.

"You were always a very well-behaved child," Bessie said.

"Yeah, I was," Julie agreed. "My parents weren't all that strict, but they did have rules, and I always stuck to them. And they warned me all the time about boys, especially the Clucas cousins and Matthew Kelly."

Bessie patted the woman's back. "I think they were right about them," she said.

"Oh, they were," Julie agreed. "But that only added to the appeal." She gave Bessie a sheepish look. "I was rather jealous of Karen Kelly in those days. She was my age, but so much more sophisticated. She'd had a bunch of boyfriends and she and Helen used to talk about boys in front of me, talking about all sorts of things that I didn't know anything about."

"They both had something of a reputation," Bessie said.

"From what they told me, they deserved their reputations," Julie said. "They used to talk about, well, sex and drinking and all manner of things. I used to be really shocked, but I tried hard to pretend that I wasn't."

"Being a teenager is difficult."

"It is," Julie agreed. "I have two teenagers now and it isn't any easier these days. It may even be harder, I don't know."

"But you were telling me about breaking the rules," Bessie said gently.

"Oh, yes, I must get on with it, mustn't I? I'm sure you have better things to do."

Bessie could think of a dozen things she ought to have been doing, including ringing John, but she didn't want to rush the woman, either. Especially not if Julie held the key to the Kelly case.

"When you're ready," she murmured to Julie.

"It was spring," Julie said softly. "I was spending a lot of time with Helen and Karen. They liked it at my house because we had horses that we could ride, rather than just working farm horses. We would go on rides after school, and the other two would start talking about the different boys and how they looked naked and things like that, and I would just blush and hope they wouldn't notice."

"How awful for you," Bessie said.

"Once in a while Susan would come along. I liked her a lot, because she was more like me. She was shy around boys, too. Anyway, one Saturday we were all riding and talking, and Susan started telling us about her new boyfriend and how she was planning to sneak away from home so she could, well, spend the night with him. She was going to tell her parents she was at Margot's house and then go and stay with him instead."

"He had his own house?" Bessie asked.

"No, but everyone was using the old Grantham farm for that sort of thing in those days. We all knew the house was empty, but they'd left some pieces of furniture behind. There were even a few beds left in some of the bedrooms and, well, let's just say they were put to use most weekends."

Bessie nodded. She shouldn't have felt shocked, but she did.

"Anyway, I was surprised at Susan, but the way she told it, she was madly in love. She just wouldn't tell anyone who the boy was, which was frustrating."

And dangerous, Bessie added to herself.

"A couple of days later Jonas Clucas caught up to me as I was walking home from school and made a few nasty comments to me about being a prude. He said something about how I'd never get a boyfriend because I wasn't any fun at all. I almost burst into tears, but then Peter came over and told him to leave me alone. He was really sweet."

Tears began to fall slowly as the woman took a deep breath. Bessie found a tissue in her pocket and handed it to Julie, who wiped her eyes before she continued.

"I couldn't stop thinking about what Jonas had said. I wanted a boyfriend more than anything else that spring. I felt like the only girl in the whole village who hadn't even been kissed by a boy. So I decided I was going to start being more like Karen. I decided to sneak out of my house and find out exactly what everyone else was getting up to at the Grantham place."

Bessie dug out another tissue, her last one. Maybe out here wasn't the best place for this conversation, she thought as Julie wiped her eyes again.

"The following Saturday I sneaked out after my parents went to bed. It wasn't a long walk to the Grantham farm, really. I took a torch and I cut across the fields. It wasn't far at all. The back door wasn't locked. We all knew that Jonas had broken in and fixed the lock on the back door months earlier. Anyway, I walked all through the house and there wasn't anyone there. After all the stories I'd heard, I think I'd been expecting an orgy in every room or something, but the entire house was empty."

She stopped and stared out at the sea for a long minute, leaving Bessie dreading where the story was going.

"I'm sorry," Julie said eventually. "This is harder than I thought it would be."

"But you may be the key to solving several murders," Bessie pointed out.

Julie nodded. "I was leaving. There was no one there, so I was going to go home and go to bed, when he came in. He laughed when he saw me there. I don't know if he was surprised or not, but he laughed. And then he offered me a drink. I'd never drunk much more than a sip or two of wine at family parties and the like. I don't know what he gave me, but I got drunk really quickly."

She drew a sharp breath and rubbed her face with her hands. "It's all a bit of a blur, but I remember him pulling at my clothes and then his hands went around my neck. He was squeezing and I couldn't breathe and then he suddenly stopped. When I heard voices, I knew why he'd stopped."

Bessie gasped. "You poor thing," she said.

"After that he was really nice to me," Julie told her. "He apologised and said he'd just had too much to drink. I didn't know what to think, really. I was incredibly naïve. He told me he wanted me to be his girl-friend and that he'd wanted to ask me out for ages, but hadn't been brave enough. Oh, it doesn't matter what he said. Basically, he flat-tered me and made me think he cared, and I pushed what had happened out of my mind. We went out a few times after that, and he was always really lovely and sweet. I more or less convinced myself that I must have imagined it because I'd drunk so much."

"But you didn't," Bessie said steadily.

Julie nodded. "It was only when the police found the bodies that I realised that he must have killed them."

"You have to talk to the police," Bessie said firmly. "You have to tell them everything you just told me. They'll arrest Jonas."

"Jonas?" Julie echoed. "But it was Peter who attacked me."

Bessie jumped off the rock and raced up the beach as quickly as she could. Doona was somewhere alone with the man. She had to ring John.

"Bessie?" Julie called after her.

"I'll explain later," Bessie called over her shoulder.

When she'd put the kettle on for Julie, Bessie had put John's mobile number down on the counter next to it. Now she grabbed the scrap of paper and punched the numbers into her phone.

"It's Bessie," she said when the call was answered. "You have to find Doona. She's somewhere with Peter Clucas, and he killed the Kelly girls."

"Are you sure about that?" John asked.

"No, but from what I just heard, it's a strong possibility. Doona shouldn't be alone with him. He was going to her house and then taking her to see the houses his son had built on Laxey beach," Bessie explained.

The sun was setting outside Bessie's window as she listened to the inspector mobilising his troops from another phone.

"Hugh is on his way to Doona's house and Constable Richards is on his way to the houses on the beach. I'm going there as well. You sit tight," he told Bessie after a while.

"Like heck I will," she said. John had already disconnected, which saved Bessie an argument.

She headed back outside, rushing past Julie, who was still sitting on the large rock.

"What's going on?" Julie demanded as she joined Bessie on her trek down the beach.

"My friend Doona had a meeting with Peter tonight," Bessie told her. "He was going to show her around the houses his son built on the beach."

"So she's alone with him in an empty house," Julie said.

"I've rung the police and they're on their way," Bessie replied tightly.

"I wish I would have gone to the police thirty years ago," Julie said.

"You were very young," Bessie said.

"And I wanted a boyfriend so badly. All of the other girls were so jealous when Peter and I were together that I told myself to ignore the incident. He was a perfect gentleman after that, you know. I even started to wonder if I'd imagined the whole thing and I definitely convinced myself that it wasn't any big deal. And now your friend is in danger."

As Bessie walked as quickly as she could, Julie took off down the beach in a dead run. Bessie knew she couldn't possibly keep up, but she kept walking, hoping that someone would get to Doona quickly.

The walk seemed to take hours, but Bessie was relieved when she could finally see the new houses in the distance. There were several police cars and ambulances parked in front of them with lights flashing against the dusky sky.

When Bessie finally reached the scene, John was just emerging from the show house at the end of the row.

"What are you doing here?" he demanded.

"Where's Doona?" Bessie asked.

"In my car," John said. "She's a little shaken up, but fine."

Bessie took a step towards the car and then stopped, her knees sagging under her. John quickly took her arm.

"Are you okay?" he asked.

"I think I may have overdone it just a little," she said, trying to smile while struggling to catch her breath.

John called one of the paramedics over and he insisted that Bessie let him examine her.

"I'm fine, just a bit out of breath," Bessie complained.

"I'll just confirm that for you," the young man said cheerfully.

Bessie sat with gritted teeth as he checked her vital signs. By the time he was done, her breathing was mostly back to normal.

"I think you'll be fine," he said. "Make sure someone gives you a ride home, though. You don't need to do any more walking tonight."

Bessie considered arguing, but the thought of the long walk home had her pressing her lips together. A ride home was exactly what she needed.

Released from the ambulance, she rejoined John, who was still standing behind the house. He was talking to someone on his mobile as she approached.

"So what's happening?" she asked as John dropped his phone into a pocket.

"I arrived just as Peter ran out of this house," John told her. "I called for backup and then went inside. Doona was there with a woman called Julie Mortimer. Apparently, she arrived in time to stop whatever Peter was planning."

"Oh, thank goodness," Bessie exclaimed. "I almost told her not to run. I assumed you'd get here before she could."

"They're doing roadwork on the coast road," John said. "I got stuck at a temporary traffic light for ages."

"And Doona is okay?" Bessie asked.

"I'm fine," Doona's voice came from behind Bessie.

Bessie gave her friend a hug and then unexpectedly burst into tears. Doona sighed and handed Bessie a tissue.

"Honestly, I don't know what you have to cry about," Doona teased.

"You should have told John you were meeting Peter," Bessie said once she'd dried her tears. "Then none of this would have happened."

"I told one of the constables," Doona replied. "And I told Peter that I'd done so. Anyway, he was just showing me around some houses."

"So what happened?" Bessie asked.

Doona sighed. "Can you take notes now so that this can count as my statement?" she asked John.

John hesitated and then sighed. "Let's move over to the office and talk there. The younger Peter has offered to let us use the space for tonight."

"Does he know you suspect his father of murder?" Bessie asked as they walked.

"Yes, but that's a conversation for another time," John replied.

Julie, looking slightly dazed, emerged from John's car as they walked past. "Am I supposed to stay here?" she asked.

"Why don't you join us?" John invited her. "I'll need a statement from you as well."

John stopped one of the constables and issued a series of orders and instructions before they reached the office. Once inside, everyone found places to sit before John began.

"Doona, I need a statement from you. Bessie and Julie can wait outside. It won't take long."

"They can stay as far as I'm concerned," Doona said. "There really isn't much to tell. Peter came over to my house as planned. He spent about ten minutes walking through it and then we talked for a short time about the changes I want to make. Then he drove me over here. Before we left, I rang the station to let someone know what was happening."

"The constable on the desk made a note of your call," John said. "You should have asked him to ring me right away, though."

"I never imagined that I'd be in any danger," Doona said. "And Peter heard me ring and tell the man where I was going and that I would ring back in an hour. I'm sure that kept me safe, if he was originally planning something."

"So what did happen?" Bessie asked impatiently.

Doona smiled at her. "Peter showed me around a couple of the houses. He went on and on about how wonderful they all were. He saved the show house for last. I was starting to think he might be right when we reached the master bedroom."

Doona stopped and took a deep breath. John looked up from his notes, concern all over his face.

"I'm fine," she said. "Nothing happened. He made some sort of joke about trying out the bed and I laughed it off. We were just getting ready to go back downstairs when the door burst open and Julie appeared in the doorway."

"Thank goodness for Julie," Bessie said softly.

"I was just lucky he didn't lock the front door behind you guys," Julie said.

"Doona, let me hear your version of events and then I'll get Julie's," John said.

"The door to the bedroom burst open and this woman I'd never seen before was standing there," Doona said, winking at Julie. "She looked mighty ferocious and she started shouting at Peter and calling him names that I'd never even heard before. Peter took one look at her and ran out of the room."

Julie flushed. "I was so angry. I never held him accountable for what he did to me all those years ago. I should have rung the police then, but I was too stupid to realise it. He must have killed the Kelly girls." She shook her head. "If I'd called the police at the time, they would all still be alive," she said sadly.

"The police might not have done all that much," Bessie told her. "It would have been your word against his, after all."

"And I wasn't even sure what had happened," Julie said. "It was all a blur."

"You mustn't blame yourself," John said firmly after Julie had given her statement. She'd told him everything that she could remember from the original attack as well as what had happened that evening. "He was obviously very clever. He managed to get away with murder for nearly thirty years."

A knock on the office door interrupted the conversation. John opened it to the younger Peter Clucas.

"I'm sorry to interrupt," he said. "I was hoping for an update on what's happening."

John nodded. "Come in," he said. "I'm sorry about all of this. Your father ran off when I arrived. We have several constables searching for him. He took off on foot, so he can't have gone too far."

"He always used to go to the old Grantham farm when he needed to clear his head," Peter told them. "He said it was peaceful there."

Bessie shivered. Doona looked at her and then patted her hand.

"We still have a constable posted there," John said. "If he turns up there, we'll have him."

"He killed those girls, didn't he?" Peter asked.

"We don't know anything for certain," John replied.

"But he did," Peter said, sighing deeply. "I've always wondered."

"Why?" Bessie blurted out.

Peter looked at her for a moment and then sighed again. "There was always something slightly odd about my father. He had secrets and I learned very early on not to ask questions. My mother, well, I think she was afraid of him. I always thought she committed suicide because she couldn't live with him anymore."

"Maybe he killed her," Julie suggested.

"She was alone, walking along a cliff," Peter said. "My father was with a group of people some ten miles away." He shook his head. "I've read the police reports a thousand times. He didn't kill her, but I think he drove her to kill herself. Officially, it was a tragic accident."

"You were quite young when she died, weren't you?" Bessie asked.

"I was nine," Peter said. "After she died, I went and lived with her sister, my Aunt Margaret, and her husband, Uncle Jerome. They raised me as their own and I had very little contact with my father, which suited me."

John's mobile made a noise. "I need to take this," he said, getting to his feet. "I'll go outside," he added as everyone started to get up.

"I hope my father didn't hurt you," Peter said to Doona. "He told me he was going to show a prospective buyer around the site tonight. I said I'd come as well, but he was adamant that I leave him alone with you. He hinted that I would be in the way of his, um, romantic overtures."

Doona shook her head. "He just showed me around the houses," she said. "I felt perfectly safe until Julie turned up and started shouting at him."

"I'm sorry," Peter said.

"It isn't your fault in any way," Doona replied.

"I should have insisted on coming as well," Peter argued. "I didn't feel comfortable about him being here alone with you, but I didn't really think he'd ever hurt anyone."

"Of course you didn't," Doona said.

"I knew he had secrets, but I always thought he had other women," Peter said, almost talking to himself. "I thought that was why my mother killed herself. I never guessed, never imagined, but somehow I'm not nearly as shocked as I should be, either. He always frightened me slightly."

"I just hope they find him quickly," Bessie said.

John's face was grim when he stepped back inside the small office. "I need to speak to Mr. Clucas privately," he said.

Bessie, Doona and Julie made their way back outside. "What do we do now?" Julie asked.

"We need to wait and see what John has to say when he's done with Peter," Bessie said.

"They must have found his father," Julie said.

"Maybe," Bessie replied.

A moment later the door to the office opened and John stepped out. "I'm going to send you all home," he said. "I'll have a constable escort each of you."

"My car is at Bessie's," Julie told him.

John arranged to have Bessie and Julie taken to Bessie's cottage. The constable would follow Julie back across the island to Peel to make sure she reached home safely.

"I'll come over when I'm done here," John told Bessie. "It shouldn't be long now."

"I'll just go to Bessie's, then," Doona said. "I'd rather not be alone anyway."

John nodded. Bessie and the others climbed into a police car and headed back to the cottage.

"Thank you for everything," Julie said, hugging Bessie tightly when they'd reached Troeghe Bwaane.

"Thank you," Doona told her. "Now that we know more about Peter, I'm ever so glad you turned up when you did."

"The police were right behind me," Julie said, waving a hand. "You would have been okay, anyway."

"I'll always wonder what he had planned for me." Doona said.

Julie climbed into her car and drove slowly away while Bessie let Doona into the cottage.

"John didn't say whether Peter has been caught or not," Bessie said as she glanced around her kitchen.

"I'll check the cottage," Doona said. "I always do anyway."

Bessie opened her mouth to protest, but Doona was already gone, walking briskly through each room, banging doors and shouting.

"No one here but us," she said cheerfully as she walked back into the kitchen a minute later.

"Thank goodness for that," Bessie said. She'd put the kettle on, now she went into the cupboard for more biscuits. The plate from earlier was still on the kitchen table and Doona idly grabbed a biscuit and popped it in her mouth.

"Goodness," Bessie gasped. "I never had any dinner."

Doona looked at her. "I didn't either," she said. "And now that you've said that, I'm starving."

Bessie found some spaghetti sauce in her freezer and set it reheating while she boiled water. A slightly stale baguette was perfect for garlic bread. "I don't have any salad," she apologised to Doona. "We'll have to have extra garlic bread to make up for it."

"That sounds perfect," Doona told her.

Bessie dumped an entire box of pasta in to boil. She could always keep leftovers for another day and she was suddenly very hungry. John knocked on her door as she was getting ready to serve.

"Perfect timing," she told him as Doona let him in. "And I've made more than enough for all three of us."

"Did you make enough for Hugh, too?" John asked. "He should be here in a few minutes."

Bessie grabbed a second baguette and smothered it in garlic butter. "We'll have to make do," she said.

She was just passing around plates when Hugh arrived. He greeted Bessie with a hug and then looked at the kitchen table. "Oh, I'm not very hungry," he said apologetically. "I think I'm a bit too nervous to be hungry."

Bessie filled a plate for him anyway, and then they all sat down and enjoyed the thrown-together meal.

It wasn't until the dishes were cleared away and everyone was enjoying biscuits that John spoke.

"I really can't stay too much longer," he said. "I have a lot of paper-work to get done tonight."

Hugh groaned. "Paperwork is the bane of my existence right now," he said.

"That's why I'm going to go in and do what needs to be done from tonight," John said. "You have enough on your plate."

"Thank you, sir," Hugh said smartly.

"But it is your case that I'm wrapping up," John said. "So you'll need to go through it all with me and it will be your signature on the reports."

"Oh, thank you, sir," Hugh said.

John nodded. "You should be very proud of your efforts," he told him. "You've solved several decades-old murder cases."

"So you're certain Peter was the killer?" Bessie asked.

"Nothing is certain yet," John said. "But after everything that's happened, I'm fairly confident that we've found the killer."

"And you have him in custody?" Doona asked.

"He's dead," John said somberly.

"What happened?" Bessie demanded.

"From what we can put together, after he ran from me, he stole a car," John said. "Apparently, he was quite good at doing so when he was a teenager, and he still knew exactly what to do."

"I would have thought that modern cars would be harder to steal," Bessie said.

"He took an older model car," John told her. "The owner had left it unlocked as well, which had to make his job easier."

"But what happened next?" Doona asked impatiently.

"I think his son was correct," John said. "He headed for the Grantham farm at a high rate of speed. I have to assume that he hadn't been there for a while and didn't realise how badly maintained the road to the farm was, but he drove far too fast for the condition of the road surface. Unfortunately, he lost control and hit a tree. He wasn't wearing a seatbelt and he was thrown from the vehicle."

Everyone was silent for several minutes. Bessie felt sad, but also relieved in a way. It seemed likely that the man had killed several women. The island was a safer place with him gone.

"We'll be searching his home, vehicle, and office for evidence in the coming days," John told them. "And we'll be questioning Jonas at length."

"It must have been Matthew that rang anonymously, mustn't it?" Bessie asked.

"I'm not sure if we'll ever know the answer to that," John said. "At this point I'm more interested in what Jonas knew. From all accounts those two were practically inseparable in those years."

"That should be an interesting conversation," Bessie said.

"Yes, I'm rather looking forward to it," John said with a grim smile.

John offered to take Doona home and she was happy to agree. Hugh stayed behind to help Bessie with the washing-up.

"I hope you're looking forward to Sunday," Bessie told the man as they worked.

"I'm too nervous for that," Hugh replied. "You don't think we're rushing things, do you? I mean, we only just got engaged. Maybe we should wait a little while to get married."

Bessie laughed. "Whatever you do, don't say that to Grace," she told him. "No doubt she has cold feet, too. For what it's worth, I think you're doing things exactly right. You and Grace are perfect for each other and I think you're going to have a long and happy life together."

"Thank you," Hugh said. "I hope you're right."

"When have I ever been wrong?" Bessie demanded.

CHAPTER 15

*B*essie found the perfect dress for the wedding at her favourite shop in Ramsey. They had a hat that matched almost exactly, and the shoe shop a few doors away had the perfect shoes. With all of that sorted, Bessie had nothing to do but read and research in the days left before the wedding.

Sunday morning was cold and wet. Bessie frowned at the rain as she patted on her rose-scented dusting powder. Even though she had a lot to do, she still paused for a just a moment to think about Matthew Saunders, the man she'd once planned to marry herself. When she opened her eyes, it was still raining.

While Bessie didn't allow herself to have any regrets, once in a while she did think about how differently her life might have turned out if circumstances had been different. She'd only been seventeen when she'd fallen in love with the handsome and clever Matthew. Bessie had never forgiven her parents for dragging her back to the island or for Matthew's subsequent death.

Weddings always made Bessie think of him, and today was no exception. She made herself breakfast and then sat and let her mind wander back in time. Over the years she'd seen a lot of marriages, both successful and otherwise, and she knew that she and Matthew would have struggled if they had married. Bessie wasn't sure she would have enjoyed being a mother, but in those days there was no reliable way to prevent repeated pregnancies. Her own sister had raised ten children, something that Bessie couldn't even begin to imagine. A knock on her door shook her out of her reverie.

"Bessie, I'm just too excited to sit at home on my own," Doona said when Bessie opened the door. "I hope you don't mind if I annoy you until time to go to the church."

"I don't think you'll annoy me," Bessie laughed. "I'm quite unable to get my brain to focus on anything at the moment. I'll enjoy the company."

"I keep thinking about my own weddings," Doona told Bessie once they were both settled in Bessie's sitting room. "I was an idiot the first time around, of course, just getting married because it seemed like the next box to tick on my life list, but the second time, well, I was so happy and so full of hope. I suppose I was more of an idiot that time, really."

Bessie shook her head. "You should never feel that way," she said. "You went into the marriage thinking you'd found the right man for you. It certainly isn't your fault that he wasn't what you thought he was."

"Hugh and Grace won't have that problem," Doona said happily. "They're perfect for one another."

"I do think they have a good chance of making it work," Bessie said.

"I just wish it wasn't raining," Doona told her. "It's meant to be bad luck to have rain on your wedding day."

"Nonsense," Bessie said stoutly. "Did it rain on your wedding days?"

Doona thought for a moment and then laughed. "Actually, they were both beautiful sunny days," she said. "Maybe I'll hope for rain if I ever get married again."

"Is there any news on the case?" Bessie asked.

"John is holding a press conference on Monday to announce what they found in Peter's home. He kept notebooks full of information about each victim. It's quite awful, really, but it does make identification easier. There were seven bodies at the Grantham farm, but it appears that he killed more than twenty women over the years. The other victims were killed in various places around the world. Apparently Peter travelled regularly."

"How horrible," Bessie said, shuddering.

"It is, but at least twenty-two families will now know what happened to their loved ones," Doona told her. "Jonas has been down at the station several times to answer questions. He's slightly less obnoxious now that he's realised that his best childhood friend murdered so many people."

"That's good to hear. I assume they can't find anything to charge him with, though?"

"John's still trying," Doona grinned.

"And how are you feeling?" Bessie asked.

"I'm fine," Doona insisted. "Nothing happened, and I have to believe that nothing would have happened. He must have known that he couldn't kill me and get away with it."

Bessie made them both a light lunch and then they changed for the wedding.

"Are you sure about the hat?" Doona asked, studying herself in the mirror.

"Absolutely," Bessie told her. "It's perfect."

Doona drove them both to the small church in Douglas where the happy couple was having a traditional ceremony. Hugh was standing at the church door when they arrived.

"Ah, Bessie, Doona, thank you for coming," he said formally.

"I'm delighted to be here," Bessie told him. "You look very handsome."

Hugh flushed. "It's pretty uncomfortable," he told Bessie. "But it's once in a lifetime."

"Or maybe not," Hugh's father said from behind Hugh. "I thought that when I married your mum and now here I am, all dressed up again."

Hugh insisted on Doona and Bessie sitting right behind his family in the small church. Doona waved to the crowd of young constables who were sitting together near the back.

"My goodness, who's policing Laxey and Lonan?" Bessie whispered as she took her seat.

"The Chief Constable sent a handful of constables up from Douglas and Castletown to cover today," Doona told her. "Everyone from our branch is here."

Bessie looked around the church and then sighed. "Even Inspector Lambert," she said softly.

Doona glanced over and then shrugged. "Hugh could hardly leave her out," she said.

A few minutes later Hugh took his place at the altar, John Rockwell by his side. Grace was only a few minutes late and as she entered the church, everyone stood up.

"She looks radiant," Doona whispered to Bessie.

Bessie could only nod in reply. Grace's dress was perfect and Bessie couldn't imagine the girl looking any happier than she did as she glided down the aisle on her father's arm. When her eyes met Hugh's an even bigger smile appeared and Bessie felt herself tearing up. Hugh looked more stunned than anything else, as if he couldn't quite believe his luck.

"You look gorgeous," he whispered loudly as he took Grace's arm.

The ceremony wasn't long, but it was very touching. The pair said their vows with so much meaning and love that Bessie actually ran out of tissues and had to get extras from Doona. At the end, as Hugh kissed Grace gently, everyone cheered. Bessie hid a grin as she noticed that even Inspector Lambert was teary-eyed as she clapped for the happy couple.

When Bessie arrived at the reception a short time later, Mary was waiting for her in the car park.

"Okay, so after our talk last night, this is what I did," she told Bessie. She opened the boot of her car and pulled out a large white box, tied up with a huge bow.

"It's perfect," Bessie said.

"I hope the card is okay," Mary said anxiously.

Bessie looked at the attached card and smiled. "I never would have done anything this nice," she told the other woman as she looked over the beautifully written list of names of everyone who had contributed to the honeymoon package.

"I'm ready for some champagne," Mary said. "I just hope they like the surprise."

"Champagne sounds good," Bessie agreed. "I'm sorry I wasn't much help with the planning. If it all goes wrong, it's all my fault, of course."

Hugh had said they were keeping everything small and as inexpensive as possible, but there was far more food and drink on offer than Bessie had been expecting. She enjoyed chatting with Hugh's family and meeting the members of Grace's family who'd been able to attend.

"Oh, you're Bessie," one of Grace's aunts said. "We've heard ever so much about you."

Bessie wasn't sure exactly how to take that, but she didn't get time to ask before she was whisked away to meet some of Grace's friends and fellow schoolteachers. Her energy was flagging by the time the happy couple cut the cake.

"We just want to thank everyone for coming," Hugh said after he'd wiped icing off his face. "I understand there are a few presents as well. We'll open them once we're back from our honeymoon. That gives us something to look forward to."

Everyone clapped and Bessie looked over at Mary. They'd planned for this, just in case.

"I'm sorry, Hugh," Bessie said, standing up. "But there is one gift you have to open now."

Hugh smiled at her. "I don't know," he said. "We were really looking forward to opening everything when we got home."

"This is the one exception," Bessie said firmly. Mary handed her the box and she passed it over to Hugh. "Rather a lot of us pooled our resources," she added. "You can see that from the card."

Grace joined Hugh and the pair looked at the card before Grace untied the bow. Hugh slowly opened the large box and looked inside. Nothing but tissue paper was immediately visible.

Grace pushed aside the paper and reached inside. She pulled out a small model airplane. She gave Hugh a confused look. He reached into the box and removed a tiny model of one of the ferries that cruises the Seine. The pair exchanged puzzled glances and then removed the rest of the tissue paper.

Bessie was close enough to see that their passports were next, on top of a thick folder. Hugh picked up the passports while Grace took out the folder. As everyone watched, she opened it and stared at the plane tickets that were on the top of the pile.

Bessie found that she couldn't keep quiet any longer. "You leave in the morning for a week in Paris," she told the shocked couple. "All of the details are in the folder, but you'll be met at the airport and taken to your hotel. There's a detailed itinerary in there as well, but we've left as much of the week up to you two as we could."

Grace began to cry as Hugh opened and closed his mouth, speechless. Grace's mum hugged Hugh's mum and they cried together as they watched their children react to the surprise.

"But what? How?" Hugh stuttered.

"We wanted to give you the perfect honeymoon," Bessie said. "Mary did all of the work. She can explain."

Mary smiled and shook her head. "It was all Bessie's idea," she said. "But then she was busy trying to help with your cold case, so I did some of the planning. But really, it was everyone's surprise. You can see from the card that nearly everyone in Laxey knew about it and contributed."

Hugh looked at the card again and then at Grace. "But we can't," he began. "I mean, we, Paris? I can't get my head around it."

"There's a list of restaurants in the folder," Mary told him. "We've arranged at each of them for you to have a lovely, romantic dinner, but you can choose which night you'd like dine at which restaurant. Obviously, everything is paid for, even the gratuity. Your hotel includes breakfast, and they do gorgeous breakfasts, I can promise you. There are a handful of gift certificates for other restaurants around the city for you to try for lunches each day. We've also booked a few sightseeing packages for you, but you can work with the company to chop and change whatever you'd like once you arrive. Please feel free to ring me at any time if you have any questions."

"The only question is how can we ever thank you?" Grace said through her tears. "I can't even imagine how wonderful it's all going to be."

"I hope it exceeds your expectations," Mary told her. "Honeymoons should be magical."

"Thank you," Hugh said gruffly. "This is the best surprise I've ever had, aside from when Grace said yes, of course." Everyone laughed.

Bessie was just starting to think about heading for home when Hugh found her a short while later.

"I don't even know what to say," he greeted her. "I'm overwhelmed."

"It wasn't much, really," Bessie told him. "I'm just glad you're pleased. We did worry you might not want to go."

Hugh laughed. "It's like a dream," he said. "If we'd have waited a year like I'd originally planned, I would have saved up to take her to Paris. I can't quite believe that we're actually going."

"You have a lot of good friends and we all wanted to see you and Grace have a wonderful start to your married life," Bessie told him.

"I'm not sure we're going to want to come back," Hugh teased.

"Of course you will," Bessie replied. "Paris will be wonderful, but the island is home."

Hours later, alone in her cottage, Bessie thought about what she'd told Hugh. The island was her home as well. Whatever had happened in the past, she wouldn't want it any other way.

GLOSSARY OF TERMS

MANX TO ENGLISH

- **moghrey mie** — good morning
- **skeet** — gossip

HOUSE NAMES – MANX TO ENGLISH

- **Thie yn Traie** — Beach House
- **Treoghe Bwaane** — Widow's Cottage

ENGLISH TO AMERICAN TERMS

- **advocate** — Manx title for a lawyer (solicitor in the UK)
- **aye** — yes
- **bin** — garbage can
- **biscuits** — cookies
- **bonnet (car)** — hood
- **boot (car)** — trunk

- **car park** — parking lot
- **chemist** — pharmacist
- **chips** — french fries
- **cuppa** — cup of tea (informally)
- **dear** — expensive
- **estate agent** — real estate agent (realtor)
- **fairy cakes** — cupcakes
- **holiday** — vacation
- **loo** — restroom
- **midday** — noon
- **mince** — ground beef (hamburger)
- **nappies** — diapers
- **pavement** — sidewalk
- **plait (hair)** — braid
- **primary school** — elementary school
- **pudding** — dessert
- **rates** — property taxes
- **starters** — appetizers
- **supply teacher** — substitute teacher
- **telly** — television
- **torch** — flashlight
- **trolley** — shopping cart
- **windscreen** — windshield

OTHER NOTES

CID is the Criminal Investigation Department of the Isle of Man Constabulary (Police Force).

When talking about time, the English say, for example, "half seven" to mean "seven-thirty."

With regard to Bessie's age: UK (and IOM) residents get a free bus pass at the age of 60. Bessie is somewhere between that age and the age at which she will get a birthday card from the Queen. British citizens used to receive telegrams from the ruling monarch on the occasion of their one-hundredth birthday. Cards replaced the telegrams in 1982, but the special greeting is still widely referred to as a telegram.

When island residents talk about someone being from "across," they mean that the person is from somewhere in the United Kingdom (across the water).

In the UK people refer to their weight in terms of stone and pounds. A stone is equal to fourteen pounds, so that someone who weights "ten stone, three" weighs 143 pounds.

When someone says "snap" they are saying that the same is true for them. It comes from the children's card game where each player takes it in turn to put down a card, and if two of the same cards are played in a row, players shout "snap." In the US, we might say "ditto" in the same context.

"Half-term" is a week-long break from school in the (approximate) middle of each term. They generally fall in October, February, and May.

ACKNOWLEDGMENTS

Thanks to my wonderful editor, Denise. Also to my incredibly helpful beta readers, Janice, Charlene and Ruth. And to Kevin, who takes such wonderful photographs for my covers.

Most importantly, thank you, readers, for continuing to enjoy spending time with Bessie and her friends.

Bessie's story continues in
Aunt Bessie Meets
An Isle of Man Cozy Mystery

Aunt Bessie meets a former acquaintance on Laxey Beach.

It's the first anniversary of Danny Pierce's death and Bessie is surprised when she sees Danny's widow, Vikky walking along the beach where the man's body was found. Vikky is back on the island with a large group that includes her new husband, his children, their wives and several business associates.

Aunt Bessie meets Vikky's new husband, Alastair Farthington, a very wealthy businessman.

When one member of the Farthington group ends up dead, Alastair wants Bessie to help investigate the murder. And he isn't used to taking no for an answer.

Aunt Bessie meets a great many new people, none of whom seem to have had a motive for murder.

Can Bessie help Alastair work out what happened before the killer strikes again?

ALSO BY DIANA XARISSA

Aunt Bessie Assumes

Aunt Bessie Believes

Aunt Bessie Considers

Aunt Bessie Decides

Aunt Bessie Enjoys

Aunt Bessie Finds

Aunt Bessie Goes

Aunt Bessie's Holiday

Aunt Bessie Invites

Aunt Bessie Joins

Aunt Bessie Knows

Aunt Bessie Likes

Aunt Bessie Meets

Aunt Bessie Needs

Aunt Bessie Observes

Aunt Bessie Provides

Aunt Bessie Questions

Aunt Bessie Remembers

Aunt Bessie Solves

Aunt Bessie Tries

Aunt Bessie Understands

Aunt Bessie Volunteers

Aunt Bessie Wonders

The Isle of Man Ghostly Cozy Mysteries

Arrivals and Arrests

ABOUT THE AUTHOR

Diana grew up in Pennsylvania, moved to Washington, DC, and then found herself being swept off her feet by a handsome British man who was visiting DC on vacation. That was nearly nineteen years ago.

After their wedding, Diana moved to Derbyshire, where her new husband had his home. A short time later, the couple moved to the Isle of Man. After more than ten years on the island, now a family of four, they relocated to the outskirts of Buffalo, NY, where Diana keeps busy writing about the island she loves and driving her children everywhere.

She also writes mystery/thrillers set in the not-too-distant future under the pen name "Diana X. Dunn" and fantasy/adventure books for middle grade readers under the pen name "D.X. Dunn."

She would be delighted to know what you think of her work and can be contacted through snail mail at:

Diana Xarissa Dunn
PO Box 72
Clarence, NY 14031

Find Diana at:
www.dianaxarissa.com
diana@dianaxarissa.com

Made in United States
Cleveland, OH
01 November 2024

10405602R00134